BUMP UP the OXYGEN

Other books by this author

Across the Tides

BUMP UP the OXYGEN

A Miranda Blight Novel

By

MARY JORDAN NIXON

iUniverse, Inc.
Bloomington

Bump Up the Oxygen
A Miranda Blight Novel

iUniverse books may be ordered through booksellers or by contacting:

iUniverse
1663 Liberty Drive
Bloomington, IN 47403
www.iuniverse.com
1-800-Authors (1-800-288-4677)

ISBN: 978-1-4759-4335-1 (sc)
ISBN:978-1-4759-4336-8 (ebk)

Library of Congress Control Number: 2012914313

Printed in the United States of America

iUniverse rev. date: 08/20/2012

. . . teach us a new terror always
which shall brighten
carefully these things we consider life.
e.e. cummings

Is it not a wonder that the greatest
tragedies,
when given time,
become the most abiding fairytales?
Christine Larson

To Holland, Katriel, Juliet and Annalise,
Little Women who will surely roar

Thank you to Bill, Kristine, Lorraine, Mark, Nancy, Shirley, Saba and a host of people over the years who have guided and encouraged me on my paths of nursing and writing.

Thank you to Mark Nixon for cover art and iUniverse for publication. A special thank you to the remarkable women from the Emanuel Hospital School of Nursing, Portland, Oregon. You have served the world with brilliance and love.

— 1 —

Lordy, the humiliation.

There I was, perched on the end of a hard exam table, buck naked, with a square of blue paper draped across the front of me, a gown of sorts. I'd accidentally torn the tie off the neck, leaving the paper to flop open all the way down my backside, my round white bottom to moon the doorway. The doctor would spot my lunacy right off.

Half an hour before, his medical assistant—trust me, she was not a bonafide nurse—tossed the paper gown at me and ordered me to take off everything. She did not smile or even look me in the eye. When I was a student nurse, I learned to meet and greet my patients with enthusiasm.

"Enthusiasm girls!" our instructor Mrs. Vic had barked. *"Enthusiasm!"*

This half-comatose creature advised me to wait on the exam table and mumbled that the doctor would be right in. Ha! Ten or twelve newborns could have popped out into the man's hands by now and he was not *right in* yet.

The stirrups sat in wait on either side of my thighs. Some kind soul had swaddled them in knitted booties of cherub pink and seraph blue. Despite the whimsy, they gave me the creeps. I dreaded that spread-eagled, raw-to-the-world position I'd have to assume for him. He would notice at once that the dark springy hair below the drape was in direct conflict with the blond curls on my head.

I'd arrived shortly after lunch, wearing a bright mauve and teal dress purchased especially for the dazzle effect. I also wore a pair of Darcy's

1

colorful panties left in the laundry on her last trip home. They rode high on my butt, with mere straps over the hips, a bit bold for me, but I'd planned to slip them on and off so quickly he'd barely have time to catch his breath—so much for impressing a new doctor with my cool good looks and sophistication.

Dr. Tormelli was chief of staff at Loving Memorial Hospital. My neighbor Lupe, a retired lab tech, had recommended him. Lupe said Dr. Tormelli submitted the most slides to detect sexually transmitted diseases, and that should put him high in anyone's book. I wondered how high in someone's book I'd go if I had sex germs crawling all over me.

I shivered from fear and the freezing air-conditioned temperature. Goose bumps paraded through the spider veins on my naked legs; my bottom fought back with nervous prickly heat. Sweat was soon trickling from the various seams in my body. This tiny exam room was claustrophobic. I wanted to jump off the table, fly at the door, fling my naked self into the hallway, roll along the corridor and beg for mercy.

Instead, I slipped from the table, grabbed a tissue from his counter, wiped the perspiration from my bottom and threw the damp paper into the trash. "Don't you think a woman of forty-something is entitled to a bit of back support?" I asked the plastic demonstration pelvis on the counter. I plunked my bare butt onto an upholstered chair and tucked the blue paper square around me as best I could. The pelvis hinted that if I were doing regular abdominal exercises, I would not need back support.

Looking around, I popped my knuckles and wondered what to do next. I'd left my latest doll magazine on the coffee table. I plucked a news magazine from the rack and was shocked to find a story about my tiny community: *Horror and Heartache in Heatherton.* It came with a photo of a striking couple.

The story reported that Tom Grenadier, who'd begun a campaign to become governor, was walking along Precipice Point Road with his wife Margo, a concert pianist, when she slipped and fell brutally to her death on the rocks below. Now the girl's mother was screaming murder. She claimed the man had pushed her daughter over the cliff, and the police were doing nothing to bring him to justice.

In the next sentence, the mother's name leapt out at me. Nora Vickerstromm. I automatically added an *RN* while I read. A Nora Vickerstromm, R.N., had been our chief nursing instructor when I was a student at Loving Memorial. During the first harrowing week of our training, some of the older students snidely called her *The Vichyssoise*, their eyebrows lifted and their teeth bared, as if she were an evil duchess or a menacing dictator, not a cold French soup. I thought it was all silliness—at first.

In her presence, we students addressed her as Mrs. Vic. It did not take long to learn that she did, indeed, spew the darkest evil from her heart, even while she was spraying *enthusiasm, girls!* from her tight red lips.

"Mrs. Vic," I said to the pelvis. "Is this the same woman? She'd be just the one to accuse a grief-stricken husband of murder. Poor fellow. He's quite handsome. I like the cleft in his chin. I think I'll vote for him."

I did not hear Dr. Tormelli enter the room. He was an impressive older gentleman, with tanned skin that would never wrinkle, a pristine white lab coat that would never stain and manicured fingernails that would never break. His blazing red dome was his only flaw, as far as I could tell, and I am a whiz at sizing up men's looks. Buddy had been a dreamboat in high school, even with a bloody nose.

Flushing with embarrassment, I lurched for the exam table. "I'm sorry. I got tired sitting up here." He tried to clasp my elbow in assistance, but my ascent was a clumsy affair. I could not help but wonder how he was sizing up me. *Premenopausal woman with hair too short, too frizzy, too yellow. Frightened green eyes. Doesn't sit where she's told.*

"So how can I help you?" He did not bother to look at my chart, but he did place another square of thin paper across my naked thighs.

"Well, you know—isn't it written down? Why I'm here?"

"Why don't you tell me anyway."

"I . . . it's hard . . . to talk about. You know?"

"I can't help you if we can't discuss your problems."

I sucked in my breath and smoothed the blue paper over my belly. "When I have . . . ah . . . my period . . . I have these cramps. Monster cramps. And they're not just in my abdomen. There's horrible pain down the backs of my legs and behind my knees."

I was beginning to whine, so I forced myself to smile, a trick I'd learned while traveling around with Mama. "Smile no matter what, honey, you have a fine big smile. Just get a grip and smile."

"The cramps started when I was about twenty. They should have settled down after I got pregnant, but nothing changed after Darcy was born—she's grown now—in San Francisco. Anyway, it's debilitating. I'm afraid to get a job."

While I blathered, Dr. Tormelli began his inspection. Eyes, ears, mouth, thyroid gland, heart and lungs. "Just take nice deep breaths," he said.

The breasts were next. Aren't they always?

As I faced him—my green eyes to his black—he lowered my flimsy paper gown to my waist, then took a step backward and stared for dimples and puckers around the nipples, he explained. I prattled on about the seriousness of my condition, about the crotch pain and the horrific diarrhea.

Dr. Tormelli laid me down. I shut my eyes and felt this strange man's hands on my breasts. The fingers were warm. Quick and searching.

"I get so frightened and weak. Sometimes I faint from the pain and all, just black out. A couple of times Buddy had to take me to the emergency room for a shot of Demerol."

"Demerol? Did that help?"

"Yeah. I liked that. It puts you into oblivion, you know?"

"Narcotics can do that." He sounded suspicious, as if he thought I was loaded with dope right now. "My husband Buddy—Dwight is his real name—anyway, we don't live together at the moment so he can't help me if I'm sick."

"Are you divorced?"

"No, but a couple of years ago we bought mobile homes and put them ten miles apart in different parks. It seems to suit us better. Dwight is here in Centerville and mine is in Heatherton, a doublewide. His is single."

"But you're still married?"

"Sort of. We go to Arby's for a roast beef sandwich and those yummy potato cakes on Saturday nights. Then we go back to his place or mine and well . . . you know."

At this point, my feet were planted firmly in the angelic-bootied stirrups. Horace Tormelli's red dome was somewhere between my legs. I could not control my blather, blather, blather, even though the doctor's assistant appeared in her near comatose way, stood at my head and took it all in. If this girl bent forward one inch, her long frizzy hair would brush germs all over my face—Mrs. Vic would have screamed at this girl. "A proper nurse's hair is to be above her collar. Always!" Actually, Mrs. Vic would have grabbed a bandage scissors and chopped off all of that germ-catching hair.

4

"Usually we go to mine," I continued, "because it's cleaner, but Dwight shines his up once in a while. I think when he has some . . . ah . . . friend over on Friday night."

"Another woman?"

"Maybe. I've seen signs. Perfume, phone numbers. Ouch!"

"Does that hurt?"

"Yes. What did you hit in there?"

"You're just tense, dear. You have a very tense little body."

His tone made me feel crawly inside. Finally, he helped me to sit up and then stepped to the sink to wash. The assistant gathered up the incriminating slides and exited.

"It's hard to grow old, isn't it?" he said suddenly, his back turned while I attempted to shove my left breast under the paper drape.

"Excuse me?"

"The aches and pains we accumulate as we grow older can play havoc. And the tensions. Marital problems are troublesome. My wife and I were divorced two years ago. We both developed unusual aches and pains. I know how that feels."

"Are you saying my cramps are due to my living arrangements with Buddy? Or to my age?"

"Could be either . . . or both." He wiped his hands on a paper towel and looked away.

"But I've had cramps for years."

"Pain doesn't always give us an accurate memory. Maybe it's worse since your marital troubles began?"

"I think maybe the cramps are *why* my marital troubles began."

"Well, not to worry. You'll be going through menopause in a few years. That should take care of it. In the meantime, you need to remove the emotion from this problem. Calm yourself down."

"Calm myself down? With cramps and diarrhea? *And the clots?* Did I tell you about the blood clots? Like golf balls, they are. I bleed and I bleed. I'm sure I must be anemic."

"Mrs . . . ." He glanced at my chart to check my name. "Blight. How can I explain this?" He pointed to his scalp, which was blazing. "My forehead is a good example. Baldness can be embarrassing. I've learned to live with it. You need to do the same."

"Learn to live with it? Baldness doesn't stop you from being a doctor, does it? Or from earning a living? I can't take care of myself here. I'm too damn sick!"

Goodness, I scared myself with that outburst. Mrs. Vic once stood me against a wall and told me I was never, ever, to disrespect a doctor—this after a surgeon threw an eight-inch-long needle holder at my head, and I asked him what the hell he thought he was doing.

Dr. Tormelli picked up a prescription pad and suggested birth control pills. I countered that hormones would give me breast cancer. I'd never survive chemotherapy. He suggested stronger, aspirin-type pain pills, but I'd tried a ton of Motrin; it would eat holes in my stomach.

He suggested narcotics; I told him I got goofy on narcotics. "And if I get a job? How can I ever pass the urine—oh, I'm sorry, I'm a terrible patient. I'm just so confused. I don't know how to live with this."

He laid down the prescription pad, stuck his hands in his coat pockets and shrugged. "There's only one other solution. There are medical grounds for taking it all out."

"Taking *what* all out?"

"Your female organs, of course. You don't want any more children, do you?"

"Of course I don't want any more children. At my age? I have a grown daughter. In San Francisco."

"Excellent. We can do something then. But let's get a second opinion."

He was scribbling a name on the pad when I at last said, "It's cancer, isn't it? I knew it. My Grandma Smothers had cervical cancer. It was awful, her dying. They stuck a hunk of radioactive material up her—"

"I don't see any sign of cancer, but we'll pull the ovaries, too. You won't have to worry about any of it." He looked at me with a curious glow, as if he were thinking about what other organs he could yank out. Maybe my brain. "We need to see if you've picked up any nasty organisms from your Saturday nights with—what's his name—Dwight?"

"Dwight. That's right. Dwight Blight. I know . . . it's a terrible name. His mother was tetched, I think. Mostly we call him Buddy."

Dr. Tormentor—for this is how I was coming to think of him—scribbled a prescription, tore it off the pad and handed it to me. "Try this for your cramps for a couple of months. It's not as potent a narcotic as what you've taken. My nurse will make an appointment for you to come in Monday morning for fasting blood work. No food after midnight."

When he turned toward the door, I called him back. "Dr. Tormelli? There's something else."

Clearly, he was eager to exit the room. He rattled the door handle.

"Could all of this uterine trouble make it so that . . . well . . . if you do the surgery . . . could you fix me so I could pee straight?"

Out he went.

– 2 –

I fretted all the way home. How could I have humiliated myself with so much blathering? Why was I so stupid as to scream about his bald head? When I was a child, Grandma Smothers sometimes accused Mama and me of being gypsies, especially when one of us would get her blood to boiling. Mine had been hissing and spewing all afternoon.

Could it be true? Were Mama and I hot-tempered gypsies? Well, yes, Mama had been dark and sultry and roamed the country playing her organ music, so maybe Grandma could make a case. But to have gypsy blood in me was a notion beyond my grasp. I always thought of gypsies as quick of wit, strong of muscle, nimble of fingers. I wasn't a strong or wily person. On Arby's nights, I could not stick my hand down Buddy's pants to snitch even one nickel.

Still, while I pulled my elderly Buick under the carport at the Morning Glory Mobile Home Park, number 48, I wondered if I should return my hair to its original chestnut.

My car was in need of a dye job, too. Her motor scolded and her paint scaled. When she belonged to Buddy, she sped along in quiet superiority, a sleek new 1981 glitzy-blue Buick Regal. Now, eight years later, I still called her the Glitz, but time and a ton of mileage had done a job on her. She needed a glitz refresher.

I've always loved the names of colors—creating them, saying them, hyphenating them so they're a bit different from paint store colors. After I named the car the Glitz, I painted all of my bathroom walls with the same glitzy-blue color. Buddy promptly cussed me out and redid the little room in Navajo white, a color I called bleached-bones-blah.

After I closed the car door, I noticed my neighbor O. Lee Olafson across the lane, sitting on his top porch step. For some reason, the unflappable Mr. Olafson looked terribly forlorn, with his head propped in his long fingers. This was not at all like Mr. Olafson, who was usually larking about, gardening, singing in his shower, playing the piano.

Olafson had thick Scandinavian-red hair and fine freckles that made me think of Sedona-red sand. His wedgewinkle-blue eyes matched a clump of bachelor buttons near his white picket fence. "Are you okay?" I called out, crunching over the gravel drive, smiling to perk him up.

"Oh . . . Miranda." He released his head and motioned me to join him on the top step of his little square porch. I sat down and brushed out the folds of my shimmering, dazzling dress.

Olafson's white T-shirt hung askew over his khaki gardening pants in a haphazard sort of way. He reached down, yanked the head off a daisy, pulled the petals off one by one and tossed them at his feet, which gave me pause to wonder. Until this moment, Mr. Olafson had always been predictable. Every weekday he drove to Centerville before seven, where he worked as an accountant for a medical research firm. He arrived home by four and puttered in his garden until dark.

No one in Morning Glory had much area for planting, but the plot around his mobile home sprouted with color all year long. He'd mapped out all of the necessary plantings, fertilizings and mulchings on a color-coded Marlite scheduling board that hung in the hall to his bedroom. A few months ago, he'd invited me in to see his school-sized whiteboard overarched by track lighting and lit up like a museum painting. Such attention to detail seemed like overkill to me.

Unlike the colorful garden, everything inside Olafson's doublewide was black and white, done in leather, glass and chrome. A piano stood in the living room, an old upright, painted shiny black. Olafson plunked down and played *Country Gardens,* a melody he often played in the evenings. It was based on an old English folk tune with a plucky kind of melody—*dum-dum-da-dum-dum, all-down-the-scale,* followed by a bouncy kind of *la-de-dum.*

Olafson and I had become quite chatty at the mailboxes since that night six months ago. As the days had grown longer and warmer this spring, I'd often listened to his music from my own garden, tapping my

9

toes against my own green grass, which was artificial and never needed fertilizer upgrades.

Two weeks ago, Mr. Olafson bought a doll I'd made to resemble Dr. Semmelweis, a European physician in the 1800s, who'd realized that doctors needed to wash their hands somewhere between cutting up cadavers and birthing babies. I'd read the Semmelweis biography in junior high and been fascinated. Because I'd never tailored a jacket, my twelve-inch rendition turned out to be very country bumpkin; Mr. Olafson had been kind to pay me twenty dollars.

Tonight he was in a totally different mood, throwing daisy petals on the ground while his shirt hung out and he grumbled about his job. Wanting to help, I nudged him with my toe and asked if maybe he had some wine. "Actually, I've just come from the doctor. I'm kind of gloomy myself."

He instantly jerked to attention and focused on me. His eyes darkened in the shadows. "Are you all right? It's nothing serious, I hope." He took my arm and ushered me inside. I was happy to see Dr. Semmelweis perched on the shiny black piano.

We took three more steps to the kitchen, where I slid onto a nook bench done in black-and-white squares. He produced several bottles of wine; I chose Zinfandel, the mildest, because I hadn't had much to eat. He served it in wine goblets with etchings of roses in the glass. He also brought out cheese and crackers on a wooden board that looked as if it had sprung from an elegant shop in Europe. I wondered if Olafson were a Dane. I loved a cheese Danish with my coffee in the morning.

After fussing about, he eased himself onto a chair across from me. I wondered how old Olafson truly was. Over fifty, for sure. He lit a fat yellow candle that sat in the middle of the table, softening the gloom in a dark space carved from surrounding cupboards.

"Tell me," he said, "you just came from the doctor. What's happening? By the way, you look pretty in that dress."

I glanced at my dazzling dress and smiled; someone had finally noticed.

"I hope you're not sick, Miranda," he was saying. "Are you?"

In truth, I did not want to discuss my uterus with Mr. Olafson. I took several gulps of wine to steady my thoughts. "I'm sure it's nothing. Just a little . . . you know . . . female trouble." I popped a cracker into my mouth while Olafson refilled my glass. The wine was as smooth as the memory of Mama's hand on my forehead.

"I had to wait in the exam room forever. It upset me . . . but it's nothing. I'll be fine."

Olafson reached over and patted my hand. He looked at me steadily. It seemed odd that a man who could fall in love with daffodils and outdated music could study a woman with such intensity. I pulled my hand back and took another sip.

"Te . . . tell me about your work." For some reason I'd begun to stutter. "Why are you so up . . . up . . . upset?"

He explained that his job was to manage grant monies in a biomedical research firm, but something shocking was going on. He poured more wine in my rose-etched glass.

I twirled the stem between my fingers. When the wine sloshed a bit, I drank enough to reduce the level to a safe zone. "Go on, I don't shock easily. I was in nurses training for almost three years, did I tell you that?" Thankfully, he did not ask me what had happened or if I'd graduated, the way most people did.

Instead, he spread his forearms across the table and leaned toward me, nudging the candle a bit. "We've gotten involved in a study for this new HIV/AIDS epidemic. The researchers are asking drug users to wear condoms during sex. But drug users aren't exactly reliable—"

"Well, of course not." I braced my forearms on the table the way he did. Our shoulders hunched forward; our wine glasses almost clinked. The candle flickered.

"Exactly! So they've decided *to pay* the addicts to use the condoms!" The unflappable Olafson's face was so close to my eyes that I could not help but notice his Adam's apple wobbling, his chin darting in and out. There were no signs of fatty folds in his neck. No thinning or dulling of his red hair. Maybe he was not as elderly as I'd thought.

He sat up straight and hit the table. It was a good thing my glass was empty. "They decided to gather up all the used condoms and express them off to a high-tech lab for some kind of experimental genetic testing—to make sure the right addict has actually used the assigned condom!"

"No! Is that a joke? Wouldn't that cost a lot of money? I read they're doing some weird testing like that on those Centerville girls, the ones who were raped and murdered by that guy in the red ski mask. Anyway, wouldn't the drug users just buy more drugs with the money they got paid?" I braced my head in my hands and peeked at him through my fingers, as if his long face dangled between jail bars. I grinned at the absurdity of this situation.

But Olafson was serious. His eyes darted, his face moved in. He was determined to convince me how dreadful it all was.

Instead, I chuckled, then belched, then slogged my way into a full-throated laughing jag.

He ignored me. "I'll tell you, Miranda, if I had the nerve, I'd walk in there tomorrow and quit. I'd start my nursery on Stony Ridge. Grow flowers day and night."

"I'm sorry, I can't stop laughing." I wiped my eyes with his cloth napkin. He stared at me in disbelief for a second or two, but then his shoulders relaxed. He sat up straight and chuckled. "I guess you're right. It is funny, isn't it? You know what?"

"No. What?"

"You look cute, giggling like that. You have an enchanting smile. Beautiful green eyes."

Whew! How long had it been since I'd received a compliment? I felt giddy and figured it was time to go home. I tried to stand up but bumped the table. I plopped back down, reached for the wine bottle to pour myself a bit more and knocked over the candle. I quickly righted the burning wax. "Oh my gosh, I could have burned your house to ashes," I said in my wine-soaked voice. "Did you know I almost burned down Loving Memorial Hospital one time?"

Olafson stared in curiosity.

"Yeah, when I was a student on the night shift. Those halls were long, dark and creepy. I answered a light for a patient who wasn't mine. She was trying to ignite a cigarette. People could smoke in the rooms back then, plus they had lights over the doors to signal the nurses—anyway, I helped her. I didn't realize—a few minutes later, I saw flickering in that room and found her on fire!

"Enormous flames shot up over her abdomen. I guess she went into a coma after I lit the cigarette. I couldn't yank the gown free. I finally grabbed an extra blanket from the chair and smashed it over her belly. I rolled myself back and forth like a crazy person. It seemed like forever until that blaze died down. The amazing thing was, the room was full of smoke, but none of the other three patients woke up."

For some reason, I then leaned close to Olafson and confessed my worst sin ever. "I never told anyone that I lit that cigarette. No one saw me."

Mr. Olafson's intriguing blue eyes rolled in amazement. I could see him thinking that one through.

"She wasn't injured," I added quickly, then squared my shoulders and sat up straight. "Just a first degree burn on her chest . . . small . . . the size of a quarter. During report the next morning, I held up that white gown with its ragged black hole and everyone gasped. My friends rushed around and congratulated me for saving a life. Even the head nurse said I'd done a good job.

"But then our instructor Mrs. Vic came by; she was the devil incarnate. 'Well, Miss Smothers,' she said in a very snide tone in front of about twenty dayshift people, 'I never did think you'd make much of a nurse, but you might make a damn good fireman.'

"Ooh, I wanted to smack her in the face."

Having made my confession to O. Lee Olafson, I told myself not to drink another drop. The floor jiggled when I stood and bumped the table again. I grabbed the candle to steady it.

Olafson took my elbow and ushered me out his door, down his two porch steps, along his little path and across to my space. The rhythm of our conversation had stopped, as if it had come to an unexpected rest in the score. The moment felt like a downbeat held indefinitely, the conductor's arms arisen, never to descend again. It seemed forever until I heard frogs croaking down along Dinky Creek. I began searching for the door key somewhere in the bottom of my big floppy shoulder bag.

At my own porch, Mr. Olafson put his hand on my arm and stopped me. "Miranda, is something *wrong* with you?"

Now this was a smack in the face. "I . . . I . . . know. It was stupid. I shouldn't have lit that woman's ciga—"

"No," he said. "I wasn't talking about the cigarette. I meant at the doctor's. You were evasive earlier. Excuse me, I don't mean to pry."

"Oh, it's just cramps. I have these monster menstrual cramps."

"Goodness, I never knew that."

"I didn't want you to. It's so embarrassing."

He took my key, opened the door and stood back for me. "Can the doctor help you?"

"Doctor Tormentor? I don't think so. Don't worry about it, okay? I wanted to find a job, but it's too humiliating. Not that it matters. Buddy takes care of me. I can stay home and make dolls." Across the threshold, I turned and blocked the doorway. I did not want Olafson following me in. "Well, thanks for the drink. I am sorry I laughed at your predicament."

He flicked a moth from my hair. "It's been nice talking with you, Miranda. Sleep well." He turned and loped back to number 47.

In my inebriated state, I headed for the bathroom as soon as I closed and locked the door. I steadied myself against the couch when I passed behind it. It was six-foot long, done up in cream and gold tweed, creating an artificial hallway to the bedrooms. I made a peanut butter and jelly sandwich and patted each of my dolls while wandering about. I'd created a whole slew of dolls representing medical people. Their various bits and pieces littered my house. While I stumbled along, guilt hit me hard. I'd never told another soul that I'd lit that cigarette. I'd planned on taking that secret to my grave.

Giving up on the evening, I did my bathroom routine, got into my floral nightgown and collapsed into bed. My guilt remained, but after a while, I heard *dum-dum-de-dum-dum, all-down-the-scale* from across the lane.

Wasn't that the most amazing thing?

O. Lee Olafson was playing me to sleep.

— 3 —

My husband Buddy Blight owned a tombstone business just outside Centerville. In addition to ordering the granite and carving the proper names and dates, he partially owned and supervised the Eternal Radiance Cemetery. When he first began chiseling granite for dead people, his occupation gave me the creeps. But I'd become used to it over the years.

Despite the doctor's dire warnings, I was with Buddy on Saturday evening, him with Horsey Sauce on his roast beef and me with Arby's Sauce and a small Diet Pepsi. Buddy winked at me while he slurped a giant concoction of sodas through his straw. I smiled back and stared at him. Even though we lived apart, I still loved Buddy's craggy dimples and gun-smoke eyes with the thick lashes. I believed his cheekbones were American Indian, although his mother Beulah denied it. At any rate, his smile always promised a lot of fun. The more we slurped, the more we looked at each other. I wondered what he was thinking.

Probably sex, by the way he began swallowing those little square ice cubes whole, shoving himself out of the booth, throwing away the trash, jingling his keys in front of my nose. "Let's go, babe. We'll use my place. The bed is better." Buddy rubbed a painful spot along his spine, just over his rump.

"Can't we go to mine? I'm always more comfortable with my own things."

"And have my tires slashed?"

"Why would your tires be slashed?"

"Let's face it, Randy. Your mobile home park is not attracting the best people."

"What . . . a few black people? And some who speak Spanish? That doesn't mean they're going to slash your tires. What's wrong with you?"

"Nothing's wrong except I live in a classier place. With no dolls. And no queer men standing in their little plots of petunias, spying on everything their neighbors do."

"*Olafson?* You're going after sweet Mr. Olafson now?" I debated walking away and then thought better of it. My period would descend in a few days and I was feeling antsy. I really needed an hour or two with Buddy. So off we went.

My Buick had trouble keeping up with his shiny black Ford pickup, racing to the upscale Sunny Glen Mobile Home Park in Centerville. His singlewide was small but very smart, with impressive tile, mahogany and strategically placed mirrors. Inside, he stood back and surveyed me, then snapped his thumb and index finger against the top of my head. "What's going on with your hair? You look like a popcorn ball, all this curly stuff on top. Or a Q-tip head."

"Don't worry. It'll grow." I brushed his hand away and scowled at him. "You're not exactly getting me in the mood here."

"Okay, let's fix that." He leaned in, kissed me and reached for my bra. Popcorn balls and Q-tips were about as much foreplay as I was going to get. On the way to the bed, I remembered Dr. Tormentor's warnings about gonorrhea and worse.

"Honey, I have a little thing in my purse somewhere." After a disorganized search, I pulled a condom from my bag, a tan shoulder bag decorated with a red and gold cable car. Darcy had sent it from San Francisco. The bag, not the condom.

"Could you . . . well . . . wear one of these? Maybe I can make it fun."

"What the hell? You don't trust me now? There's nothing wrong with me unless you gave it to me. That's why I do it with you. So I don't have to wear one of those damn things. And you sure as shootin' won't get pregnant again—you could barely do it the first time."

Oh, he could be mean, dastardly mean. Buddy knew I'd always longed for another baby, a hope I'd eventually give up on. But at this moment, when he stood before me in his white Hanes underwear, with his jock muscles bulging from the grave digging—well, what could I do? I gave in and had sex. This was our habit—a nasty insult smoothed over by the warm blessing of sex.

Before he fell asleep, he mumbled something about me moving back in with him if I could not trust him living apart. It was a bluff. Buddy did not want me and my nursy dolls—his spiteful name for them—sprawled over his suede sofa any more than we wanted to be sprawling there.

While he snored, I lay on my back and stared at the ceiling. He turned abruptly and snuggled close. I rubbed his forehead as if we did this every night. "Honey, do you remember Mrs. Vic?

"Buddy? Can you talk to me a little? Do you remember Mrs. Vic?"

"Hmm?"

"Mrs. Vic. Remember? From Loving Memorial?"

"What?" He sat up quickly and stared at me. "Mrs. Vic? What about her? What have you heard about that woman?"

"Nothing. Why are you so excited?"

He scratched his head. "You woke me out of a sound sleep. What about her?"

"Is she the one whose daughter fell off the cliff? Did you make a headstone for her?"

"Why?"

"I was reading about it in a magazine. Is she the one?"

"How the hell do I know?" Buddy belched and grabbed a bottle of Tums from the nightstand, stuffed a fistful of tablets in his mouth and made a face chewing. "Why can't you ever just have sex and go to sleep? All the time it's this yakking."

"It's important to me, Buddy. Did you bury Mrs. Vic's daughter?"

"I don't know. Maybe she's in the mausoleum. Damn, I never had to get up and pee like a woman in the middle of the night." He cussed all ten steps to the bathroom. The poor fellow. He had no experience in growing older, as I did. The gray hair, the acid reflux, the nighttime bathroom urges. They'd all hit him so suddenly. The toilet flushed and he shuffled out, still mumbling. He flopped down beside me and turned away.

I slipped from his bed and began to dress.

"What are you doing?" he asked. "Are you going home?"

"Yeah, you're too cranky and you've got heartburn."

"Well good grief, it's the middle of the night."

"It's only eleven o'clock. And why didn't you tell me?"

"Tell you what, for Pete's sake?"

"About Mrs. Vic. Her daughter. Getting killed and being put in Eternal Radiance."

"Oh hell, Miranda, aren't you ever going to be finished with that part of your life? You know talking about Mrs. Vic will only upset you."

"What upsets me is our entire ludicrous situation. This is just plain bizarre, the way we end this in the middle of the night. Living apart is more insane. I can't even remember why we separated in the first place." I hooked my bra and yanked my sweater over my chest. "But now that I have my own home, that's where I'm going."

"Fine. Leave. Go home to your nursy dolls and your sappy neighbors. That won't last long. In the end, you always get hungry for what I've got."

"Ha!"

"*Ha!* back at you. And lock the door on your way out. Watch your tires!"

I slammed his door, roared my engine and drove too fast on my way north. I scanned the hood for steam and overheating. The Glitz burped the entire route but we made it just fine, past the Centerville city limits, over the Dinky Creek Bridge and on into Heatherton. Number 48 never looked better or safer. I surveyed my roomy doublewide, with my relaxing gold tones in the living room, my whiff-of-coffee-brown Barcalounger and gossamer-wings carpet, worn but clean. The kitchen linoleum swirled in orange and vanilla; it reminded me of an old-fashioned 50-50 ice cream bar. Everything was safe and yummy, as it should be. I reminded the dolls that they were proper nurses, not Buddy's nasty nursy dolls.

One of my first creations was Clara Barton, who'd founded the American Red Cross in 1881. The real Clara had been a courageous woman during the Civil War, not a nurse, but one who'd cared for the wounded with wild derring-do.

My Clara was made of porcelain, which I'd painted and then glazed at a Centerville doll shop. She stood twelve inches tall and was dressed in your-royal-highness-blue. She wore ruffled pantaloons and a starched apron of maiden-white, with a red cross appliquéd on the bib. She strode about in Mary Poppins' shoes with tiny mother of pearl buttons at the ankles. Clara's chocolate-cherry hair was glued to her head, parted down the middle and pulled up into ringlets over either ear. Her face was not delicate or beautiful. Rather, her broad dark eyes, heavy cheekbones and thin smile showed strength and determination far beyond anything I could imagine. I so admired her.

Most of my dolls were medical people. After Clara, I'd fashioned Florence Nightingale, who never needed an introduction, and then the Curies, Madame Marie and Pierre in their happy days, before horses and radium did them in.

I'd also created various versions of Sue Barton, a fictitious nurse created by Helen Dore Boylston, who'd written seven books until the dedicated Sue Barton had accomplished almost everything a skilled nurse could hope to accomplish, including marriage to the handsome Bill Barry, M.D. When I was in junior high, the Sue Barton books had strongly motivated me to become a nurse. I'd flubbed up on that nursing bit a few years later, but now I'd successfully created all seven stages of Sue Barton's lofty career in doll fashion.

After reassuring my friends of their worth, I moved on to a basket where my newest creations lay; they were *Little Women* replicas, who were not medical people at all, but Poor Beth had been ill and the others had taken such good care of her. I loved those March girls. I'd even cut off Jo's lovely chestnut curls. To make up for it, I was creating a gown of exquisite red silk, with a slim skirt for the modern, independent Jo. I'd cut my hair as short as hers, but I was not independent and certainly not exquisite.

No indeed. I was a Q-tip head.

After I finally fell asleep, I experienced a nightmare almost too gross to tell. Mrs. Vic stood tall before me, draped in a heavy, priestly black robe with a large metallic cross adorning her bosom. She smirked, growled and took a step toward me.

I tried to slither and scream, but I lay paralyzed on an iron bed in a black-walled hospital, waiting for my female parts to be yanked out. I was desperate to go home, to keep all of my bits and pieces. But my mouth refused to open and my arms and legs would not move.

Before she reached me, she herself was sucked into a hot, steaming hospital laundry, into the cauldrons and Mangle irons; she floated helplessly along the assembly line until she emerged bleached, ironed and starched into a white uniform, white stockings, white shoes, a batwing white cap over her drizzly white hair, the Celtic cross still on her chest. Mrs. Vic stood over me like an albino ghoul inside my black cranium, her watery eyes tattooed with pink rims.

As soon as she regained her momentum, she leapt from the laundry and came at me with an enormous stainless steel tray packed with tiny paper medicine cups, each brimming with pills and syrups, all unlabeled, with no colored tags noting each patient's name, room number or proper medication. I was aghast when I realized she was going to force someone else's deadly concoction down my throat.

And yet, I could not move, scream or fight back.

The tray of meds faded but the metal cross on her chest did not. That dearest symbol of Christianity suddenly became a huge, multi-armed thermometer, its longest leg bearing a rectal tip. I knew instantly where she was going to insert that—

I awoke trembling and gagging. I stumbled from my bed and flipped on lights while I traveled into the bathroom. Sleep would be impossible now. I made myself a cup of tea and inched backward into the protection of the Barcalounger. I picked up a doll dress on the table and tried to rethread a needle. It was no use.

I wondered what on earth God could be thinking of me. I longed for the 8:30 a.m. service at the Reverend Bob's Community Church. I needed to ask forgiveness for the desecration of my dream. Those images had come from my own brain. I'd transformed a holy cross into a huge and disgusting rectal thermometer.

Lordy, I was a broken mess of a soul.

Surprisingly, the world was still revolving when I left my house in the morning. I put Clara Barton on the Glitz's front seat; Clara was the best of all my medical people to chatter with. She seldom interrupted.

While I drove, I relished the beauty woven into my village of Heatherton. The rising sun transformed the grasses, shrubs and trees into diagonal streaks of green, as many shades of green as in a fanned-out color sample book; muted-purple pavements waited for traffic patiently, like liturgical banners waiting for a bit of spirit breeze.

Long ago, a set of twins named Salt and Pepper created the twin burgs of Heatherton and Centerville. One twin was blond, the other dark, which must be why their mother plunked such absurd names on them. Legend says the two feuded over everything but could not stand to be separated for even one day.

Salt Heatherton founded Centerville at the exact center of the universe, so the natives bragged. There was no world beyond.

The city stood upright on a totally logical grid across the valley floor. All the Avenues ran east and west, and all the Streets crossed north and south, First through 64th in both directions. To the west, rose gentle hills that long ago sprouted a lovely pine forest. Now the area was an enormous community of ranch-style houses. Buddy and I lived there while Darcy was growing up, at a time when I believed my life would spread before me in contentment like the amber waves of endless grain we sang about in school patriotism class.

Pepper Heatherton purchased all the turf north of Dinky Creek, primarily hilly, waving land that led up to the Stony Ridge Mountains, which were actually tall hills with animal-like rock formations: rhinoceros heads, elephant rumps, panda bear paws. Contorted and scraggly trees struggled into existence here and there. Trickles of shiny water drooled from mouths and nostrils in the stone during any significant rain.

Heatherton lay at the base of this zoological frolic, and Pepper's streets ran in a totally disorganized fashion. The east-west routes generally followed the contour of Dinky Creek, but the cross streets tangled like sewing threads dropped on the floor. They were primarily named after flavorings—Rosemary, Vanilla, Sage, Curry and my street, Lavender Lane.

The flavors blended here and there or ended abruptly as Route 71 wound down into town from Stony Ridge. The locals called this long, treacherous highway Panic Place. They'd seen many a deadly crash at its twists and turns. When Panic Place entered Heatherton, it celebrated its notoriety by creating a raucous-flavored intersection, a hefty brew with Bourbon Boulevard, Whiskey Avenue and Scotch Street.

The Reverend Bob's church sat smack against this intersection. For about a century, the church people fought with the city people to change those names. The churchgoers finally had to give up. Cleverly, they hired a bagpipe band, held a concert on the green and argued that the street names helped them remember and honor the old country.

After trying out all the churches in Heatherton, I'd written my name on the attendance card at the Reverend Bob's and was planning a three-bean salad for his congregation's Fourth of July picnic.

The Reverend Bob was a good-looking fellow, close to my age. When the pulpit light beamed on his head, his light brown curls shone like a halo. His hands were large and he knew how to use them. During the sermon, he spoke about God's love and care for us—not so much about

God expecting us to go forth and save the world. Just the look of him quelled my nightmare and took the edge off my guilt.

But on the drive home, I had a moment's relapse. I thought about Buddy. Obviously, our dual-trailer-park marriage was not working out as well as I'd imagined. Romance could not bounce back simply by putting space between Buddy and all my sewing rigmarole. Instead, I should probably drop by a church more often, maybe St. Mary's, with its candles to light and benches to kneel on. I needed divine intervention to help me love my husband unconditionally and completely. I'd sworn an oath, after all.

"But then, who wrote those oaths?" I asked Clara Barton.

"Probably a host of elderly monks walled off in distant Alpine cloisters," she answered.

"So what would those men know about male-female relationships anyway? Shoot!"

Ready to kick away my gloom, we began singing. *Amazing grace, how sweet the sound* . . . While the sun moved from a glancing blow to a direct hit on the Glitz, I listened to Clara harmonizing perfectly. God bless her. Clara Barton, founder of the American Red Cross, was an essential voice in my choir.

At that time, I could not imagine just how essential Clara Barton would prove to be.

— 4 —

I am no good at fasting.

If I were in prison, I'd never make it on a hunger strike. One hour in—before we could even achieve a good heartrending photo op—I'd be clanging on my bars, begging for a metal tray of lardy grub. Some time ago, a doctor diagnosed me with hypoglycemia. Low blood sugar. He said I should never, ever, skip meals.

On Monday, I arose at the crack of dawn to be the first person in line for my fasting blood work. The laboratory was not crowded and I was called fairly soon. There was the usual nightmare of urine sample cups and tubes of blood, but I made a firm resolve to pee straight and stifle my screams. I soon left with a cotton ball squeezed over the puncture hole in my arm.

Various medical offices, labs and Loving Memorial Hospital had all been jammed into the south end of Centerville. In the 1930s, a family named Loving lost their only child to polio. The story always broke my heart. A brand new hospital emerged in the child's memory, however, and all the townsfolk agreed that Loving was an excellent name for a place of healing.

Driving from the lab parking lot, I continued to squeeze my arm over the cotton ball and hold my elbow above my heart. While I thought of the lost child, such doom and gloom descended upon me that I paid no attention to where I was. I'd once lived nearby, but nothing looked familiar. I could not find the North-South Highway to Heatherton.

Sitting at a traffic light, I noticed a dreary, three-story structure on the corner that looked like something from a Grimm's fairytale. The once-painted house was lost in a tangle of shrubs and vines; overgrown bushes completely hid the entrance. With the exception of a long wooden ramp made from fresh lumber, the place looked familiar, but I could not think why.

Still waiting, I wondered how soon I could obtain the results of my lab tests. My slides were probably crawling with sex germs. I asked Clara Barton if she'd worried about pools of blood spilling across Civil War battlefields. Might they contain gonorrhea and syphilis? Did she even know about such things? She said she knew but had neither time nor inclination to worry. No, of course not.

Eventually, I moved on. While searching for the large green interstate sign, it came to me. "That was Mrs. Vic's old house! I'm sure it was. I don't suppose she lives there now. She's probably up in the snooty hills with the Grenadier clan. Trust me, Clara, that woman's getting herself into a big mess if she's shouting murder at such a powerful family."

Lost in chatter, I had to brake suddenly at the railroad tracks; the dinger was dinging and the gate was dropping down. We sat and waited for a long train of dusty orange boxcars to chug two blocks forward, one block back, on and on. Groaning, I realized my arm was still on high. I was driving one-handed—of all the stupid—

I brought my arm in front of me and cautiously removed the wad of cotton still clenched tightly. There was no gushing of blood, but I bent over the puncture wound and shuddered at the growing purple discoloration.

Just then, the driver behind me honked his obnoxious horn. I looked up and saw that the crossing gates had already lifted. I jumped, terrified that he might pull out a gun and shoot me in the head. We'd had two drive-by shootings in Centerville lately. My foot hit the gas.

Unable to spot the interstate sign, I decided to take surface streets to Heatherton. The route was extremely poky, considering traffic lights, ambulances, pedestrians and children at school crossings, but I had nowhere else to go. While the Glitz burped along, I worried that I did not need modern highways with six lanes and cloverleafs to whisk me off to Nowhere.

Eventually, I came to the Pine Woods Mall, where three stalwart virgin pines grew proudly at the entrance. A weathered buckboard stood artistically under their branches. Several years earlier, I'd found work as a receptionist for the Centerville Chamber of Commerce. Part of my job was to explain the perfect street grid to tourists and direct them to the photo opportunity in front of the dazzling mall. But during the entire three months, not one tourist was interested. I'd never advised even one parent about the possibility of a splendid Kodak moment. When the civic leaders handed me a pink slip, I was off the hook.

That's about the time my father-in-law also ran out of luck. Blight Merchandise had carried on a booming downtown business before the Pine Woods Mall sucked up all the shoppers; but with the mall's arrival, Mr. Blight closed the downtown store and graciously retired.

His wife Beulah, on the other hand, sprouted wings. First, she opened the Red Blossom Mall in Heatherton and inserted a fancy little boutique. Then she branched out with a second shop in the Pine Woods Mall in Centerville. Before we knew it, she got herself named Mall Manager for the entire Pine Woods enterprise. Beulah Blight was a force to be reckoned with, hustling around on her Mall Manager's electric cart. You could see her coming from most any direction, garbed in her parrot-colored outfits, platinum pageboy and dangling wooden earrings from Brazil.

Despite my mother-in-law's existence, I decided to run in, exchange some shoes for Darcy and maybe find myself a lifesaving breakfast in the food court.

Whoever designed the mall parking garage did not have Salt Heatherton's sense of the compass. This structure was a maze of seesaw ramps and pillars that ran up and down like some crazy card maze your Uncle Bud would erect. Each section sported a fruit type: apricots, grapes, bananas. If you parked your car in strawberry, you were supposed to remember the color red. I tried it a few times, but somehow—despite my fetish for color names—I always forgot my fruit. Today, I parked way up on the rooftop and the light of day. Here the spaces ran at an angle, with no pillars to watch out for, no produce to remember.

Because Darcy's favorite shoe store was on the bottom level, I had to sneak down with great care. Luckily, it was close to the elevator. By hugging walls and charging entrances, I was able to reach the shop, exchange the shoes and pop back into the glass-enclosed lift without running into Beulah.

But while the elevator swooshed me up to the third level, my fasting blood sugar plummeted. I hurried to the food court with shaking knees, a nauseated gut and a woozy head. Sadly, I could find no pancakes, eggs, waffles or biscuits in the food court. And before I could even buy a pretzel or an Orange Julius, here she came, careening around the corner in her spiffy little cart. Spotting me, she cut off my escape.

"Miranda! I had no idea you ever shopped here!" She stopped a little beyond me, then spun backwards to meet me face to face. Lined us up perfectly.

"Sometimes," I said awkwardly. "I like the shoe store and . . . and breakfast. I'm hungry. I'm hypoglycem—"

"*Hungry?*" she snapped loudly. "At ten in the morning? I suppose you're on your period again. Goofy with the drugs." Beulah's facial bones were bold and primitive. I often imagined her with a long ivory spear sticking into one nostril and jabbing out the other. Her voice could pierce the far reaches of a jungle, all the way to Macy's.

Beulah grabbed the shoe bag, poked her nose inside and complained that she hadn't heard a word from her granddaughter in months, even though I knew Darcy had sent her a birthday card a few weeks earlier. Before I could argue, the official pager on her waistband began to buzz. Without saying goodbye, the Mall Manager switched on her cart, maneuvered her little wheels into *GO* and whizzed away.

Forgetting food, I hurried back to Clara, drove down all the zigzag ramps and then sped north until I crossed the bridge at Dinky Creek and came into Heatherton, where all the streets went catawampus and all the names were totally zany. I drove up to Exotic Eggs and instantly smelled bacon, strong coffee and the remains of hash browns from the breakfast crowd. I captured a fine table by the window and ordered a three-egg omelet covered with a rich béarnaise sauce. I figured I'd earned it.

The view of the valley was excellent. I spotted the university on the far side of Centerville. Squinting, I could make out the library tower, a good place to research medical people for my doll collection. Switching views, I located my street but could not find number 48 at the end of Lavender Lane. Too many trees dug into the Dinky Creek riverbed, which ran like a properly raging river in winter but whittled itself into a spineless brooklet during summer.

Dinky was a good name for me as well, I thought, savoring the extreme cholesterol omelet. Except for memories, there was nothing much to discuss with the dolls. The ceramic ladies were all worn out from hearing about my failed attempts to be a nurse, a wife, or even a health-care manager of my own body, what with my blood sugar fiascos and my monster cramps every month.

Driving home, I continued to see blood, even Buddy's nosebleed in study hall when he'd gushed all over his geometry paper. Clara wondered what practical advice I'd offered the hemorrhaging chap, but I'd only giggled while he hauled himself down the aisle, head up, nose pinched, red blood splattering on his white buck shoes. The study hall teacher had snapped at me. "Well, Miss Smothers, if he hemorrhages to death, I suppose you'll have hysterics!"

I did not laugh at Buddy for long. After one date with the football hero, I glommed onto the light in Dwight Blight's eyes. Yessiree. Clara had never married and did not think much of my confused relationship with Buddy Blight. Her serious countenance made me remember Dr. Tormentor's warning. I wondered if Buddy was dangerously full of nasty germs. I wondered if we should continue eating Arby's potato cakes together on Saturday nights.

I wondered if, honestly, I could give up the sex.

— 5 —

"Once when Mama and I were on the Greyhound, a gigantic boulder rolled down a cliff and almost plunged us into the abyss." I said this to Mr. Olafson while we drove up the Panic Place highway. I was trying to give a hint about speed. "I've been terrified of going over cliffs ever since."

Olafson did not slow down.

Panic Place was an apt name for Route 71. If I'd had an ounce of sense, or maybe just a teeny inkling of what was to come in the next weeks, I would have paid attention to every stone, tree, twist and turn when my friendly neighbor invited me to look over his property on Stony Ridge. Enormous boulders lay in wait far below; the flimsy guardrail on that precarious two-lane road gave me no comfort at all.

We came to a four-way stop far up the hill. "This is the intersection with Precipice Point Road," he said. "Out that way is where that young woman fell off the cliff. The mother thinks her son-in-law may have pushed her daughter over the edge."

My stomach curled over itself like burning paper. I envisioned that lovely pianist flinging headlong into those stones, smashing herself to bits. I also thought of Mrs. Vic, which upset me in other ways.

I quickly changed the subject and told Olafson about the childhood game I'd played whenever Mama and I had found a new town. "All the buildings came two by two, like Noah's Ark. A Chevron on the way in, a Texaco on the way out. The Piggly Wiggly here, the A&P there. Now

28

we have the Red Blossom Mall on our end of Heatherton and the Dinky Creek Splurge near Scotch and Bourbon. Nothing's changed."

I did not tell him, however, that I was a child on high alert for danger, maybe neurotically so. I always figured there'd be a marauding band of teenagers at one end of town and a second gang of menacing thugs at the other.

Instead, I poked fun at Beulah Blight and the fiasco at the grand opening of her Red Blossom Mall. "The painter left the L off the BLOSSOM sign. People instantly called it Beulah's Red Bosom Mall. They've ridiculed her ever since. And that pink color? She told us to imagine elegant clusters of Moroccan blossoms. Instead, Buddy calls it titty-pink. I go for nipple-parfait."

Olafson let out a huge roar. I kept my eyes from the gorge and continued talking. I told him that my father married my mother before being shipped overseas, but he was killed in the war. He was brought home in a box, which somehow seemed appropriate, because I was born in a box.

"What?" Olafson said.

"Yeah, Mama went out walking in the woods, got caught in a thunderstorm, sprained her ankle and plunged herself into labor. She spotted an empty packing crate on the side of the road, crawled in and gave birth to me. Grandma was at the Ladies' Aide meeting and Grandpa was with the Hog Society. They found us on their way home, sitting in the weeds at the edge of the forest. Bonding."

Olafson's eyes were open wide. "Your mom was something else."

"After that, we moved every year. She played the church organ as Evelyn Smothers by day and the piano bars as Evie Lyn Bedlo by night. We usually managed to stay in one place long enough for me to pass another grade in school. But by May, the church people would figure out the bar connection. There'd be a terrible ruckus and we'd come hightailing it back to Grandpa's for the summer. In the fall, we'd take off and do it all over again."

In response, Olafson told me that his mom was a goofy but practical Norwegian lady. All the men in the family had been named Ole Olafson. She added Lee to his name and registered him in school as plain Lee Olafson.

"All the kids teased me anyway, so I figured I might as well use O. Lee Olafson. Actually, I like Ole better."

I said *Ole* and imitated his Norwegian lilt. I liked the way the word puckered in my mouth. By the time we conquered that mountain road, Ole Olafson no longer seemed so elderly to me, but he was still an odd duck.

About fifteen miles farther, Ole turned the car into a tight stand of evergreens where a *No Trespassing* sign hung askew on a ramshackle bridge. After a few good bumps, the lane opened onto a meadow alive with wild flowers. From where we parked, the scene looked like artwork from France, with dabs of cadmium yellow, viridian green, vermilion red. I could imagine a maiden in ankle-length muslin taking a turn among the field of wildflowers, a Monet parasol over her shoulder.

The sky was cloudless and vivaciously blue. A yellow and tan butterfly settled onto Ole's shoulder. Its colors perfectly matched the plaid in his shirt. The insect paused and then fluttered to the far side of the clearing, where a weeping willow's long branches shimmered and bent low, as if the tree were eager to double dip the water supply.

Ole bent down, scratched his fingers through the dirt and came up with a handful of dark soil. "An eon or two ago there must have been a lake here. Maybe marshes. This soil is rich, a banquet for plants. I searched far and wide for this spot."

We ate lunch at a two-seat picnic table he unloaded from the back of his station wagon. The food was yummy: potato salad, homegrown tomatoes, orange muffins. He'd even brought his rose-etched wine goblets. While we ate, I decided it was good for a lone man named Ole Olafson to occupy himself so happily with his horticultural hobby. Evidently, flowers provided the only color in his life.

After lunch, he showed me where every greenhouse would be situated; I wondered how many Marlite scheduling boards would be required to organize it all. "Hey!" I blurted out. "Maybe I could come up here and be your salesperson. You'll need a little shop to sell your plants from."

"You're hired," he said, pumping my hand vigorously. "You could sell your dolls from here."

"Hmm, with little red wagons so shoppers could haul their plants around. We could call it Blossoms and Dolls."

Ole chuckled. "Come with me. I have one more surprise for you." We entered a woodsy area and plowed through a lot of scratchy underbrush. Fortunately, I was wearing blue jeans and a red San Francisco sweatshirt—also a gift from Darcy. I hoped there was no poison oak lurking about. You can't imagine how I could break out from head to toe with poison oak. Lordy, the cortisone cream I'd already gone through.

Gradually, the taller trees thinned a bit. A couple more steps and we entered a clearing. A gray, beaten-down cabin stood maybe fifteen feet away. "This looks like the witch's house," I whispered. "The one who tried to eat up Hansel and Gretel."

"Yes," Ole answered softly. "I don't think even a witch would want to live in this tangle now. It must have been a prospector's cabin. You could find minerals along the creek beds in these hills a hundred years ago. Even a little gold."

"Are we going in?"

"Do you want to?"

"I don't know. Is it safe?"

"I think so. Just watch where you step. A lot of the floor is rotted through."

I climbed carefully onto the porch and tested every board before putting weight on it. The door was off the hinges. Ole swatted cobwebs from the entrance. The place was too dark to see in and too musty to breathe in, but we entered anyway. In the far corner, the roof had caved in and the rain had rotted the wall and floorboards. Huge pine branches had scratched through the opening, wiping out any trace of daylight.

After my eyes adjusted, I saw a stone fireplace that stretched from the uneven floor to the drooping roofline. I reached out and touched its heavy stones, blackened with soot and traced with green moss. "Could you build a new cottage right around this fireplace? It could be the shop with the red wagons and the blossoms. Maybe titty-pink and nipple-parfait."

Ole was too busy looking up and down to laugh at my humor. He poked his head under the blackened chimney, reappeared and brushed soot off his hands. "I had no idea the cabin was here when I bought the land. I can't save the wood, but this fireplace was built to last." He patted the stones the way I had but stopped when something wobbled. "Here's one that's loose. It jiggles."

I poked my nose near the fireplace while he tugged, until the rock slid into his hands. He looked at it and gave a low whistle, then bent a little to peer inside the opening. I stood on tiptoes and tried to see over his shoulder. "Looks like there's a hidey-hole in here," he said.

"You mean hidden treasure? Did we find a secret compartment? Maybe the Salt and Pepper twins hid a stash of money up here."

Ole straightened up and nudged me back a few steps. "Be careful. The Salt and Pepper twins may have left nothing but recluse spiders. I'm not reaching my hand into that hole to find out."

"I bet something's in there. Maybe gold. Where did the twins get all their money from anyway? Do you have a flashlight in your car?"

"I think so, wait here." As soon as he was gone, I tried to peek in the hole, but it was far too deep and black. I sneezed from the dust and pulled a cobweb from my hair. I thought about our distance from medical care, should something come hissing at my ankles, nipping at my fingers or crashing down on my head. Dashing outside, I looked for a long stick to poke in that hole.

The world was very silent with Ole gone. The woods were as much a coffin as the cabin, the air as quiet as six feet under, the aroma as heavy as a shroud. Occasionally, a bit of breeze ruffled one tree branch or a bird chirped in the distance. I had no idea where actual danger lurked. One dark bush was covered with green berries, another with red. Ripe or not, I figured they were all poisonous.

By this time, I needed to pee. I blazed my way into a clump of trees, found a barky stump to squat against and went at it, tugging at my jeans to keep them free of the wayward stream. Once, when Mama and I had an old car and stopped to take a break, I looked up from my tree and saw a strange man peeing behind his tree. After that, I was always on my guard for men in the forest. I figured there'd be one sneaky-eyed lowlife here, another dangerous character over yonder.

While I zipped up, I listened to the world around me. I could not hear any cars out on the road, which must not be far—or was it? Was I somehow turned around? Why was it so quiet?

At the cabin, I found a small branch on the ground, broke off its extra twigs and admired it as a good poking stick. Unwilling to reenter that eerie place alone, I plunked down on a log to wait and held the stick before me like a weapon.

Spiders, poisonous vegetation, men behind trees.

Where was he? *Who* was he, for that matter. I really knew nothing about Ole Lee Olafson. What if it were all a cover? Ole's goofiness? His oddness? His Norwegian-ness? You heard about neighbors like that.

Salt-of-the-earth types who snuck out at night to rape, bludgeon and murder—what on earth was I doing here?

Through an opening in the trees, I spotted a distant hill with the blue sky behind it. Whenever I would become frightened on my travels with Mama, she'd looked for the highest place around. If there were no hills, a silo or weathervane would do. She'd quote a Bible verse from the Psalms. "I will lift up mine eyes unto the hills, from whence cometh my help. My help is in the name of the Lord."

"Are you okay?" Ole pushed his way from the bushes and stared at me huddled on my log, brandishing my flimsy spear to fend off evildoers.

I glanced up at this man's broad, sweet smile. My imagination had gone totally amok. "Yes, I'm fine. I found a good poking stick." I handed over my weapon and smiled as best I could.

"You're a better scavenger than I am. I couldn't find the flashlight anywhere. Sorry." Inside, Ole went to work with the poker. I could hear it hitting the sides and bottom of the hole, maybe ten inches down. "There's a good-sized compartment here, but I don't think there's anything in it." He brought out the stick and brushed his hands. "Probably never was."

"Shoot. We should have found something in there."

Ole replaced the stone, then took out a pocketknife and marked it with an X. "Rich soil is the treasure up here, Miranda," he said, helping me to the doorway.

"I'm going to the library and read up on the Salt and Pepper twins anyway."

"Come on. There's one more thing to show you."

Outside, Ole grabbed my hand and led me around back, near where the roof had caved in. He pushed aside a tangle of thorny vines until we spotted the oddest collection of junk. It was something like an old potbellied stove with rusted pipes sticking out of it every which way, many others broken on the ground—a heap of iron oxide that smelled a bit like blood.

"What is this?" I asked, shivering.

Ole laughed. "It's an old still. We can put that thing back together and make our own moonshine up here."

"Do you know how to make moonshine, Ole?"

"No, but it might be fun to learn."

After a few minutes of kicking debris with our sneakers, we turned and made our way back toward the car. When we reached the Reliant, he leaned against the door and looked at me for a long time. I brushed at my sweatshirt and batted at my hair.

"I like watching you, Miranda," he said

"What?"

"I said I like watching you. You remind me of that butterfly we saw earlier. Sometimes you flit around . . . a certain turn of your head . . . you're quite luminous. Your light shines through."

"Wow, I think I need a soda pop." I dove into the cooler and came up with a Sprite. "Want one?"

"Are you going to divorce Buddy sometime?" He continued to lean against his car, hands in his khaki pockets.

I pulled the aluminum tab harder than I needed to. "I don't know. I haven't thought about it. What difference does it make?"

"How are you going to move on with your life?"

"What life? I just have my doll hobby. Darcy's never home."

"Yes, but you're very clever . . . titty-pink and nipple-parfait." He chuckled and kicked the ground.

"I was just being silly."

"Miranda, don't you have a clue as to how talented you are? Doesn't it ever occur to you that you could be doing something with yourself? What kind of control does this Bud character have over you? Has he wiped out your brain and all semblance of self-esteem?"

The soda can froze halfway to my mouth. I stared at him. What would Olafson know about marriage, anyhow? Or about commitment, or how relationships have a way of holding you captive, digging into your bone marrow and never letting go.

The butterflies flew right out of this day. "Look, thank you for being concerned. I know my arrangement seems odd to others. But it's fine for us. We just need space to work out some tangles."

I finished packing up the lunch supplies and hauled the cooler to the car. He continued to watch me. Again, I wondered who this person was, whose primary decorating color was black. And why was I with him in this isolated spot? After all, he *could* hack me up in little pieces and stuff me in the potbellied still. No one would ever find my body.

Instead, Ole smiled, picked a dandelion and handed it to me. "This is just the first of many flowers I will give you from this land."

"Hmm . . . listen; what with all this fresh air, the sun and the wine, I'm kind of tired. Do you mind if we head back? Darcy is calling this evening."

On the way home, we came to a stop and then slowly crossed the intersection with Precipice Point Road. I studied an enormous boulder that jutted from the hillside. Some savage force far beyond my comprehension had sliced this mammoth stone right down the middle. I closed my eyes and listened to Ole ramble on about classical music, colorful plants and his dream for an abundant garden on his Stony Ridge utopia.

Some savage force must have sliced Margo Grenadier right down the middle, as well.

It seemed probable that Buddy was slicing me.

— 6 —

Monster cramps attacked my gut the following Saturday night. By Sunday morning, I could do nothing but curl up, clutch my belly and whimper. In desperation, I took a large dose of ibuprofen one hour, alternated with a large dose of Dr. Tormentor's super pills the next, followed by an extra dose of both for good measure. When the diarrhea and clots began, I figured the only doctor who could possibly save me now would be Dr. Kevorkian.

By noon, the explosions of pain leveled off, but my head felt disconnected from my body. Tottering to my feet, I fastened an old terrycloth robe over my nightgown. The faded blue fabric had a bleach stain on the front in the shape of a cockroach, but it was okay for the couch and the heating pad.

All sorts of doom and gloom bullets whizzed through my mind. Fearful of a heart attack, I counted my pulse. Fearful of cancer, I poked at my breasts and abdomen—all the places they warn you about—looking for lumps and bumps. Fearful of AIDS—well, I had no idea what to do about AIDS. Fearful of dying of an overdose, I wondered when to call 911.

Ole knocked on the door just as I began to doze off. And there I was, a cockroachy stain on my robe, hair a tangle, teeth unbrushed. I opened the door only a crack. I told him I had the flu and shut the door in the poor man's face.

I dropped back onto the couch and hugged the heating pad to my tummy. Heat helped more than anything. In my bygone-glorious-married days, I sometimes pressed tightly to Buddy's rump and absorbed his body heat. But Buddy always became sick of my whining. Once, when I had cramps right after sex, he threw a doll across the room and cracked open her head. I suppose he felt helpless or maybe even responsible for my pain. Sometimes I actually felt sorry for him.

While I was thinking I should eat something, Ole's footsteps shook the porch again. I'd forgotten to lock the door, and he barged right in with a pot of something hot. It smelled like chicken soup, a delicious aroma at any other time of the month.

"Ole, please, I look just awful." I shoved the heating pad under the afghan.

"Don't worry about how you look, Miranda." He took over my kitchen and soon brought me a bowl of soup with oyster crackers, then perched on the edge of the recliner and waited eagerly for me to slurp it up. It was homemade and delicious.

"So, Miranda, I took the afternoon off yesterday and drove up to the property. Found my flashlight and explored the fireplace hole. It was empty. I'm sorry, I should have invited you, but considering how you have the—"

"You've been thinking about that fireplace?"

"Well, sure, haven't you?"

At that moment, Ole's hidey-hole was the last thing on my mind. I stood up, shooed him across the room and out the door.

A million dollars? Who cared?

Resettling on the couch, I asked Clara Barton what hymns she thought I should write in my Bible for my funeral service. Should we have a bagpiper march through the gloaming of Eternal Radiance? Playing *Amazing Grace*?

Lordy, I was on a pity pot. Trying to get a grip, I turned on the TV and found a rerun of *Designing Women*. There was Suzanne sitting at the top of her grand stairway in a fur-trimmed negligee, clutching an enormous rifle while her watch pig snorted at her feet. I laughed out loud and slurped up Ole's chicken soup. He was such an odd man, Ole Lee Olafson, with his lanky body and feminine ways.

At three in the morning, I dreamed about Suzanne's pig. It looked just like Poppy, Grandpa Smother's fat old sow on the farm, who would squeeze under the latticework of the front porch and let out dreadful moans when Grandma had her time of the month. Grandpa was furious because he had to do all of Grandma's barnyard chores. When I was staying there, I smeared peanut butter and jelly on homemade brown bread for him, morning, noon and night. He was never particularly grateful, but he ate it.

I don't recall taking anything up to Grandma. Imagine her lying up there all alone, her husband bellowing so loudly that the whole county knew about her most private secrets, the pig picking up her pain and moaning with her.

I never took her one cup of homemade chicken noodle soup. Not even an oyster cracker.

Dr. Tormelli had suggested I have a second opinion regarding surgery; his referral was to a Dr. S. A. Azadi. Initially, I was leery of the name Azadi. It sounded like a man from the Middle East with fiery black eyes, heavy dark eyebrows, maybe even a turban. On the other hand, I'd been very impressed by Queen Noor, an American girl who'd married a handsome Jordanian king. And I was always harping on Buddy about his intolerance; maybe it was time to start practicing what I preached.

The consultant's office was lovely; it was not the teal-mauve-gray combination of every other office in the late Eighties, but rather a comfortable beige and yellow, with lavender as an accent color in silk flowers and wall hangings. A smiling nurse called each patient by the first name only, unlike so many who yelled out, "Mrs. Blight." Everybody in the county knew the Blight name, what with Beulah's Boutique, Blight Fine Headstones, Inc. and the Red Bosom Mall. Nobody recognized the name Miranda. In nurses training, we students had to call each other *Miss This* or *Miss That* or put a nickel in the name-dropper jar. Sir names were a matter of respect in those days. By this time, first names were a happy matter of privacy.

"You can have a seat in her office," said the friendly nurse, who sported a genuine R.N. pin on her lapel. "She'll be right in. She likes to meet her patients before the examination."

A woman? Goodness. I'd never had a female physician.

I liked Dr. Azadi as soon as she stepped through the door. She had salient-gray hair and sympathetic brown eyes. We sat in comfortable chairs while I remained fully clothed in a sweet sundress of green and plum. My hair was now light brown with a few blond highlights; I called the effect summertime-aglow. The length was more pleasing also, not so kinky curly. I'd dabbed my cheeks with flirtation-pink powder and my lids with whimsy-green eye shadow. I felt pretty, soft and sensible, even while I spewed out my goofy medical history.

Dr. Azadi leaned forward and looked interested. It was easy to tell her about the pain, the previous treatments, and why I was not living with Buddy.

Finally, in the exam room, her nurse provided me with a thick white gown that was surely fabricated from actual tufts of cotton; she covered me with an equally sufficient sheet that would swish in a sudsy laundry at the end of the day. I did not wait on the end of the table for more than a minute or two. Following the exam, Dr. Azadi sat me up and handed me pain pills in case I had cramps from her poking. She said I'd had enough pain in my life. I dressed and we finished up in her office, me fully clothed.

"You do need surgery," she said. "You have the classic symptoms of severe endometriosis and a couple of very large fibroids. I'll be happy to write that I agree with Dr. Tormelli's opinion."

I stared at my hands, then looked up and gulped. "Do you think I could have cancer?"

Dr. Azadi smiled. "I doubt it. Endometriosis isn't life threatening, but it can be terribly painful. I've never seen a woman who deserved surgery more than you do."

"So could you do it? I don't want Doctor Tormelli."

"Yes, I'd be happy to. But do you have private insurance? You don't need prior authorization?"

"No. That's one thing Buddy's done right. We have easy-to-use health insurance."

"Okay, let's get you set up with the hospital."

"Which one?"

"Loving Memorial gives the best care. Do you know it?"

Of course I knew it, inside and out. I could only hope that Mrs. Vic was no longer dominatrix of that world. I took a deep breath and smiled at Dr. Azadi. "Thank you so much. You know, sometimes I've actually wanted cancer, just to get this mess out of me."

Dr. Azadi stood up, came around the desk and touched my shoulder. "Miranda, I promise, you'll feel like a new woman. But do you think you could stay away from Buddy for a while? Since we aren't sure of his other sexual partners?"

"Is that an order? An official pronouncement? Can I tell Buddy that the doctor says I can't—you know? Otherwise, he'll stomp and swear and finally talk me into it."

She looked at me with concern. "We need to work on this, Miranda. This dependence you have on Buddy. Maybe some counseling?"

"Oh, I had a psychiatrist once, to see if the pain was all in my head. He didn't help much, just charged a lot. But I have a friend who shares your concerns for me." I remembered Ole's words on Stony Ridge and squirmed.

Dr. Azadi looked at me a moment and then glanced at her watch. I'd spent a long time with her. I debated asking the other question, the one about the urine thing, but that would just launch me back into fool mode. Likely, the surgery would clear up all of those annoying issues. I decided to let her off the hook on whether or not I'd be able to pee straight when all of this was done and over with.

– 7 –

"Of all the damn fool times to be driving someone to the hospital, this is the damnedest. Midnight. I still can't believe it." Buddy hit the steering wheel with his fist while speeding south along the six-lane highway, which was nearly empty.

"It's because of the insurance," I explained for the third time, after learning that my health-care coverage was not so easy to use after all. "My hospital day begins at 12:01 a.m., so I'm not billed for an extra day. I'll be able to stay three full days after the surgery. I figure I'll need every bit of that time."

I tried to sound calm and rational, but I had to agree with Buddy. Midnight was a creepy time to be entering a hospital. Even with the highway lights, the overall feeling was darkness. The moon had cruised with the sun all day and both had disappeared by nightfall, leaving a heavy layer of black clouds. It had rained earlier in the evening for the first time in a month. A slick sheet of oil coated the pavement. We could not see it, of course, but television reporters had warned us about it on the news. I began gnawing on my index finger.

When I was a student nurse, patients arrived at the hospital in broad daylight on the afternoon prior to their surgeries. This gave us all afternoon and evening to *prep* them, which meant, in the case of an abdominal hysterectomy such as mine, giving enemas-till-clear, potassium permanganate douches—deeply purple, messy things—and then shaving and scrubbing until the women resembled plucked chickens. They were

41

properly sterile and sedated by the time they arrived in the OR the next morning. Two hours ago, I'd done my own prep at home—one Fleet enema, a body scrub in the shower, a mini-shave, and even a clear-colored drugstore douche under the watchful eye of my frothy-white angel doll, who stood guard on a shelf over the toilet.

Buddy arrived during all of this, but he paid no attention to my body prep then or to the oil slicks now. He rode on people's bumpers until they hit their brakes. When our only option was to leap over the next car, he would twist the steering wheel so sharply that we'd almost bounce into the next lane. Then he'd dash ahead without warning.

He was doing it now. He quickly caught up with three cars that were blocking all three lanes in front of us. Buddy sat on one bumper after the other, but could not maneuver around. He royally cussed out the other drivers.

"Buddy, calm down, please. There's not a time deadline. They're not going to send me home, like 'oops, your surgery is canceled, Mrs. Blight,' if I arrive at 12:15 instead of midnight."

"There's a deadline for me. I have an early job tomorrow." He blinked his brights in one driver's eyes. Getting no response, he swerved behind the next car in the lineup.

"Buddy, it's slippery out here. Please, I'm nervous enough as it is."

"Well, you should be," he said, spotting an opening and darting through, leaving the dawdlers far behind. "Just last week I was hearing on *Twenty-Twenty* or *Sixty-Sixty*—one of those damn shows—how dangerous hospitals can be, especially surgery. They showed this woman went in for a hysterectomy, they got her wide open on the table and she just conks out. Goes into a coma from the sleeping gas. Now they have her plugged up to one of those breathing machines, stored away like a sack of potatoes in a nursing home. Her little kids were right there on the TV screen, crying and sobbing. Her husband was arguing with the judge about pulling the plug."

"Dwight Blight, shut up *please!*"

"Seems to me it's a silly chance to take for a few little pains once a month. You'll be hitting that menopause stuff before you know it."

"Can't you just slow down? I'm getting nauseated."

"How about I pull off at this next exit and we turn around and go home? You move back in with me and I'll help you every month, I swear. You can stay in bed with a hot water bottle on your stomach, and I'll bring

you tea and rub your back. I miss your goofiness, if you want the truth."
He headed for the slow lane.

"No! Don't you dare. Just keep going, Buddy. Get me to that hospital.
If I conk out from the anesthesia, who's to care anyway? You'd have another
woman lickety-split, and Darcy is perfectly well off in San Francisco.
Neither one of you needs me any longer."

"Hell, Randy, don't start talking like that. I hate it when you feel sorry
for yourself like that."

"Here's the exit. How I remember this street." I was lost in nostalgia
for a moment, being in a truck with Buddy at midnight, scurrying back
to Loving Memorial.

"Don't know why you'd consider going back to this place after what
those bitches did to you. You should have married me after high school
like I wanted. I was crazy about you, babe."

"Of course you were, Buddy. Just pull into the front parking lot there.
You don't have to go in with me. They'll be giving me a sleeping pill right
away so you can go on home. You have your big job in the morning."

"You sure you don't want someone to help you? Hold your hand?"

"No, I think the nurses will take care of me just fine. You can call
tomorrow in the afternoon. They'll tell you if I'm out of surgery. Dr.
Azadi promised she'd take good care of me. I'm not going to end up on a
respirator."

He pulled into the deserted parking lot. Ours was the only vehicle.
Eerie cones of light crept over the dark concrete at the base of each
lamppost. Buddy turned and stared at me. He ran his strong thumb along
my cheek. I almost weakened and let him kiss me, but I feared he'd talk
me into going home with him.

"Doctor who?" he said suddenly, pulling his hand away. "Azadi?
Sounds like an Arab name to me."

"What difference does that make? Samire Azadi. I think it's a lovely
name."

"A woman? And an Arab? An Arab woman is going to—"

I conjured up Dr. Azadi's calm face and her woman's practiced hands
that were going to save me. Without trying to defend her, I hurried
through a kind of tuck and roll out of Buddy's huge truck, then dashed
to the entrance. I had in my grasp a pink plastic bag from the Giggles
and Whispers store at the Dinky Creek Splurge. It contained not only my
hairbrush and toothbrush, but also a dazzling foxy-lady-pink nightgown

and matching fuzzy slippers. I'd also squeezed in my not-so-foxy-lady-pink housecoat of seersucker—from home, but without bleach stains.

Buddy roared off before I was even in the front door. He'd be ranting about women and Arabs all the way home. Maybe he *would* hit an oil slick. Maybe *he'd* be the one to die, not me. It would serve him right. I'd collect all his life insurance money. Then I wondered.

Did Buddy still have life insurance?

Before my surgery, I tried to prepare myself for ghastly pain, a dire inability to pee, or even Buddy's prediction of death from anesthesia. But I never imagined the worst. Dry heaves.

My session in the OR was at 9:00 a.m. and I was back in my room around 3:00 p.m., yet not fully conscious, still slogged down with hefty drugs. Soon after, the first violent puking began. The siege continued all evening. I would drift off, surface to a haze of awareness, be sickened by the swell of nausea, then twist and spasm like a captured fish. Within seconds, I'd gag and cough up green bile. While my newly seamed muscles went into each spasm, I knew my incision would rip apart. The pain was excruciating.

My face felt like cement; I could not pry open my eyes to find the call bell. The only way to signal the nurse was to bang my head against the side rail until its metal parts clanged from the shaking. I could not use my emesis basin, which was plastic, disposable and noiseless. I remembered being a student nurse, when stainless steel was standard issue. Shiny metal emesis basins got your attention right away if a patient hammered one against the metal side rail. This puny mustard-colored thing I had now was doing me no good at all.

Finally, I heard an angel. She said her name was Kathy—Kathy with a lovely, soothing voice. She heard my bars rattling and came quickly to hold my head, rub my back and reassure me that my layers of stitches and staples would remain woven together. At some point, she pulled crumpled flannel surgical blankets from around me and washed my face. The cooling freshness brought a bit of relief.

Too soon, Buddy's voice replaced Kathy's. By this time, I could lift one eyelid just a tad and acknowledge his presence. He actually held my hand for a bit, but I kept falling asleep, until another wave of nausea hit my gut. Forcing my head up and over the basin, I heaved and then moaned in pain.

"Buck up, old buckaroo," Buddy said. "Relax, it'll be easier."

Old buckaroo? My eyes were shut, but I could hear just fine.

I suddenly wondered where God was in this anguish. During my life, I'd turned up at the Methodist, Presbyterian, Roman Catholic, Christian Science, Lutheran, Episcopal—and even three times—the Jewish houses of God. And now the Father in Heaven seemed to have forsaken me and left me with Buddy instead. But not for long. After the next heaving, Buddy gave up and went home.

I listened to Nurse Kathy try to soothe the patient in the next bed—she'd been wheeled in after my surgery. She was a nasty woman from the sound of her, who yelled for attention all evening. In the end, Kathy must have mixed a powerful brew of sleeping pills and tranquilizers to shove down that woman's throat.

Before Kathy went off duty at 11:00 p.m., she sat me up and dangled me on the side of the bed. Dangling was a routine post-op procedure—sitting the patient on the edge of the bed and letting her legs dangle down. I found it more dreadful than the deep breathing and coughing I'd been struggling with. I could not get my eyes open and relied on Kathy's hands to guide me, her voice to encourage. "Hey, darlin'," she said cheerfully, as if we were on a lark in the park. "Remember, you aren't going to have any more cramps. Ever again. You're all done forever."

After she left, I silently apologized to God for being angry with him. I also thought how nice it would be if God were a woman like Dr. Azadi or Angel Nurse Kathy. It was a comforting sort of thought, the first one I'd had all day. Soon after, I slept.

— 8 —

Dr. Azadi came in sometime around dawn. She inspected my wound and listened to my abdomen with her stethoscope. "Just ice chips today," she advised the nurse. "Let's wait for some bowel sounds before she has food."

I could not protest and went back to sleep.

When I next awoke, the nausea was gone and I opened my eyes. I raised the head of the bed so I could wash my face and brush my teeth, but I could not use the bedpan—it was too nerve-wracking. My bladder clamped shut, fearful of its own bad aim. Bags of glucose water had been dripping into my veins for twenty-four hours, and now the dire inability to pee was upon me. While I whined and moaned, my nurse Melvin set to work uncovering me.

Melvin was a small fellow dressed in white scrubs, who had a way of flinging his head backward to flip a swirl of yellow hair from his round, springy eyes. Melvin's eyes were always lunging at me, as if he were constantly amazed by my appearance. After removing my unused bedpan, he insisted I get up and go to the bathroom, an act that involved pushing my IV stand into the tiny room and maneuvering around it. Even sitting on a toilet, I could not pee. The pain was quite incredible.

I became dizzy when I strained to encourage the flow. I clutched a handrail and yanked the chain on the emergency call bell next to the toilet. The small pale room closed in on me; I felt as if I were sliding down the toilet, swirling deeper and deeper into the mire of my life.

46

Eventually, Melvin poked his daffy head through the doorway and zeroed in. "How's it going, honey?" His eyes looked ready to gobble me up.

"Arrrgh," I uttered, tugging the gown over my bare knees.

He reached in and turned on the tap to let me hear the sound of tinkling water.

"Please, Melvin, I'm in agony here. Can't you put in a catheter?"

"Oh honey, you're not as bad off as you feel. They cathed you twice on the night shift. I'll get to you as soon as I can." He flipped his hair and backed away.

The nasty woman behind the curtain took my side. "For heaven's sake, see to your duty, young man. Get an order for a Foley cath and shut this woman up." What an ugly voice she had. But her demands got action.

After I was back in bed, a highly efficient Filipina nurse named Ida arrived and inserted a Foley catheter into my bladder. She inflated a tiny balloon to keep it in place. A continuous yellow drip began flowing into a plastic bag hanging from the side of my bed. The relief was amazing.

Dreading the idea of Melvin giving me a bed bath, I begged Ida to help me wash a little and maneuver the IV bag so I could get into a fresh gown. The shapeless hospital garments were made from thin, lethargic-blue fabric with a slightly brighter pattern of—oh, who can describe such utilitarian and uncheerful material? At that point, I was just relieved Melvin was nowhere around. After Ida left the room, I fell asleep.

Sometime later, I woke up with a searing pain in my arm. I must have been moaning a lot because my roommate was yelling in a deep throaty voice, "I insist upon a private room. I stated clearly when they brought me in here that I wanted a private room." Her bed was near the door, with a curtain between us; she sounded like a very scary old broad.

I opened my eyes to determine the problem. A large tumor of IV fluid, ripe with searing medications, was swelling my arm from wrist to elbow. The needle had evidently ripped through the vein, and the fluid was infiltrating into the soft tissues. I grabbed the call bell and wondered why the black IV box hadn't rung an alarm.

We did not have such sophisticated equipment in my day. I once saw a woman who developed a terrible infection after her IV infiltrated. Her skin and muscle sloughed away. The arm became gangrenous and had to be amputated. Remembering, I shuddered and inspected my own fingers to see if they were swollen and turning black.

No one answered my call bell. No one answered my roommate either, who continued to storm about her private room. I figured they were avoiding us because I was so whacky and she was so bitchy. I wanted to holler from deep in my throat the way Miss Bitchy Roommate hollered. Instead, my voice was screechy and frantic. "Somebody please help me! Ida, Melvin!"

I knew the sound did not travel past the curtain. Hers did. "Get the administrator of this goddamned hospital in here and I mean stat!"

With the force of a punch to the gut, I recognized that voice. My roommate was Mrs. Vickerstromm, R.N.! The evil duchess. The cold Vichyssoise French soup.

Nobody responded to our pleas, but I had to do something. I reached across to my left side and looked for some kind of control knob to stop the flow. I finally figured out the shutoff gismo and, biting my lip, rolled it over the tubing. Then I ripped off the bandage and yanked.

On hindsight, this was not a smart maneuver. A thin-gauge catheter had been inserted into my vein, not a tiny needle that I could have pulled out quite easily. Once I began yanking, there was no turning back. It seemed like at least ten yards of the stuff had been threaded into the deep recesses of my body. It stung while I pulled, but I dared not stop. After I freed the final bit of tubing, I waved it through the air in a victory celebration. Unfortunately, the shutoff valve was not completely shut off. Instantly, 5% Dextrose in Water sprayed recklessly over my bed and me. In complete panic, I tried to pinch off the flow but was all thumbs. I hollered with more drama than my roommate was providing.

Melvin was soon at the door, demanding to know what the hell all the commotion was about. I screamed about my IV, while Mrs. Vic hollered about her private room. When Melvin came tearing around my bed, he slipped in the puddle of sticky IV fluid and sprawled in a heap under my urine collection bag. Trust me, Melvin was not having a good day either.

Before he could stand up, Mrs. Vic yelled at him through the curtain. "Young man, call the hospital CEO and tell him to get his fat ass up here. Stat! I want to know why I'm being so blatantly tortured and ignored!"

Melvin scrambled to his feet, grabbed my IV bag and righted it to stop the flow. While he inspected my arm, he snapped at her that the CEO was not available at the bloody moment. There would be no private rooms until somebody kicked off, but if she continued hollering, no doubt someone would kick off, so there should be a private room and soon. I won't repeat what Mrs. Vic barked in response.

Poor Melvin. He got me fixed up with a dry gown and changed my wet sheets before he ran away to deal with his own pants, which had become rather see-through in the dampness and all. He was wearing bikini-red briefs under his thin, white scrubs.

When Melvin was dry and tidy again, the poor fellow returned and gave me a walloping injection of painkiller. Thankfully, the lunch hour, as well as my former nemesis, spun into oblivion.

But from somewhere in my narcotic-induced sleep, I heard another commotion. Mrs. Vic was on the phone. "Listen to me, you damn son of a bitch, you stay away from here. You come within two blocks of this hospital, I'll kill you. Don't rely on me being an infirm old woman." The receiver clicked down and then she hollered, "Melvin, come in here."

Melvin responded quite promptly. "I want a security guard on this floor," she demanded. "He's threatening again. He'll sneak in here to silence me, I know he will."

"Ah, he just wants to visit with you, honey," Melvin said. He'd evidently been given new orders to be sweet to her. "Bring you candy and such."

"Visit? Ha! Get me a guard in here pronto! And don't call me honey!"

Melvin's footsteps trailed away and the room became quiet, except for her clattering around with her drinking glass and muttering under her breath. I soon heard heavy male footsteps. "So, ma'am, you're worried about being murdered? Really, I don't think that's likely."

"You don't think? Why the hell don't you think? He'll be here any minute. He'll probably blow my head off. Maybe that next woman's too."

It took a second to realize she was talking about me. I looked about for the man who was going to blow my head off; at the same moment, the guard poked his head around my curtain and smiled at me.

I recognized him as Jackson, the good-looking security guard who'd been on duty when I was admitted two nights before. He was about thirty, with shiny black curls and honey-colored skin. Wonderful shoulders, great in a uniform. He'd been the only person in the large, empty lobby when Buddy dropped me off. Jackson had run over to hold the door and then, with great pizzazz, he'd punched my ID number into a computer at the desk. "Ah, here you are, just as predicted," he'd said. "Miranda Blight. You'll be in room 327, after we get you checked in."

Room 327. Jackson had not warned me that I'd be sharing room 327 with this wild woman who thought she was being murdered. Now I wondered if I should return to the admitting station and start over. Better yet, just go on home, as Buddy had suggested.

Instead, Ole Olafson stuck his red head around my curtain. He smiled as if I were as beautiful as a Barbie doll. He came clutching a vase of fresh flowers: pink snapdragons, purple iris, a bountiful-red rose beginning to blossom. He'd attached a handwritten note about getting well real soon. Oblivious to the scene he'd just walked through, he asked how I felt.

There was no explaining how I felt, so I made a wry face and thanked him for the flowers.

Ole said he'd left work early to visit me. He also said I was looking pretty good, all things considered. Meanwhile, the hospital administrator arrived on the other side of the curtain. I could tell he was a high muckety-muck by the way he spoke quietly, in a deep, diplomatic voice.

Mrs. Vic told the CEO that she had no confidence in that Jackson fellow, who was nothing but a gullible security guard. She wanted the state police brought in to protect her. Ole glanced at the curtain. I did not know if I should ask him to sit down or just what I should do with Mr. Olafson. I wriggled from my side to my back and tried to fluff my hair. I longed to brush my teeth.

Ole was in no hurry to leave, but our silence was strained compared to the odd conversation going on a few feet away. I finally asked if he had a pen.

"Sure, I think so." He reached into his jacket pocket and handed me a slick rolling writer. I put his get-well card on my overbed table and scribbled on the back as best as I could.

> *That's Mrs. Vic. We talked about her driving up the mountain.*
> *She thinks her son-in-law is going to come in here and kill her!*
> *Maybe me too!!!*

I was exhausted writing this much, but I watched Ole's eyes go into action. He glanced at the curtain, back at me and mouthed the question *really?* To which I nodded yes.

Nurse Kathy was back on duty and appeared with a new IV setup. She stepped into the bathroom to wash her hands and called out over the running water, quite loudly, "I'm sorry, Miranda, but we need to start this over again. You need fluids."

"Miranda?" The curtain flew back. My roommate and I were suddenly in plain view of one another. You could almost smell the ozone from all the electrical sparks shooting to and fro.

"Miranda? I've only heard that name once in my lifetime and I'll never forget it. Who are you? Are you my Miranda?"

All of us in the room—nurse Kathy in blue scrubs, the hospital CEO with matching tie and handkerchief, Ole with his curious blue eyes, even me in my post-op yuck—all of us turned toward Mrs. Vic and froze. We were stunned by her appalling rudeness and the glint of nastiness in her evil eye while she scrutinized me. I thought maybe I was hooked to a respirator and in a coma. Maybe this is what happened inside your head when you had brain death.

I stared at her and was utterly amazed. Mrs. Vic was a wrinkled and worn old woman. Her shoulders and arms were larger than I remembered. They were encased in a layer of soft flesh that jiggled below the capped sleeves of her own drab hospital gown. Her lips had shrunk to nothing, whereas her nose and earlobes had grown into tulip bulbs. Her eyes, once sharp as steel, looked like pale blue milk. Her hair, formerly pulled into a tight bun under her nursing cap, was now short and frizzled, clamshell-gray near the scalp, bleached into beeswax-yellow at the tips. Mrs. Vic had always walked upright, her arms swinging at her sides, her nose leading the way. Now she just looked collapsed. Actually, she was a holy mess.

But that voice. Nothing was old or deteriorated about that voice. This crone was Mrs. Vic, all right.

I don't know how long we were frozen, but finally Nurse Kathy had the good sense to unfreeze us. She soothed Mrs. Vic while the administrator scrambled away. "Miranda's tired," Kathy said. "You can become acquainted later." Swish, swish with the curtain.

Ole stood by my bed and looked amazed. I could see questions clicking across his brain. He probably wondered why I had not told him I knew Mrs. Vic. Instead, he looked at me and winked, pulled up a chair and sat down.

He picked up my sore hand while Kathy poked and threaded the IV into my right arm. After my fluids were dripping again, Ole went into the bathroom and dampened a washcloth, then sponged my face and fluffed my pillow. He gave me ice chips to suck, found my hairbrush in the drawer and smoothed my hair a little. He just whispered *shh* when I tried to protest. I leaned against the pillow and sighed.

I wanted to ask him if he could hum the Humperdink song, the one from the *Hansel and Gretel* opera about the fourteen angels at your head. Mama would often sing it before she went off to work in the saloons. But with Mrs. Vic listening, I dared not ask him. So I closed my eyes and imagined Ole playing it on his piano. I heard Mama's voice as she sang along.

When at night I go to sleep, fourteen angels watch do keep . . .

Every fall, Mama and I traveled by Greyhound to her new job. At my insistence, Grandpa dropped us off at the bus depot half an hour early. We hopped out, blew him a kiss and shoved through the heavy swinging doors. Mama spent the next thirty minutes in the coffee shop, perched on a red stool at the counter, having coffee and a doughnut, charming all the men.

I scrambled off to the ticket window to find out what number I should stand under. Marching directly to that doorway, I stood on top of the yellow mark that said WAIT HERE and plopped down my little suitcase for emphasis. The case was small and square, the size of a woman's traveling cosmetic box. Its color was gray, with a red lid that gave it pizzazz.

The other passengers grew nervous. All kinds of ticket holders sat on their benches and fidgeted. They tried to ignore me, but as the black clock on the wall ticked along, they began to shift in their seats. If they could not be first in line, maybe they should be second or third.

As soon as two or three old ladies waddled up behind me, a mother with two babies would appear. Elderly couples and the old men followed her. Last in line came the soldiers and sailors, toting hefty duffel bags, chewing gum, stubbing out cigarettes. The end of the line and the back of the bus suited the military just fine.

Mama sauntered over at the last minute, flashed a smile at the troops and took her place smack dab in front. She was fresh, relaxed and lovely. A moment later, the bus driver arrived and swung open the door. We stepped across the yellow WAIT HERE line into the outdoor boarding area, a place that made me gag with the smell of stale cigarettes and bus exhaust.

As a child, I was well aware of the dangers around me; I understood what the word *carcinogen* meant. I knew exactly how to catch cancer.

Finally, the baggage man heaved our luggage into metal compartments beneath the bus. But I held onto my suitcase. Mama traveled with one big case packed full of our clothes and immediate necessities. Earlier in the week, she'd shipped a box that contained bouffant wigs, fancy dresses, our warm winter coats and all of her sheet music. She had two piles of music, one for the church, *Sweet Hour of Prayer* and the like, and one for the bars. Mama's face could change from angel to sorceress the minute she switched beats. *Blue moon, you saw me standing alone . . .*

My favorite seat on the bus was on the right side, over the wheel toward the front. I usually found it waiting for me, even if the bus arrived from somewhere else with plenty of passengers already on board. The seat was a tight fit for an adult, but a great place for a kid's feet, high on the shiny hump of gray metal. When I grew taller, my seating arrangements changed, but I always dashed for my footrest seat prior to that. It became the place I fit into, my tiny spot in the world that I alone fully appreciated or enjoyed, the place I felt secure. The wheel-well hump of the Greyhound bus was my true family home.

I tucked my gray and red suitcase under the seat. It always contained my current doll, a new Jumbo coloring book and exotic Crayolas like persimmon and magenta. I became so enchanted with color names that my imagination went wild. Attending church so often, I thought of my little suitcase as Good-Friday-gray, the lid as Pentecost-Sunday-red.

I also toted my favorite *Little House on the Prairie* book for that year, although by junior high, Laura Ingalls Wilder had to move over for *Sue Barton, Visiting Nurse,* or whatever Sue Barton was up to on that trip.

For the first few years, I carried along my baby doll Janie Belle, who was named after a book I loved by Ellen Tarry. It was an intriguing story about a poor baby left in a trash can, rescued by Mrs. Ora Looka and the postman, taken to the hospital and saved by Nurse Moore and a team of impressive doctors—Dr. Great, Dr. Big and Dr. Little. In the end, the baby was scooped up and loved forever by Nurse Moore, who was also called Janie Belle, only no one at the hospital knew that just yet. I was inspired to become a nurse the first time Mama read me *Janie Belle.* The Sue Barton books cinched it.

Janie Belle's wooden arms, legs and head rotated in small round sockets; I could do all sorts of baby things with her—walk her, sit her, burp her.

During second grade, I turned Janie Belle into an acrobat. I forced her into performing summersaults and cartwheels like those I'd been doing on the farm. One day I pulled back her arms and legs, bent her head forward and snap! Head, arms, legs, all popped off her body. Sturdy wire hooks snapped like springs and would not squeeze back into place. From September until Christmas, I carried around poor little Janie Belle's various body parts in my Good-Friday-gray suitcase. Mama replaced her with a Raggedy Ann doll that year. She said a cloth doll could bounce right back even if it was folded, bent, packed, sat on or squashed.

I never quite loved Raggedy Ann, and I've never made a cloth doll, come to think of it.

Late in the evenings on our bus rides, when it grew too dark for Mama to read her murder mysteries, we cuddled under her jacket while she recounted family stories. Her mother died when she was a baby, and so she traveled around with her father, a preacher who spoke at tent revivals. When I asked if his wanderings meant we really could be gypsies, she said he preached the gospel, not folklore. Mama learned to sing and play on his portable box organ. After he died from a heart attack when she was ten, Mama lived with her aunt who owned a feed store at the southern end of the Heathertons' valley. This brought us to the scandal, the story I loved best.

"Tell me about the scandal, when you met my dad," I begged frequently.

"Beau Smothers? That green-eyed charmer? His first name was Gary but we all called him Beau. We met in algebra class in ninth grade. I was head over heels in love from the very first day, but he ignored me and went for Peggy Greene the Make-out Queen. She was a senior, of all things. In those days, boys did not date older girls. But Peggy was loose. They sat in her parents' car out behind the Dairy Queen and necked. She had to drive, which was terribly scandalous at that time—a senior girl driving around a freshman boy—girls never even called boys on the telephone.

"Anyhow, I spied on them once. He looked to be the best kisser in town. And I wanted to be the one kissing him."

"So how did you get him to kiss you?" I whispered.

"It took me a whole year. I tried winking, teasing, flaunting myself in his face, but Beau was too big for his britches. He grew so early in life. He was six foot tall by the time he was fourteen. A wonder to behold on the basketball court."

"Did you go to all his games?"

"As many as I could. But we lived in the country and my aunt was teaching me the piano. She insisted I practice two hours every day. And isn't it good that I did?"

"Yeah, but how did you get my father from the older woman and stop the scandal?"

"I bought a pair of falsies and a tight sweater. I wore bright red lipstick and pierced my ears. I joined the cheerleading team and jumped higher than anyone else. My legs were much longer and prettier than Miss Rob-the-Cradle's. One day I turned cartwheels clear across the gym floor, right in front of his face. My long legs finally captured Beau Smother's attention."

"And he broke up with the make-out queen and loved you forever and ever until he died?"

"Yes, he did, sweetie. Some day you'll meet him and see for yourself."

"Will you do cartwheels for us, clear across heaven?"

"Oh yeah, honey, clear across those pearly gates."

— 9 —

The next morning, Melvin waltzed into our room and swished open the curtain between our beds. "Ah good, you two look much brighter today." He trotted to the window, opened the blinds and flooded the room with light. He sat us upright in our beds and tossed us washcloths to freshen our faces. After he carried in the breakfast trays, he lifted the shiny heat-retaining domes with great anticipation, exposing our morning meals. I was craving bacon, eggs and a delicious Dunkin' Donuts maple bar; Melvin uncovered thin gruel and herbal tea. Before I could complain, he bounded out the door.

So there we sat, my archenemy and I, in our crumpled sheets and our lethargic-blue hospital gowns, with breakfast trays on our overbed tables and an unused television mounted on a platform high on the wall between us. The window and the bathroom door stood blandly on my side of the room. An amazing garden of get-well bouquets blossomed on her side. I took it all in with short, sideways glances.

"Turn around here so I can look at you," she soon demanded.

Like a new recruit at boot camp, I turned obediently and tried to smile. "Hello, Mrs. Vic."

"Yep, you're the one. God, how you've aged."

"I'm sorry." I picked up my spoon to swirl the gruel.

"You're sorry? Sorry for what?"

"For aging or whatever. I'm sorry about your private—"

"Don't bother with apologies now. When I think of what this hospital has become—I should have encouraged you to stay in training, Miranda. You could not have done any more harm than these sad sacks are doing now. That sorry fellow in here posing as a nurse. I didn't think he'd ever get that Foley cath in you yesterday."

"He did the best he could under—"

"Ha! I doubt you'd be a very good judge of that."

Obviously, Mrs. Vic had not mellowed with age. Instead, she'd lived her entire life by intimidating people. I could barely speak but I tried to be polite. "Look, Mrs. Vic, it's good to see you again, but I've had major surgery here and I'm afraid—"

"What did you have? Abdominal hyst? They do too many of those damn things nowadays, to my way of thinking. Who'd you have? Horace Tormelli is the best man in town, everybody knows that."

"I had Dr. Azadi."

"A woman?"

"She's been wonderful."

"I'd certainly never have a woman cutting on me. I've seen too many of them in the OR. Give me a man with large, well-trained hands, no jitters—a woman? I'm disappointed in you, Miranda. No wonder you don't feel well. Horace Tormelli's patients are up walking the next day, urinating, bowel movement right on schedule. I remember when that man arrived directly from medical school. God, he was handsome. He'd often stop in my office for a cup of coffee after he'd been up all night. I recognized his medical genius right away."

"He's bald now," I blurted out, but she did not react. "Why are you here, Mrs. Vic?"

"You can't tell?" She waved at all her equipment, including a motorized wheelchair in the corner. "A little cardiac fibrillation. Absolutely nothing to worry about. I had a minor fainting spell after a confrontation with Tom Grenadier, my murdering son-in-law. He would have finished me off if we'd been alone, but a friend was with me. Thank God she called 911. Now I have a pacemaker. Of course I have the best cardiac surgeon in Centerville."

"I'm surprised you're not in intensive care." I twisted to see if I could grab the curtain between our beds, but Melvin had shoved it all the way to the wall.

"Intensive care? Good God, girl, do I look like I need intensive care? Do I look critical? Do I sound critical? I can assure you, there's nothing critical about me."

"That's good," I murmured while gagging down my little puddle of gruel. "What about the wheelchair?"

"You don't know about that? Honestly, Miranda, don't you read the newspapers? The car accident was written up in all the major papers. Well, you never did keep up, as I remember.

"It was never an accident, of course. He tampered with the brakes on my car. He knew Margo and I were catching on. That was his first attempt to kill her. I was driving her down from their home in Pine Woods when my brakes failed. Smashed right into a tree. My daughter survived that disaster. I was his only victim. Severed my spinal cord at lumbar three. Severed my plans for retirement, as well. I'd made arrangements to travel . . . follow my daughter's career.

"She was a prodigy, you know. Gave concerts around the world. Horowitz heard her play. Said he'd never heard anything like it. My daughter astonished Horowitz. Imagine!"

Mrs. Vic was suddenly quiet, except for some blowing of her nose. While she occupied herself with her tissue box, I located the button to recline the head of my bed. When I was nearly flat, I scooted as carefully as possible onto my side, away from her and toward the window. I closed my eyes and tried to visualize the car accident that had severed her spinal cord. Perhaps she'd been yakking at her daughter and not paying attention—pitched into that tree all by herself. Maybe she'd bonked her head at the same time. A brain injury seemed likely to me.

"Did you ever hear her play, Miranda? No, I suppose not. You don't look as if you've been to many concerts. Damn, where am I supposed to put my dirty tissues? Don't you remember how I taught you girls to make discard bags out of brown paper sacks and pin them to your patients' sheets, first thing after taking their vitals every morning? That little pop-eyed bugger comes bouncing in here—wouldn't know what a discard bag was, I don't suppose. Even you knew that.

"And who was that man in here yesterday? The one with the homegrown flowers? That wasn't a Blight, surely. I prefer Bentley's Floral Gardens, myself. But I don't suppose you use Bentley's too often."

At that snide remark, I debated the moves necessary to yank out my new IV, jump over my side rail, leap onto her bed and throttle her. Fortunately, Melvin reappeared and interrupted us both.

While I was still revved up, he coaxed me down the hall to a small room with a shower. He hung my urine and IV bags on hooks planted in the tile, then eased me out of my gown, which had to be pulled over my IV tubing and bag. He tried to cover me with a flimsy towel while he adjusted the spray, but I was not at all comfortable with a male nurse.

Before scuttling away, he assured me that water could run right over the raw staples. It was just as well. I could not imagine Melvin lugging basins of hot water to give bed baths every morning. I couldn't see him changing the sheets with the patients still in bed, the way I had once been able to do. Mrs. Vic would undoubtedly demand a female nurse to help her with such personal care. Obviously, she could not trot off to take a shower.

When I was tidy and in yet another lethargic-blue gown, Melvin ordered me to walk up and down the corridor pushing my IV stand and carrying my urine bag. "Let's pump the good air deep into your lungs, honey. Get all the anesthesia out."

"But it feels really stupid, shuffling up and down this long corridor carrying a pot of liquid gold over my arm. You ought to try it sometime."

"Stop whining, Miranda," Actually, Melvin was right. The medical world now realized that surgery patients recovered more quickly if they ambulated a bit. In my day, we kept patients in bed way too long—six weeks for a heart attack. We did not allow those patients to raise their arms above their hearts. I can't describe how embarrassing it was to be eighteen years old, brushing a forty-year-old businessman's teeth—those men were all so adorable. Their teeth? Not so much.

When Melvin finally let me return to the room, Mrs. Vic had been carted away to X-ray and physical therapy. I collapsed in my rumpled bed and let the morning narcotics soothe me. Pain-free and alone at last, I fell asleep, but not for long. Dr. Azadi stopped by. She wore her green scrubs from surgery. She checked my incision and told me I was doing just fine.

"Can I go home? Please?"

Dr. Azadi raised an eyebrow and studied me a moment, then sat carefully on the edge of my bed and patted my hand. Nothing was terribly amiss, she explained, but they'd discovered that over the years a lot of menstrual blood had seeped backward into the muscle layers of my uterus, causing inflammation, bogginess and pain. It also explained the large clots and overwhelming diarrhea. The official diagnosis was *adenomyosis*.

I took a deep breath and smiled. My misery had not been coming from my disturbed, psycho-neurotic brain after all. "And you didn't find any cancer?" I asked.

"No cancer. Now stop fretting, Miranda. We'll remove the catheter and the IV right after lunch. You can walk more today. Go down to the solarium for a bit. But you were quite ill from the anesthesia. We need to observe you at least one more day."

She stood and inhaled the sweet smell from Ole's red rose, which had come into full bloom this morning. "I think this is the loveliest rose I've ever seen," she said.

When she smiled, I thought she must be the loveliest doctor I'd ever seen, even in hospital-green scrubs.

— 10 —

Melvin removed my tubes after lunch. Lark-free, I wriggled out of the hospital garb and slithered into my foxy-lady-pink nightgown and slippers from the Dinky Creek Splurge, along with my pink seersucker housecoat from home. I could instantly sense my new wellbeing.

I smiled at passing nurses and inched my way along the hall. The solarium was located on the crossbar of an H connecting the Med-Surg Tower and the Perinatal Pavilion. The room was full of green indoor plants and molded white furniture, with teal and mauve cushions scattered every which way.

Despite my new zest for life, I fell asleep before I could watch two minutes of *General Hospital.* After a bit, a loud sudsy commercial awoke me. When I returned to room 327, Mrs. Vic was fast asleep, halfway sitting, snoring lightly, exhausted from her morning's exertion.

Beulah called while I prepared for visiting hours. She asked if I'd received the basket of toiletries from her boutique; she apologized for not having time to visit. I quickly assured her that it was quite all right—Beulah was the last person I wanted to see in room 327. Hanging up, I compared the Mall Manager with the Bitchy Roommate. I wondered if becoming cranky and snide with age was inevitable, like gathering fat around your middle.

Before I knew it, my neighbor Lupe Gutierrez arrived with a yellow mum done up in gold foil and a pink ribbon. For the umpteenth time,

Lupe apologized for sending me to Dr. Tormentor in the first place. I shushed her before Mrs. Vic woke up and began another diatribe.

Soon after Lupe left, Buddy stopped by with an overflowing basket of pink roses. Actually, they were from Bentley's but likely snitched from a fresh grave. As soon as he was out the door, a volunteer brought in a beautiful gloxinia plant from Darcy, wired by a florist in San Francisco.

By late afternoon, I'd collected a nice bunch of flowers. The sun came around to my window, and its rays danced over the many colorful blossoms. I could not compete with Mrs. Vic's blooming galleria, but neither did I have to hang my head in shame.

When the supper trays arrived, I ate my mashed potatoes and Jell-O in peace because two elderly nursing cronies had come to sit with Mrs. Vic. I tried to ignore them even though she was whispering about me. One of the old gals got up and closed our dividing curtain halfway, but I could still hear them. Mrs. Vic was soon harping about her murdering son-in-law. She told them she'd hired a private detective to find some missing evidence. I wondered if real people actually hired private eyes. Evidently. She said he was the best in town. He was costing her a fortune.

I finished my food in no time and lowered my bed, while her voice grew louder. "Margo called me the morning she died. She said if anything happened to her, I should check her father's grave. It was such an odd thing for her to say because he's on the top level of the mausoleum. I'd just had the attendant place new silk flowers up there for him. Before I could ask what she meant by *grave*, she hung up. That was the last I ever spoke to my daughter." Mrs. Vic's voice stuttered on the last words.

"Isn't she up there next to him?" one of the nursing friends asked.

"Yes she is. There was no love lost between Ed and me, but he adored Margo. It seemed only proper to put them together. I had quite an argument with Tom about it. He wanted her buried in the Grenadier plot."

While the friends made gurgling noises in response, Mrs. Vic did her nose-blowing business, which seemed to be her pattern whenever she spoke about her daughter.

"Did I tell you I found him pillaging my house the day I had this fibrillation episode? He still had a key! Said he'd been worried about me when I didn't answer the door. Mabel Harstaad was helping me in the bathroom. You remember Mabel, my rehab nurse?

"Anyhow, when we came out, there he was, down on all fours under the elephant, searching for the money and the evidence Margo had been gathering. I can assure you, there's nothing hidden in my animals. Why would he be under the elephant if he were so concerned about me? I tell you, I'll trap that conniving rat if it takes everything I have to do it."

The snarl in her voice made me shiver. I wondered about an elephant in her house and figured it was some sort of carved footstool. I could imagine her handsome son-in-law down on the floor, trying to figure out what she was up to. What courage he had. If he could put up with this woman for an in-law, he could surely run the government. I wondered how a person would go about joining his campaign team. With no more cramps to slow me down, I could enter politics myself. It might be a very exciting life.

My phone rang and I reached to answer it. "Hi Mom, how are you?"

"Oh, Darcy, I'm so glad to hear your voice. I'm okay, I guess."

"A lot of pain?"

"Well, yes, but I've been too preoccupied to notice."

"Preoccupied? About what?"

I pulled my pillow over my mouth to block the sound. "I've been lying here thinking about going into politics," I whispered. "And people crawling under elephants. How are you, dear?"

"Elephants and politics? Aren't elephants Republican? I thought you were a Democrat. My gosh, Mom, what kind of weird drugs are they giving you? Anyway, I have great news. I have a new boyfriend. He's what you'd call a hunk. He jogs five miles every morning. And he's a CPA. He's going to be very successful. Last night he took me to the opera. It was great. I've never been to an opera, have you?"

Darcy was a pretty girl, with a tiny waist, dark curly hair and mystical green eyes like my father's. I could visualize her all dolled up, attending an elegant San Francisco opera. I had an instant vision of Cher in *Moonstruck*, Loretta shedding tears during *La Bohème*. "I'm so happy for you, darling. What did you wear?"

"Jeans and a black blazer."

"What?"

"It's okay, he wore the same thing. We drove over on his motorcycle. Our seats were way up in the starving student section. We blended perfectly."

"If he's a CPA, couldn't he afford a car and decent tickets? Didn't you want a lovely red gown like Cher's?"

"Percival says it will be more fun to learn about opera if we start at the top and work our way down. Did I tell you his name is Percival?"

I imagined this Percival character arriving in Heatherton with a long grubby ponytail, torn jeans, a leather jacket and an earring in one ear. I could see him shaking hands with Buddy. "Darcy, are you sure we'd approve of a Percival?"

"Don't worry, everyone calls him Percy."

Percy? Percy and Darcy? What a combination. When I was pregnant with this child, I was reading *Pride and Prejudice* and was madly in love with Mr. Darcy. I decided to name my baby Darcy whether Buddy liked it or not, which he didn't. Maybe now my choice was coming back to haunt me.

"You'll love him," she was saying. "By the way, I can come home next week and help you."

"Be sure and bring a snapshot of him, okay?"

"Okay—Mom? Your voice is slurry. Don't you have any idea what they're giving you for pain?"

"Something strong, I guess. My voice is slurry? I am woozy when I stand up, but the pills are easing the pain today."

Darcy chuckled. "Mom, you need some sleep. I'll hang up now so you can rest. I love you. I'll see you soon, okay?"

"Okay. Please try and come next week. I'm not supposed to lift a finger."

After we hung up, Ole appeared. I did not want him anywhere near Mrs. Vic, and so I eased myself from bed, put on my pink robe and asked him to walk with me to the solarium. While strolling with Ole, I was mightily relieved that the urine bag was not hanging over my arm like a Gucci-gold handbag.

Ole's eyes twinkled and he wore a mischievous grin. As soon as we sat down, he pulled out an Arby's bag from under his windbreaker. "What did you have for dinner?"

"Bland, bland stuff." I stared at the bag and sniffed it. "Ole, do you have crunchy potato cakes in there?"

"You told me once they were your favorite food."

"Yeah, but I'm not supposed to eat that stuff right now. It gives you gas."

Despite my protest, I was drooling.

"Gosh, I'm sorry," Ole said. "It was just an impulse buy."

"And a very sweet thought." I opened the bag and handed him a roast beef sandwich, taking in the aroma. "Did you eat dinner yet?"

"No, but I also brought you these." He reached in his pocket and pulled out several sheets of paper, copied from magazines and newspapers. "I was looking for more information on my Stony Ridge property. I found this at the library."

The articles were about Tom Grenadier and Mrs. Vic's daughter, with a feature story about her concert tour of Germany. *Margo Grenadier.* She was beautiful. I wondered how Mrs. Vic could have given birth to such an amazing daughter.

"It seems your Grenadier fellow is a distant relative of the Heathertons," Ole said.

"Which one, Salt or Pepper?"

"Salt, I think." We both chuckled. Without much thought, I began to nibble on a potato cake, just around the edges. "His grandmother was a Heatherton," Ole added.

"So his family goes back to the beginning? They don't seem like the kind of people to produce murderers."

"These articles tell only the good they've done. But I learned from a doctor who periodically drops by our lab that Grenadier's maternal grandfather was Dr. Embers, former head of the medical board here at Loving Memorial."

I was listening to Ole, but the potato cakes were wonderful. I figured one would not hurt me. I'd been hungry all day.

"It seems the old guy was snitching his patients' morphine. When your friend Mrs. Vic found out, she had his surgical privileges revoked. She tried to have him fired, but flunkies on the board came to his defense. Not much later, Dr. Embers died in a boating accident. That was the public version, anyway. On the inside, they believed it was an overdose. Maybe Mrs. Vic didn't want her only child married to Dr. Embers' grandson. The lingering animosity, even guilt for his death."

I leaned back and ate another potato cake, then drank some of Ole's Pepsi. Real food was amazing.

"So the way I see it," Ole said, "her daughter had trouble with her marriage, then had a tragic accident. Naturally, the old lady started blaming someone in the Embers' clan."

I unwrapped a roast beef sandwich. "Or Margo threatened to leave the guy. Maybe he used drugs like his grandfather. Maybe he and Margo actually fought while they—we don't know how she fell off that cliff."

We were both quiet a minute, thinking and eating. After a few bites, I set down my food and chuckled. "Look at us, sitting here like characters in an Agatha Christie novel."

When two elderly couples came into the solarium, we stashed the Arby's bag and began to watch a rerun of *Green Acres*. We were very close on the settee. I could feel the warmth of Ole's arm next to mine. Casually, he reached over and picked up my hand. His grasp was strong, warm and pleasant, even though I could feel a callus here and there. I chattered to keep the mood light.

"Just think, Ole, when you retire, you can go up to Stony Ridge and fix up your cabin and lakebed the way Lisa and Oliver did on *Green Acres*."

Arnold the pig waddled through the unfinished wall of Lisa's bedroom. It reminded me again of Grandpa's clairvoyant pig, and I told Ole how Poppy had come upstairs in the middle of the night, got into my room and pressed her slimy, cold nose to my cheek. "I woke up screaming my head off. Jumped so hard in the middle of my bed that I broke the slats. Mattresses and featherbeds crashed to the floor. When Grandpa and Grandma came running in and switched on the light, there was Poppy, bouncing off the furniture, flinging her fat self against the walls, squealing, snorting, on a wild frenzy to find the doorway out."

I laughed, remembering the astonished expressions on my grandparents' faces. Laughing hurt my incision, so I let go of Ole's hand, grabbed a throw pillow and jammed it against my belly for support. "Poppy ran squealing through Grandpa's legs and down the stairs. That old man didn't know whether to cuss at the pig or me.

"Grandma stood there in her long flannel nightgown, a teeny smile at the corners of her mouth. Grandpa was in his red long johns, running upstairs and down for half an hour trying to pry Poppy out of the house. He finally used a pitchfork to prod that animal out from under the stairway. He was not happy when he stomped in to rebuild my bed at three in the morning."

Ole laughed out loud, then took a large white hanky from his pocket and blew his nose.

"So when all the commotion died down and I went to the bathroom, there it was, my first period. The pig knew!"

While I laughed at my own story, other couples stared at us. I pressed the cushion more tightly into my belly. "Oh my, that sad old couple. I've never seen the humor until tonight. Maybe it's all the drugs. Darcy says my voice is slurry. Is my voice slurry, Ole?"

"Maybe a little. But you need to laugh, Miranda. It helps with the healing." He picked up my hand again.

I wanted to sit there all night and chatter nonsense with Ole, but the PBX operator announced that visiting hours were over. With my gut screaming for rest and my voice slurring, I headed back to bed.

At the door to my room, I stopped and peered in. Mrs. Vic's nursing friends were gone, but now she was speaking with a man I hadn't seen before. "I wonder if that's the private eye she hired?" I whispered to Ole.

"Listen in, if you can. That fellow looks as if he knows all her secrets." Ole held my hand a moment and gave me one of those long searching looks that I could not understand. Then he left me alone with Mrs. Vic and her guest.

Before lowering myself into bed, I used the bathroom, brushed my teeth and smoothed down my hair. Coming back into the room, I caught a better view of him. He was middle-aged, with a bit of gray hair. Everything about him looked square—his brown suit with broad shoulders, his wide face with a boxy jaw, his hands with fat fingers and hefty knuckles. He looked like maybe he'd worked his way up from prizefighter.

I lay down behind my curtain and tried to listen. They were talking about money rolling over and insurance policies, but I could not hear enough to put it all together.

Unable to figure out their conversation, I reviewed my own situation. Ole was right. Laughter was good for me. Mama and I had giggled a lot on the buses.

Buddy and I were also very silly, in the beginning. Sometimes he took Polaroids of me making goofy faces. He called me his peanut face or his slithery motor oil face, something ridiculous. We thought it was hysterical at the time.

On the one-year-anniversary of Mama's death, he dared me to try marijuana. I'd ached for my mother that day and needed to release the tension. In the evening, Buddy dragged me down to his basement party room. I barely got the hang of the grass and giggled more than I inhaled. I only did it that one time, but it was the most fun I ever had with Buddy Blight.

I could hear Mrs. Vic clearly now. "I found a key to a diary in Margo's bedroom after she died. I've never found the book it might unlock. But that slime bag was crawling around under my elephant's belly last week, looking for something."

The man cleared his voice as if to change the subject. "Tell me again what your daughter said the day she died."

"She called that morning and said, 'Mom, I've learned something too horrible to talk about. If anything happens, go to Daddy's grave.'"

"To his grave?"

"I don't know whether she meant the mausoleum or the entire cemetery. But by God, I'm going to find it, if we have to dig up every rigor-mortised body in the place."

I'd been to the cemetery with Buddy a zillion times. I'd been in the mausoleum too. I enjoyed sitting and thinking among the marble columns. Now I could visualize Margo and her father Ed side by side on the top level, their names on gold plates, with vases of silk flowers anchored above.

Silk flowers. I spoke before I thought about it. "Did you look in the vase on your husband's vault?" I called out. "A person could hide something in there. There's a long pole in the flower room you can use for moving those vases up and down."

"What?" they both asked. The man came over and pulled back the curtain.

"I'm sorry, I know this is none of my business, but I couldn't help hearing and . . . and you said you put silk flowers in his vase. A lot of people do that in the mausoleum. Your daughter could have hidden something in there. But then . . . it was just a silly thought, I suppose."

Mrs. Vic organized herself. "Miranda, this is Mr. Sebastian Cross. Miranda lives in Heatherton. In a mobile home park, I believe she told me at breakfast. A doublewide."

Lordy, she was snide.

Mr. Cross was polite. He came to my bed and shook my hand. "Hmm, maybe I need to peek in Ed's flower vase." He looked at me and winked. "Well, young lady, if I ever get to—which park are you in?"

"Morning Glory, number 48." I said it flippantly, knowing Mr. Sebastian Cross would never call on someone like me. He smiled before turning back to her. I sensed he shared my belief that she was plumb off her rocker.

Before Mrs. Vic ridiculed me further, Kathy arrived with my sleeping pill. After she left, I watched my roommate perform her evening ritual, which involved a lot of grunting, groaning and bossing around another nurse. In a desperate need to protect my vital organs, I managed to turn all the way onto my abdomen, despite the incision. Drifting off, I thought again about Ole and the intense looks he sometimes gave me. I could still feel the strong grip of his hand with mine. A warm and tingly sensation wriggled under my incision. Something like romance, but maybe—

Without warning, I burped potato cakes. Then I knew. That warm and tingly feeling wasn't romance; it was a giant wave of nausea and a new round of spasms. I had to scramble for my mustard-colored emesis basin. And in a terrible gush, I heaved up the bag of potato cakes.

I'm sorry, Arby's, I love your food. But honestly, I should have known better.

Two days after surgery.

– 11 –

"You were vomiting in the night," Dr. Azadi said, after I'd endured another breakfast of gruel and Jell-O. "And you have an elevated temp. We need to watch this, Miranda. I'm not sure why you were vomiting. One more day, I'm afraid."

In the meantime, Mrs. Vic bossed me around whenever I got up to use the restroom. "Miranda dear, since you're up anyway, would you mind pushing this overbed table out of the way? And bring me a glass of fresh water; I'll just rinse my teeth." She'd been saying *Miranda dear* since dawn, which made me furious. She'd also stated that my worsening condition was due to the fact that Dr. Azadi was a woman, what else could I expect?

By lunchtime, I was ready to pull out the roots of her clamshell, beeswax hair. The nurses had again rolled up our beds and propped us in front of our heat-retaining dishes. I put on the noon news so I would not have to listen to Mrs. Vic gripe about hospital food. While she hollered over the intercom for a better lunch, I watched the gloomy stories unfold.

Someone was mugging senior citizens while they strolled away from bank teller machines. The man in the red ski mask had raped again, an exchange student from Mexico this time. Juveniles were ransacking mobile homes in Heatherton, a story that hit close to home.

Maybe Buddy was right to worry about someone slashing my tires. The nearby woods would be a perfect hiding spot for a marauding gang of teenaged thugs.

70

Had I remembered to lock my door? I was about to pick up the phone and call the Morning Glory manager when the face of Mrs. Vic's son-in-law appeared on screen. I tried to turn off the TV, but I was not quick enough.

"You leave that on," she snarled and then watched intently.

It occurred to me that Tom Grenadier looked much like the drawing of Prince Charming in my Cinderella coloring book. The prince was an old-fashioned royal figure that I'd colored with Crayolas of the time: his tunic in red violet, his knee britches in green blue, his eyes and hair in brown overlaid with burnt sienna. I'd used *flesh* for his wide tender lips and then changed the name to *peach* long before the crayon people did so officially.

The current prince was very polite. He said he was terribly sorry that his late wife's mother was under so much stress; he was taking every step to ensure her care and comfort. However, Mrs. Vic's farfetched accusations would not deter him. The woman had no concept of reality whatsoever. Continuing his bid to be governor of our great state, he would use whatever talents he had for the good of the people, as his father and grandfather had done before him.

It was a short segment, but so much tension seeped from Mrs. Vic's body that I almost choked on the poisoned air. As soon as the report ended, she hissed at me. "Turn that damn thing off."

We finished the meal in silence. I quickly lowered my bed, got the curtain closed between us, wriggled onto my side and turned from Mrs. Vic.

"I suppose you believe him," she called out a few minutes later.

I shut my mouth.

"Miranda? Answer me. I know you're not asleep."

"What?"

"Do you believe him?"

"I don't know anything about him."

"Well, you had no trouble thinking of that cemetery last night. Can't you make some kind of judgment today? Do you think I've made up a story like this? Can't you trust me? You and I were close once."

"Close? I was a student. You were a teacher. You consider that being close?"

"Of course it's close. There's nothing closer than a pupil and her mentor."

"Oh no, you were certainly not a mentor. Look, I'm sorry about your daughter. I have a daughter too, and I'd die if something terrible happened to her. I can imagine you must be devastated, but I need to rest. I want to go home. I can't talk about this anymore."

Fortunately, Melvin came in with our 1:00 p.m. medications. Mrs. Vic made nasty comments about all the drugs I must be taking and then bragged that her thinking was as clear as a bell. She said her murdering son-in-law was grabbing at straws to imply she'd been addled by a few pills. "Is Jackson on duty this afternoon?" she asked Melvin. "Get him for me."

When Jackson ambled in, I rolled over and peeked at him from under my covers. So adorable, I thought, all bronzed and blazing. He'd hitched his fingers in his security guard pants, and he was chewing gum as if there were no problems in the world. He glanced at me and pulled the curtain, cutting me off. For a moment, I allowed myself a flimsy fantasy. What would it be like to kiss a man with such honey-brown skin and sweet-peachy lips? I'd been raised to believe this was forbidden territory for a white girl like me. Even so, I wondered.

With that, I thought of Darcy and her new boyfriend. What nationality was this Percival, anyway? What did Darcy know about her new love? What if Percival were some kind of weird psychopath and ended up killing my daughter? How would I react? Would I be able to sort out who was telling the truth and who wasn't? Heavens no. I'd be out of my head with anguish and rage. I'd be way nuttier than Mrs. Vic.

Renouncing such terrifying thoughts, I let myself sink into a heavy nap. I was soon jolted awake by a harsh metallic clanging near my bed, as if Mrs. Vic were slamming together two stainless steel domes from our food trays. "Help me, damnit!" she roared over the racket. "He's going to kill me! Get the police. Call security and get him out of here!"

Terrified, I tried to sit up too quickly. The incision pain pushed me back. I shoved my fist into my mouth to stop my own scream. Remaining on my side, I looked at the floor. Charcoal-gray trousers and polished black shoes showed under the curtain between our beds. I was certain those feet did not belong to Melvin-the-nurse or Jackson-the-security-guard.

"Calm down, Nora," a man's voice hissed just above my head. His shape and bulk pressed backward through the hanging cloth. I could have goosed him through the thin curtain.

72

"I'm not going to hurt you," he said emphatically. "I'm concerned about your welfare."

He sounded concerned to me, the way a dutiful son-in-law should sound.

"Police!" she boomed again. "Get the state troopers in here before he kills me! I mean it. Get the hell out of here!"

While her outburst continued, his shoes scampered away. At the same time, glass exploded against the doorway, a crescendo of broken glass that cascaded downward in diminishing sounds. *Crash. Jingle. Chime. Tinkle. Jangle-jingle-clink.*

A moment later, Melvin dashed in through the carpet of glass on the floor.

"Did they stop him?" Mrs. Vic barked.

"For crying out loud, settle down. You can't be throwing flower vases at the—don't you dare. Don't you dare pick that up. Really, Missus, I think your medications are getting the best of—come on, honey, give me that glass." Melvin's voice lost all of its enthusiasm for outstanding patient care.

"Don't you honey me. Get Frank Armstrong up here. Head of security. And I mean STAT!"

Melvin's footsteps retreated to the continued sound of broken glass crunching under foot. Holding my breath, I pulled back the curtain just enough to catch a glimpse of her. Mrs. Vic looked like a wild woman; her eyes, cheeks and hair were all charged with madness. "Those nincompoops! They have to watch the stairwells, not just the elevators. He's tricky. He could hang a stethoscope around his neck and march right back in here. He'd have no trouble posing as a doctor. I'm the only thing that's keeping that man out of the governor's mansion and he knows it. He wants me snuffed out. If he can't do it himself, he'll hire someone else. My God, he could have walked right in here, shot me and strolled out again. He could have killed you too, Miranda!"

I pictured myself shot to death—the blood, the gore, nothing but bone fragments for Buddy to put under my tombstone. Stress hormones surged from my toenails to my hair.

A moment later, Frank Armstrong, head of security, crunched through the debris into our bizarre scenario. "Come on, Nora Margaret, calm down. Don't let your imagination run away with you. We're taking every precaution."

73

"My imagination? Don't you tell me about my imagination. You've known me since I babysat you. Haven't I always made sense? I want everyone searched who comes on this floor. *Everyone*, Frank. I'm trying to save lives here!"

Frank Armstrong was evidently her old buddy. While he tried to placate this Nora Margaret—I'd never heard that full name—I slipped from my bed, put on my robe and slippers and picked my way through the glassy debris. A janitor with a broom and dustpan brushed past me, followed by Melvin with a syringe on a tray. "Something for your heart, Nora honey," he said while I made a break for it.

Reaching the nurses' station, I propped myself against the counter. A prickling sensation shot up my legs into my bowels and bladder and then on up to my incision. "Who's . . . who's in charge?" I could barely whisper. I was either going to poop, heave or faint. Maybe all three. Several nurses ignored me and went off in three different directions.

I began to hyperventilate and grabbed my chest in real panic.

"Can I help you?" a ward clerk finally answered, although she did not look up from her computer screen. She seemed deeply involved in her learning curve.

"Who's the charge nurse? I need to talk to her." Suddenly, tears gushed down my face, my voice choked, and my heart went into some kind of freakish attack. I figured shock was dead ahead.

The ward clerk looked up, noticed my approaching crash, then stood, hurried around the desk and propped my shoulders. Assuring me that everything would be all right, she took my arm and led me to the office of the charge nurse. A plaque outside the door read Eileen Collins, R.N., M.S.N. Administrative Nurse IV.

Ms. Collins wore a three-piece, navy-blue business suit with a burgundy bow tie, almost identical to the hospital administrator's. She was so far beyond a wash-and-wear uniform that it was hard to believe the R.N. initials remained in her title. Her light brown hair fell into a perfect pageboy, and her dark eyes straddled a fence between professional concern and hard-nosed practicality. If she knew Mrs. Vic was throwing such a tantrum, she did not seem worried. Obviously, Eileen Collins maintained distance from her patients, both physically and emotionally. "Let's discuss your problem, Miranda," she said, handing me a tissue, indicating a chair opposite her desk.

I did not want to sit down. I wanted to cry out that Mrs. Vic should be *her* problem. "Doesn't anyone around here think that maybe the woman has gone over the edge? That she might be terribly upsetting to me? Don't you care what happens to me in that room? Get that crazy old woman away from me! Please!"

Ms. Collins frowned, handed me another tissue, then turned and dialed the phone. She wasted no time with chitchat. Instead, she whispered into the receiver and then swiveled around and said Mrs. Vic would be given a private room. I could wait in the solarium. She was sorry for the inconvenience. Before I could mumble thanks, Eileen Collins ushered me out the door.

I sat in the solarium and glanced at another daytime TV hospital love scene. I sincerely hoped this was not the reality in a modern medical care facility. I also imagined a young Mrs. Vic dallying with Dr. Tormelli in the linen closet, but the thought was too creepy to maintain. At last, a pink lady appeared and informed me that all was clear in my room.

The housekeeping staff had been very busy. My bed was smooth and turned down, the bathroom shone and the towels were fresh. Bed number one was done up with crisp new linens, beautifully free of wrinkles. Best of all, Mrs. Vic was not in it. Not a trace.

"Gracias, gracias," I said to the woman who'd done all this work. She grinned at me and patted my bed. I wanted to hug her and slip her a thousand-buck tip, but I simply returned her smile and slid into the sanctuary of fresh sheets. I was more than ready for a quiet nap.

At 5:30, Buddy showed up. At 5:35, Ole walked in. The two of them stood eyeing one another while I told them about my meltdown and Mrs. Vic's relocation to a private room.

Neither of them responded. Finally, Ole handed me a brown paper bag.

I worried for a second about deep-fried food, but I pulled out Clara Barton instead. "This is wonderful," I said, giving my doll a big kiss. "It's the nicest thing that's happened all week." I pulled at the ringlets over her ear and let them curl around my finger. "So thoughtful of you, Ole." I smiled at him and kissed Clara again.

"Good God," Buddy moaned, turning away and looking out the window. "Those damn dolls!"

Ole ignored him. "I remembered where you hid the door key and invaded your house. Hope you don't mind—"

"Is everything okay at home? I heard teenagers are breaking into Morning Glory homes."

"Ah ha! So you heard," Buddy said, pouncing on the idea. "I warned you!"

"Don't worry," Ole countered. "I've been watching your place. It's fine."

Buddy glared while I wondered what to do about this threesome we had going. A lie might be the best way out.

"Hey, you guys, I appreciate your coming to visit, but my fever has gone up again. I'm having chills." I pretended to shiver and tucked the blanket under my chin. It was a corny ploy, but men can be so gullible. "Buddy, could you find a nurse and bring me another blanket? Then go see about the bill? I should go home in the morning.

"Ole, can you take away my dinner tray and add fresh water to my flowers?"

Buddy wore down first and kissed me goodbye, a smacking, impressive kiss. Technically, I still belonged to him and he knew it. He headed for the door.

"He's a good-looking fellow," Ole said, watching him leave. "Don't you suppose he has girlfriends?" He looked absently out the window and avoided my scowl.

"Ole, please, I . . ."

He turned slowly. "I'm sorry. It's just that seeing you two together, well, now I can understand why it's so hard for you to leave him. He's macho, the kind of guy women fall for." Ole sat on the edge of Mrs. Vic's former bed and rubbed his big thumbs together.

I nodded at that bed and changed the subject. "You should have seen how crazy she was. She went berserk when her son-in-law came to visit. I feel sorry for that man, Ole. Sorry and scared to death."

"A security guard is questioning everyone as they come off the elevator. She has this hospital wrapped around her little finger, doesn't she?"

"She held power here for a lot of years. She was supervisor of all nursing before she retired. Evidently she still is."

Ole remained perched, in no hurry to leave. The sun was behind the building. The room grew dark in shadows. We did not add lights.

"What did she do to you, Miranda? Tell me what happened."

"I don't like to talk about it."

"You need to." He pulled a straight-backed chair to the side of the bed, straddled it backwards and rested his face on his arms. There was so much intensity in his eyes; I was thankful we were alone.

"She kicked me out of training. It was humiliating. I suppose that's why I married Buddy so quickly. To save face. In those days, you weren't allowed to stay in nurses training and be married. Not until the last three months."

"But why kick you out? What did you do wrong?"

I shrugged, and then a wild explanation popped into my head, likely drug induced. "Did you ever hear of Pussy Galore?"

"Aah . . . Pussy Galore of James Bond fame? Why?" Ole looked puzzled.

"I don't know . . . it's the word *galore*. Doesn't *galore* mean an abundance of?"

"Yeah but, an abundance of—"

"*Thumbs* Galore," I interjected quickly, realizing what he was about to say. "Thumbs Galore was me. I had no mechanical skills, and nursing is all about mechanical skills. I couldn't shake down the mercury in my thermometers; I had to sneak them into the dorm at night and practice. I couldn't slam-dunk a syringe of gunky antibiotic into someone's butt without hitting the bone. I could not even insert and fasten the cufflink-type buttons into my uniforms when they came back from the laundry every week. Our dresses and aprons were Mangle-ironed and stiff as boards. They could stand on their own. There must have been a couple dozen buttons up and down the front of the dress and holding the bib and apron together, and I was all thumbs."

"But Miranda, that's not enough to be kicked out for, surely? Not knowing how to button your dress?"

"My first injection? I bent the needle into a ninety-degree angle. And the surgeries? Surgery was an abomination for me. We did not have chemo drugs for cancer patients in those days. It was all slash and burn. Slash with every surgery, then burn with radiation. I had a man—they cut off his penis. Gave him estrogen and his breasts grew, his voice got high. Became a eunuch right before my eyes. Never once did Mrs. Vic help with the emotional impact, on him or me.

"The term *burnout* was certainly not in our vocabulary. We were only eighteen years old. We worked from 7:00 a.m. to 7:00 p.m., with a few hours for class in the middle. We ran up and down the hallways dressing horrid wounds and watching IVs like hawks. There were no black monitoring boxes in those days. And giving out meds? Wham! One mistake and you kill a patient. No ICU either. The critical and the dying were all lumped in with the recovering and the living. We got burned out. Most of the girls survived it, but me? I was grand and gloriously expelled."

Ole handed me my water glass and I took a sip—my voice was getting dry—but I was on a roll.

"I've heard that people who go into caregiving professions do so because they grow up thinking they have to be the caregivers of the world. That was me. I took care of my mother. She earned the money with her music, but I found us the seats on the bus. I shooed us into and out of the rest stops on time. More so, the older I became. Maybe that's why I wanted to be a nurse, I don't know. I do know it was shameful to be expelled in my third year. A dishonorable discharge for Thumbs Galore. If I'd graduated, I could be supporting myself right now. Nurses are making a lot more money—I could have learned."

Ole held up a hand to halt me. "Hmm. Maybe you need to forget Mrs. Vic right now. Just give it—well—I wouldn't join her son-in-law's campaign team if I were you." He surveyed my vacated room. "Are you definitely coming home tomorrow?"

"If my fever stays down."

"I thought you said it had gone up?"

"I lied so you guys would leave. I was nervous with both of you here at once."

"Will you need a ride?"

"No thanks. Lupe is coming for me. She promised to help me out until Darcy arrives."

"Okay. I have some errands in the morning, but I'll check on you when I get home. I'll bring over hot food. Don't try to make your own meals."

"Thanks, but I have dinners in the freezer. I'll be fine. Please don't worry about me."

He stood up, leaned over and kissed me goodnight, a neighborly kiss on my forehead. Ole knew I belonged to Buddy Blight and could never break free. I'd taken an oath, after all.

Those monks in the Alps had me pinned to the wall.

— 12 —

I once read that before an Indian carved a totem, he would study the wood and commune with it until he felt its spirit. I did the same with my dolls. After Ole left, I tucked Clara Barton under the covers with me; she was my totem of strength and compassion. When I rubbed her smooth porcelain, I felt thick sinews in her thighs, strong bones in her spine, a proud lift to the muscles in her neck. Clara Barton had all the courage I lacked. I felt it in my fingers.

I began making dolls after Buddy inherited a small house from an elderly woman who required a headstone. When he discovered that his new-found real estate was worthless, he came stomping home in fury. "That dump is not worth one cent. Everything's broken and full of g-d-dolls. I'll have to pay some idiot more than the damn place is worth, just to haul it all off!"

I insisted Buddy let me go see it. At first sight, that dismal gray house was a mess. A broken window, a moldy shower, a stopped-up sink. Broken-to-pieces dolls everywhere. Eyes here, hair there, noses, fingers, unraveling cloth bodies. It was utter carnage.

But among all the rotting materials, I discovered a trunk full of reasonably good velvets, satins and laces. I also found one decent Singer sewing machine that could whipstitch, zigzag, hem and button. "Oh, Buddy, this is wonderful," I said, ignoring the melted doll I found in the oven. Buddy beat his fist on the wall and cursed.

And then I discovered two lovely porcelain dolls packed between two pillows on the closet floor. Their gray and brown muslin dresses were a bit frayed, but their china faces were in perfect condition. When I examined them, I found tiny labels on the undersides of their skirts. One doll was *Miss Jane Bennet*, the other *Miss Elizabeth Bennet*. I whooped with excitement.

For two weeks, I scavenged everything of use in that old woman's house and lugged it home. I decided to reread *Pride and Prejudice* while I carefully dissembled the dresses adorning Lizzy and Jane. I found enough fresh muslin to make them new frocks in brighter blues and purples. Ripping seams, I imagined myself to be Lizzy Bennet sitting in her parlor with a sampler on her lap. I took to saying "I am all astonishment." That's also when I decided to name my coming baby after Mr. Darcy. Both words—*astonishment* and *Darcy*—upset Buddy.

While I reminisced, the elevator spewed out mobs of visitors. I lay in my dimly lit room and watched family groups swarm the hallway. Some were amazingly large and strong, especially clans from the various ethnicities. When one of their own was hospitalized, the others hovered around. Chattering groups became intense forces for healing; clucking grandmas, clinging children and spicy chickens in pots of simmering broth became their drugs of choice.

My family, however, had no clucking grandmothers, no lively kids, no contraband pots of chicken stew. My family was slipping farther away each day—Darcy so far away physically, Buddy so far away emotionally. Everyone else dead and gone.

"Mrs. Blight, I have a special delivery for you." A volunteer flipped on my light and handed me a box of chocolates done up in a gold ribbon. I scrunched my eyes in the sudden light and thanked her, then raised the head of my bed so I could read the attached note.

> *Dear Miranda,*
> *Please accept my apology for the abominable way I behaved toward you. I am truly sorry. I never meant to upset you. I need to see you in my room, 301, past the nurses' station. It's very important for me to talk to you.*
> *Fondly, Nora Vic*

I shoved the box to the floor as if it were crawling with poisonous snakes, then wadded the note and shot it across the room into the wastebasket. The phone rang and I prayed it was Darcy. "Where are you?" Mrs. Vic growled, not bothering with a pleasant hello. I dropped the receiver as if it were a deadly reptile.

She called again and I was afraid *not* to answer. "Miranda, come down here right now. I wouldn't be asking if it weren't important."

"Why?"

"I can't tell you over the phone, you ninny. Now get down here before I raise a ruckus."

Lordy, another ruckus. "All right, give me a minute." I hated myself for giving in, but soon I was nodding at the security guard stationed just outside room 301.

"It's okay, she's waiting for you, go on in." He was a grizzled, tough-looking fellow who seemed perfectly capable of stopping a murdering son-in-law.

Mrs. Vic's private room was plush with new furniture and an arbor of rosebud wallpaper. Heavy draperies framed the windows, which offered a sparkling view of the Centerville lights at night. Her bed was a slick new piece of hospital equipment fashioned from molded plastic, even the upper body side rail—nothing to bang or clang here. Bentley's flowers bloomed everywhere, but there were no visitors. It was 7:30 p.m. and Mrs. Vic was as alone as I was. She had no great healing force of a family either. No old grannies, no little urchins, no exotic pots of chicken stew.

Actually, Mrs. Vic looked a bit pathetic in her floppy hospital gown, dwarfed by all the impersonal floral arrangements. A leftover applesauce container and a smudged glass of water sat on her overbed table. She was awash in scattered, crumpled Kleenexes. No discard bag.

"Are you feeling better now?" I asked. "This is a very nice room. And the guard is right outside the door." I automatically grabbed up the used tissues and applesauce cup, brushed crumbs from her table and straightened the silent phone.

"It's fine." She waved away the room. "Miranda, sit down a moment, I need to talk to you. Not there—that chair's much too soft for someone who's post-op. You ought to know that. Sit in this firm chair."

I sat where I was told.

"Perhaps an apology is in order. I didn't mean to frighten you today. I was just so horrified when that man came slithering into our room."

"That's okay, but I think this is better for you . . . the privacy . . ."

"Yes, well, I've been thinking it over since you blurted out your notion about the cemetery last night. Tell me more about yourself. You have one child? A grown daughter?"

"Yes. In San Francisco." I sat stiffly and cautioned myself not to trust her. She'd be calling me *dear* again.

"I'm sure you miss her."

"I do! An empty nest is a lonely place."

"Ha! Tell me about it."

I cringed at my insensitivity. Mrs. Vic had lost a daughter, after all. Forever.

"Tell me about her, dear. What's her name?"

"Darcy."

"Darcy Blight?"

"Yes, Darcy Blight."

"Don't be so huffy. What does she do? Does she work?"

"She's an accountant in San Francisco. For Bales and Haley, I think."

"So she's intelligent then? And perhaps as pretty as you?"

How weird. Was I actually impressing Mrs. Vic? In my foxy-lady-pink gown?

"I have a brother in the Bay area," she said. "Maybe you could look him up, if you visit your daughter. He's crazy though. Nutty as a fruitcake. Tell me, Miranda, about the two men who have been visiting you. I know Dwight Blight, of course. But who is the other?"

She stated the request nicely, which calmed me a bit. I tried to describe how interesting Ole was. "He has a nice piece of property up on Stony Ridge. He's going to put in a nursery. Maybe someday he'll be growing flowers for Bentley's."

"Yes, I expect he will. This morning I was looking at the flowers he brought you. The rose was quite elegant. Do you have a job now that your daughter's gone?"

I told her about the dolls and she listened. "I might sell them in Ole's shop when he gets it up and running," I said. "He brought Clara Barton tonight, to keep me company."

"Clara Barton? Founder of the American Red Cross?"

"Yeah, I like medical people. I research them. I also have a set of Sue Barton dolls. I read all the books in junior high."

"I see. And you have the Clara doll right here . . . with you?"

Good heavens, what a trap. She was simply playing with me, dangling me like that horrid urine bag at the end of a long catheter tubing. "And you don't live with Buddy anymore?"

"No. But really, I have to go back to bed."

"So you're all alone? And Ole is the neighbor?"

"Mrs. Vic, there's nothing between Ole and me. I don't think he's that kind of fellow. He plays the piano. Classical music."

"A pianist? Hmm. That just shows you can never judge a book by its cover. Look at my son-in-law. Wasn't he charming on the noon news? Don't be fooled by charm, Miranda. It will cut you down every time. By the way, I need a friend like you."

"Excuse me?"

Friends? She had us being friends now? I stood up to leave. "I'm going home in the morning, Mrs. Vic. It was good to see you, and I'm very sorry about your daughter. But good night." I began to walk away.

"Miranda, come back here."

Boing! I'd had enough! I turned and stared at her. "Mrs. Vic, don't talk to me like that. I'm not your student any longer."

"No, but you are my friend. Please, come here."

"Why do you think you can growl at me one minute and say pretty please the next? And you expect me to do it!"

Despite my gutsy words, I obeyed and returned to her bed. She grabbed my hand and squeezed. Her dry, cold palm was lined with hard calluses, likely from pushing the wheels on her chair. "Because he has connections. Everywhere," she whispered.

There it was. Tom Grenadier again.

"Sebastian Cross hasn't called me yet tonight," she went on. "He was going to call after he went to the cemetery, but he hasn't. He's been watched, I'm sure of it. I can't trust anyone, Miranda, not even that guard out there. He could be bribed. And Tom knows all my friends. But he doesn't know you. He'd never think of you. I'm sure he'll come back tonight and sneak in here, maybe bribe the guard."

"Mrs. Vic!"

"Hush! Listen to me." Genuine fear lunged from her eyes. "Go get your doll, Miranda. That Clara Barton person."

"What?"

"The Red Cross doll. Please, dear, please!"

I still can't believe I did it. She turned me into her robot every time. I tottered all the way to my room, snatched Clara Barton from under the covers and hobbled all the way back to 301. "Just a little walking," I said to the guard. "It's good for me."

Mrs. Vic did not admire Clara Barton, even though I pointed out the exquisite little buttons on the shoes and the long lashes glued to the eyelids. Instead, she grabbed my doll and poked at every item of apparel; she lifted up the skirt, raised the petticoats and poked her finger down poor Clara's lace-trimmed panties. Huffing, she worked off the doll's left shoe without unbuttoning it.

She then ordered me to open the top drawer of her bedside table and fetch her cosmetic bag, which was lumpy with items from home. She removed a small jar of rouge, unscrewed the lid and pulled a piece of aluminum foil from inside, then unrolled a tiny key. "You heard me talking about the diary to Sebastian Cross. You guessed about the cemetery. But I . . . I haven't heard from him. Put this key in the doll's shoe and don't tell anyone, do you hear me?"

Well, my goodness, why not? I dropped the key into the shoe and fitted it back on Clara's foot. My fingers felt as clumsy as they had with the uniform buttons; they worked not at all like an expert doll maker's.

"Can you squat down, Miranda, with your incision? Bend at the knees?" she asked, while she grabbed Clara Barton and inspected the security of the shoe.

"Squat down? Of course not. I'm not supposed to—"

"I need you to get something from under the battery of my wheelchair. Can you squat down for just a minute? I'm certain you can, if you apply yourself."

"Under the battery of your wheelchair?"

"Shh! He may have had this room bugged. Why did it take so long to transfer me?"

"I think you watch too many melodramas, Mrs. Vic."

She whispered, "Miranda, listen to me. Go to my wheelchair, squat down, bend at your knees. Feel under that big black battery box. It's taped there. Get it for me. That pink froufrou outfit of yours isn't too tight, is it?"

Froufrou? Apply myself? For spite, I bunched the fullness of my gown and robe above my knees and squatted. My abdomen and thighs went into painful spasms, but I squatted anyway. When I reached under the wheelchair, I was shocked. Something hard and metallic was indeed affixed with tape to the underside of the battery box.

"Be careful," she hissed. "Don't cut yourself."

I felt the object and looked up in disbelief.

"Get it! Get it!" she mouthed.

I had to pull hard at the tape, amazed she'd been able to work on anything so close to the floor. Eventually, the object was in my hands and I prodded myself up. I knew what it was, yet I gasped as I stared at a very wide, very sharp butcher knife.

Mrs. Vic motioned me with wild, waving arms and an open, soundless mouth. I went to her bed, the knife in my outstretched hand. She grabbed it from me and swished it back and forth a couple of times as if she were Zorro, catching its glint in the light. When these antics were completed, she slipped it under her pillow.

"Thank you," she said, bringing out her hand, fluttering me away. "And Miranda, don't breathe a word of this to anyone. Keep that key secret as if your life depended on it. If you alert anyone, I swear I'll have my revenge. For starters, I'll see that your friend never has his flower field. Don't ever doubt what I'm capable of. Tom Grenadier may have the entire state behind him, but I can play hardball just as he can."

"Okay," I whispered, retrieving Clara Barton from Mrs. Vic's bed. "But you can't keep that knife here. Someone will find it. Or you'll be hurt. You'll roll on it."

"I'll do no such thing. And no one will find it. It's my protection, that's all, in case that bastard sneaks in here—why Miranda, you're positively white as a ghost. Go back to bed, dear, and don't worry about a thing. You know me. I always have everything well in control."

I could not move.

"Go on, before you faint or something. Now remember, dear, mum's the word. Don't ever forget old Mrs. Vic can make anything happen. By the way, you look very pretty in those nightclothes." Her phone rang. She lunged for it and quickly shooed me away.

Till my dying day, I'll see Mrs. Vic lying in that rosebud room, fire and fear shooting out of her milky eyes while she waved that nasty butcher knife under my nose. I could visualize her rolling into Morning Glory in her power wheelchair, whacking faces off Ole's flowers with her dagger as she sailed by. She'd go after my dolls when she reached my space. Then she'd chase after me.

Heading back to my room, I clutched Clara to my chest. A couple of the nurses stopped me at the desk to admire the doll. They touched her gently, examined her, oohed and aahed over her. *Please don't let them look in the shoe,* I prayed.

The wall clock showed that it was only 9:00 p.m., but I asked for my sleeping pill. Extra pain pills too. The nurses suddenly decided I did not look too well, despite my lovely gown. Was I spiking a temp again? Sending me back to my room, they gave me more care than I'd received all week. For some reason, having the founder of the American Red Cross in my bed made a difference. They wanted to be near her. I'd never thought such sensible professionals could be lured by the childish notion of dolls.

Just before I fell asleep, I wondered if Mrs. Vic could pull that knife out from under her sheets and whack off the head of an unsuspecting, task-oriented nurse who might be bending over to take her vital signs. And if she did, would I be an accomplice to murder? After all, I was the one who'd squatted down to obtain the murder weapon.

An accomplice to murder? How many years would I rot in prison?

Lordy, all I'd ever wanted was freedom from menstrual cramps.

— 13 —

The end of our second year in nurses training, we rotated to the night shift—11:00 p.m. to 7:00 a.m. Because patients often died in the predawn hours, our main task was to prevent those deaths, or at least be aware of them. The first day of night-shift nursing class, Mrs. Vic stood over us and stared with her sharp blue eyes until we bit our nails, crossed our legs and tried not to pee our white nylon panties.

Then she turned on me. "Why must you always . . . always check with your flashlight until you actually see the tiny rise and fall of the blanket on each patient's chest? Miss M. Smothers, do you have any idea?"

"Because," I gulped, "the patient might be dead?" I longed to look away, but her imperial-blue eyes came at me like ice picks.

"Cessation of breathing! Ex-pired. Yes, dee-aad." She shouted the word, then whispered, "I had a careless student once, a sloppy nurse who, despite my best efforts, was interested only in her boyfriend, Miss Smothers."

Why was she picking on me? Probably because I'd missed curfew the week before, when Buddy's truck had a flat tire. At 10:00 p.m. the dorm had been locked, and near midnight I had to wake the dorm mother to get back in.

Mrs. Vic rumbled on. "That sloppy girl twirled her flashlight like a baton over her patient's inert form. And in the morning? In the light of day? What did she find? What did I find? And the charge nurse and the doctors? What, Miss Smothers?"

"A body?" I asked, squirming on the points of those ice-pick eyes.

"Rigor mortis! Stiff as a board." She'd pronounced the dreaded words in a low, slow and ghoulish tone, like Digger O'Dell, the creepy undertaker from Grandpa's old radio program, *The Life of Riley.*

Remembering the words *rigor mortis*, I recalled the nightmare I had a few weeks before surgery. I felt the same paralysis now as when Mrs. Vic had dangled her huge, denigrating cross-thermometer in front of my eyes. I was awash with terror.

Eventually Clara Barton got me under control and we went to sleep, until something equally ghoulish crept into room 327. I sensed it at the edge of slumber, yet I could not get myself fully awake. Feeling a warm pressure on my hand, I forced open one eye and saw heavy fingers clasping my wrist. I opened the other eye and realized that a man's hand was holding my arm; another hand was shining a pocket flashlight onto my ID wristband.

When I squirmed a bit, the light disappeared. My arm was dropped.

"What is it?" I drawled. "Is it time for medication?"

"No, go back to sleep. I must have the wrong room."

I raised my head and opened my eyes. The light from the hallway allowed me a glimpse of a man wearing a lab coat, carrying a tray of tubes and syringes.

"Who are you looking for?"

"Ah, Nora Vichy . . ." He slurred her name and stopped in the doorway.

"Is something wrong with her?"

"No. No. We just need to . . ."

I sat up on my elbow. "Are you sure she's okay, because . . ." Had she stabbed herself with that butcher knife? Why else would she require lab work in the dead of night?

He snapped at me. "She's fine. Just tell me where she is."

"They transferred her." The light was behind him as he stood in the doorway, and so I could not see his face.

"Which room?" he whispered urgently.

I was so confused. Was this a middle-of-the-night terror or could it be the murdering son-in-law masquerading in a white jacket? Could it be possible that Mrs. Vic was neither crazy nor brain damaged after all?

I'd never spoken to a murderer, and I stumbled on my words now. "I . . . I'm not sure. You'll have to ask the nurse." When he stepped back and the light glanced off his face, I realized I'd gone completely bonkers. This guy was much younger than Prince Charming on television. He wore dark-rimmed glasses and his hair was as drab as worn shoe leather. Whoever he was, I was certain he could not possibly be her son-in-law, murderer or not.

"Who are you?" I asked, wide awake now, aware of how disoriented I'd been.

"Go back to sleep." He raised a finger, then turned and disappeared along the hallway.

I fumbled in the sheets for my call button and punched it reluctantly. A voice responded over the speaker. "Can I help you?"

I hated intercoms. I did not want to blurt out nonsense over a crackling microphone for everyone to hear. During my student days, we ran ourselves ragged all night long answering lights over the patients' doors.

While I tried to think what to say, I glanced at my clock and noticed that it was 11:00 p.m. The nurses should be at the desk for shift report. They'd surely notice a strange man strolling by, carrying a tray loaded with syringes.

"I'm sorry. I hit the bell by accident," I said.

"Are you okay?"

"Ah . . . yes . . . just a dream."

"Go back to sleep. Everything's fine."

I eased myself off the bed, put on my pink robe and slippers, and held onto the walls until I reached the door. I could see to the far end of the dimly lit hall. A security guard slouched in a white chair in front of 301. He held reading material in the glow of a small table lamp. Could a lab tech have gotten past him without raising suspicion? Could the guard be asleep? Or bribed?

But if someone had snuck into her room, she would have been screaming bloody murder by now. All was quiet along the hospital corridor. Had I hallucinated the entire incident?

I stood frozen in the doorway, easing off a fingernail with my teeth. Maybe he was hiding somewhere—in a utility room, under a patient's bed, behind a laundry cart. Maybe he'd invade my room again if I went back to sleep, though why, I had no idea.

I returned to my bed, picked up Clara Barton and ran my finger across her shoe. The outline of the key was still there. I glanced frequently toward the door, ready to pounce on the call button. I finally gave up on sleep, raised the head of my bed and turned on the TV.

Despite my fear, my sleeping pills took effect. The next thing I knew, another person was standing over me. This time I woke up fully cognizant. A black nurse stood by my bed. She smiled, then quickly poked a thermometer in my mouth and flipped off my TV. Another smile and I recognized her.

She was Miss Joanie Sampson, the first black girl ever admitted to the Loving Memorial School of Nursing. I had not stayed in touch with ex-classmates, but I was thrilled to see her now. She was the only one in our class who could laugh down Mrs. Vic.

Her nametag said *J. Anderson* so she must be married. She wore a scrub outfit from the Perinatal Pavilion; the lively fabric bounced with floppy-eared pink and blue bunnies. Staffing had evidently floated her to our unit due to a lull in the baby business tonight.

"So it really is you, Miranda." She took the thermometer from my mouth, then leaned over and hugged me. "I haven't seen you in an age, girl. What have you been up to?"

"Marriage, a daughter, cramps and a hysterectomy. What about you?" My voice was hollow and droopy, hers bright and full of energy.

"About the same, except I still have all my parts. I've been working here ever since graduation. Nightshifts are easier with my kids at home. Have you been nursing?"

The question startled me. How could she have forgotten my disgrace?

"I never finished," I said, stumbling on the words. "Don't you remember? I married Buddy Blight instead."

Joanie laughed a big daytime laugh that had no part of this quiet, low-voiced, scary night. "Heavens yes, now I remember. Seems in those days you could only see the light in the blight." She stretched it out. Liiiiight in the b-liiiiight. "That's what we all used to joke about, remember?"

"Blight is right. We're separated now."

"Didn't you have some run-in with Mrs. Vic?" She rolled her eyes and motioned with her head toward the other end of the hall. During this talk, she managed to check my incision, take my blood pressure, count my pulse, straighten my sheets, fluff my pillows and admire Clara Barton. Now she stood by quietly, looking down at me.

I squirmed. "Yes . . . she asked me to leave."

"I remember that now. None of us could figure it out. You just disappeared into the night, like the Gestapo marched in or something. Several of us went down to her office the next day and demanded to get you back, but she slammed the door in our faces and refused to discuss it. We tried calling your grandparents, but they said you were sick, not to bother you. Then we read in the paper you were married to Buddy Blight. We couldn't figure out why you didn't invite us to the wedding."

"There wasn't a wedding. We just went away and—"

"Well, we all thought it was terribly romantic. You were the first one of us to be married."

"Thanks," I said sarcastically. "My grandparents never told me you called. I wanted to talk to you all, but I was too embarrassed."

"Really? That's a shame. What'd you do to rile Mrs. Vic so much, kill a patient or something? We thought maybe you were so enraptured with Buddy Blight that you forgot to shine the light on some old geezer and he woke up with rigor mortis."

I looked at Joanie's bright open face and sparkling eyes. I half sighed, half laughed. She was awfully close to the truth, but I could not tell her. I'd never told anyone. "I could never do anything well enough to please her. Joanie, is she all right?"

"The crazy madam? Personally, I think she's nutty as a fruitcake. She can't walk, her heart's giving out on her, her mind's chock-full of paranoia, but her mouth works just fine. She's scheduled for a psych eval tomorrow, but I doubt she'll cooperate. Eileen Collins gave her a lecture about scaring everyone to death after you broke down in tears today."

"You heard about that?"

"It's in your chart, baby."

"What next? You must all think I'm as bonkers as she is. Well, I'd better ask. Did Mrs. Vic need blood work tonight? A little bit ago?"

"Blood work? No one said so during report."

"Was a lab tech up here? Looking for her?"

"You've been having crazy dreams, girl. All that hooey they gave you at bedtime. Don't take any more of that stuff. Just use Tylenol now, okay?"

I figured Joanie was right about me dreaming up the man, but I knew I had not dreamt the knife episode earlier in the evening.

"Joanie, I have to tell you something. You have to promise me you won't discuss this with anyone. Promise?" A sudden commotion in the hallway prevented me from asking her to crisscross her heart. A nurse ran by, spotted Joanie and hollered, "Need you, babe. 332's coding."

Joanie was gone.

I watched the entire nightshift run to room 332. A male attendant dashed past, pushing the crash cart. An ER doc followed hot on his heels. I figured they'd be frantic in that room for a few minutes, squirting chemicals into a flaccid heart, slapping electric paddles on the patient's chest, performing all the heroics I'd seen on television but never learned myself, not even in a CPR class when Darcy took swimming lessons. I was too scared to try.

With the entire night crew in room 332, I had a clear shot to room 301. I donned my robe and slippers and then hobbled as fast as I could down that long dim hallway. I remembered my student days, moving from room to room and shining my flashlight on each mound until I could see it breathing. I remembered the doorway of the four-bed ward and the terrifying flickering behind the curtain, the big round comatose woman I'd lit on fire, the dashing in and rolling over and over her flaming belly.

I wondered what I was doing with this nighttime trek. Igniting or extinguishing?

Frieda Dorflander, an aide who'd been here since my student days, almost caught me as I passed the nursing station. "Going somevere, Miz Blight?" she asked, in her threatening German accent.

"Ah . . . nowhere. Just pacing. Couldn't sleep. Heard the commotion. Have a cramp in my leg. Need to walk a little." I leaned forward and rubbed my thigh, and even stomped on my leg a few times for good measure. Surgery pain ripped across my belly, but my act fooled Frieda.

When the phone rang softly, I slithered by.

With each bit of pacing, I inched toward Mrs. Vic's room. Jackson was the lucky security guard on duty. I was surprised to see him, but the staff probably had to double up with Mrs. Vic on board. He looked up at me with his adorable grin. "Hi, Miranda," he whispered. "How come you're not sound asleep?"

"Too much commotion," I whispered back. "And bad dreams. I thought a strange man was looking for her. But nothing unusual is happening?"

"Not a thing. She's sleeping like a baby."

"Ha!" I said. "I can't imagine that."

He shrugged. "Go on, have a look. Do you good to see her so peaceful."

I bit down on my lip to keep from smiling. He'd played right into my hands and not provided much security at all. *I am all astonishment,* I thought to myself, trying to lighten my mood.

The room was shadowy, but the light from the bathroom was on, the door ajar. I could see her just fine. The head of her bed was at a forty-five degree angle. I tiptoed closer, until I stood over her the way the phantom of my nightmare had stood over me. Her mouth was partly open; she snored at a medium pace and volume. Wisps of yellow-gray hair lay across her pale forehead. Her gown twisted around her muscular arms and chest. There was no sign of a knife.

I moved closer to her bed and very slowly, hardly daring to breathe, I reached over the plastic side rail and placed my hand flat on her sheet. If she woke up, she'd bellow like Poppy the pig or pull that knife out from some fold in the bedding and rip me to shreds.

Telling myself to hurry, I crawled my fingers near her shoulder but found nothing. I wondered if her nurse had discovered the weapon when giving bedtime meds. Mrs. Vic moaned and twisted a bit. The pillow wriggled with her; I spotted something dark underneath.

After the next snore, I put my hand flat on the sheet and held my breath until I could feel the hard smooth handle of the butcher knife. I curled my fingers around it, pulled gently, and watched the shiny steel blade slide from beneath her pillow. I breathed deeply, as when I'd gone into Darcy's bedroom and removed some contraband from under her sleeping head. I'd once found firecrackers under her pillow. Buddy had brought them home from an Indian reservation. Imagine. A seven-year-old child sleeping on cherry bombs.

Mrs. Vic snored on while I retrieved the butcher knife, held it up and stared at it. The bathroom light sparked off the blade. I remembered Grandpa slaughtering the pigs and Grandma decapitating her chickens. I summoned their courage. I held the knife in both hands and suddenly felt giddy with power. How easy to plunge this weapon into Mrs. Vic's heart. I angled the sharp point directly over her chest.

This woman, who had so ruined my life.

I felt my heart pound and even heard it lub dubbing. It would be such a reward to rip her wide open. If I could set comatose patients on fire and conjure up rectal crosses, I could surely butcher . . . I knew how to butcher . . . I closed my eyes and saw streaks of blood red and trophy gold flash inside my eyelids.

Revenge. That's what I needed. Revenge. An eye for an eye . . .

I don't know how long this insanity lasted, but at some point, I slipped the knife under my robe and clutched the handle through my pocket. I tightened my grip while the steel blade slid along my foxy-lady nightgown. It ran hard against my thigh, the tip pointing downward. I backed away step by step, then turned at the doorway and escaped. I sucked in my breath and forced myself to speak. "Yes," I said to Jackson, "she's sleeping like a babe."

"Can you get back to your room okay?" he asked, looking up. "You look a little shaky."

"I'm o . . . okay. Thanks." I began a long confused stumble down the hall but somehow walked upright past the nurses' station. The code must have ended one way or another. A couple of staff were charting under fluorescent desk light, but Joanie was nowhere in sight. "You done pacing now, Miranda?" Frieda asked, as I hobbled by.

"Yea . . . yes ma'am."

Reaching my room, I leaned against the hall for support. The dizziness and confusion made me wonder what exactly had happened in room 301. I'd been standing at Mrs. Vic's bedside with the knife raised . . . and then what? I could not remember. What had I done, influenced by all those terrible drugs turning me upside down?

Ignoring my own room, I snuck into a small utility kitchen two doors down. The knife was clearly too full of clues to dump in the trash or put on the dirty dish tray. I spotted a space between the refrigerator and counter—two inches of dark concrete that looked like it had never been cleaned. If I slid the weapon in there, no one would locate it until the next century.

I pulled the knife from under my robe and stared at it in the bright kitchen light. I expected streaks of blood but it was as slick as a whistle. I looked under my robe to check for blood on my gown or thigh, but I must have washed it off.

I continued to stare. *What in God's name had I done with this thing?*

"You need something, Miranda?" Joanie's voice made me jump.

I tried to hide the knife behind my back but guilt spread over my face. She filled the entrance and stared at me.

Joanie's eyes grew wide. I could not fool her, so I slowly pulled the weapon from behind my back and handed it to her. "I went to see Mrs.

Vic. She had this with her, in her bed. She didn't wake up. I took it. I think I might have killed her."

"My God, this was in her bed?" Joanie stared at the object in her hand. "And you think you *killed* her with it?"

"I don't know. I'm so dizzy." I slumped onto a kitchen stool and buried my face in my hands.

"You killed her? Mrs. Vic? You think you killed her?" Joanie rotated the blade back and forth; sudden bursts of light reflected my wickedness. Then she said, "Well, there's no blood on this thing. Is there blood on you?"

"No." I showed her my clean hands and gown. "But I could have washed it off in the bathroom. I wanted revenge. What if I have amnesia and can't remember doing it?"

Joanie studied me hard and shook her head in disbelief. "Wait here." She put the knife behind the door and left me on the kitchen stool. I wondered if a hysterectomy could actually land me in a prison for the criminally insane.

She was not gone long. "She's okay . . . sound asleep. But what's wrong with you, Miranda? And where did you get that thing?"

I blurted out the crazy story with great relief. By the end, I was somehow rooting for Mrs. Vic. "I don't want the hospital to know about this, Joanie. Can you imagine what would happen? They might even lock her up. I really don't want that for her. Please, let's just hide it and never tell anyone."

Joanie and I stared at one another. We'd been terrified of Mrs. Vic, but she'd been our teacher. In our youth, teachers had been sacrosanct, the essence of our lives. Regardless of our feelings, we'd learned remarkable things from teachers. Most graduates of Loving Memorial learned how to be great healers of the world's ills. Joanie's bright, wide-awake eyes and my dull, half-comatose eyes came to some kind of agreement. Quickly, she slid the metal into the slot by the fridge. We listened to it clink onto the floor. "Miranda, if you ever tell about this, I'll lose my job. Maybe my license."

"And if you tell Mrs. Vic I took that knife, she'll have my head on a platter."

Joanie ushered me back to bed and tucked me in. She probably wondered why I took Clara to bed with me, but by this time, Joanie was either too polite or too tired of my escapades to ask.

— 14 —

I once read that professional nurses in the Seventies and Eighties discarded their caps because they saw them as signs of servitude. Modern nurses like Eileen Collins were eager to create a legitimate profession; within a few years, nurses had reinvented themselves. Soon, only elderly patients in nursing homes insisted that registered nurses in starched white caps dole out their medications.

When I entered training as a Probie, I joined my classmates on probation from September until March. During this period, we wore aprons over our dresses but no bibs and certainly no caps on our heads. Mrs. Vic and her staff taught us to give simple patient care in Nursing Arts lab. After a few weeks, we trotted up to the floors to care for actual sick people. The night before this Great Event, we ran all over the dorm asking one another: would *you* like a bedpan? Would you *like* a bedpan? Would you like a *bedpan*?

With amazing luck and some bluffing, I passed probation. By the first of March, I earned the right to wear a bib with my name pin attached, Miss M. Smothers, S.N.—Student Nurse. I could finally anchor a starched white cap to my head.

Every nursing school had its own cap: some dull, some cocky, some with seagull wings; most had black stripes to denote seniority and buttons in back to create the shape of a cap. These were a cinch to put together after laundering. The Loving Memorial caps had no stripes and no buttons. Each began as a stiff, white, flat rectangle that had to be measured, marked, pleated and fastened with white bobby pins to form the proper head-hugging shape.

We practiced for weeks and argued endlessly about proper measurements. When our caps were finally perfect, they were sent to the church in preparation for our Capping ceremony.

On a Sunday afternoon in early spring, a Greyhound bus arrived in front of our dorm. Out we came, sixty-five nervous, excited young ladies, two by two. When we marched onto the bus, we swished at every step. People stopped to stare at our parade of white shoes and legs, heavy blue-and-white-checked dresses, white aprons with bibs, hair lifted high off our collars. We wore no earrings or nail polish to trap germs, only wristwatches for counting pulses and small gold crosses tucked discreetly under our bodices. We anchored bandage scissors between the back buttons of our aprons, which gave us a look of great medical purpose. People used to say, "Aah! The nurses are coming!"

With all of us lined up alphabetically and me being a Smothers and at the end of the line, it took some clever maneuvering, but I managed to be the first girl to climb onboard. Finding the seat over the wheel, I avoided wrinkles by pulling the tails of my apron forward and over my lap. With an amazing sense of satisfaction, I put both of my polished white duty shoes on the rising metal, and then I asked God to part the clouds and let my parents look down. For a few moments on the ride across town, I was in my true home on the Greyhound bus.

At the church, we marched with serious decorum into the imposing Gothic structure. Mrs. Vic and the other instructors sat on chairs across the front of the sanctuary, a flock of white nurses pure as doves, each with a tremendous sense of infection control. No nail polish. No earrings. No hair below the collar.

The organ played while we swished down the red-carpeted aisle. Proud parents sat up taller and turned sideways to witness this prized moment. The nurses are coming! I do not remember many of the hymns, remarks or prayers that day. But I remember Mrs. Vic standing like a preacher at the lectern, sweetly telling our families how courageous and wonderful we all were, and how thrilled she was to prepare us for such a noble calling. Turning her sharp eyes on us, she said that we should never see problems in our nursing careers, only challenges. She also said we would never receive an adequate monetary reward for our countless hours of hard work. Instead, we would receive our rewards in heaven.

At last the organ gave the cue, and carefully rehearsed, we arose as one body, sixty-five young women who solemnly processed toward the altar.

When I heard my name called, I ignited from within. I could have walked on water while I climbed three steps, crossed to a padded bench and knelt in front of Mrs. Nora Vickerstromm, R.N. I bent my head and felt the arrival of the angelic-white cap onto my short hair. Her hand was firm on my head and I trembled.

A second instructor anchored my cap with two white bobby pins, and then I stood, stepped before the hospital chaplain and received my Florence Nightingale lamp. My candle of service to the ill and the maimed burned with self-sacrifice, emphasized when we recited the Florence Nightingale Pledge and sang our memorized hymn: *O Master let me walk with thee, along the paths of service free . . .*

People applauded when we ran from the church. We cried, hugged and yelped a bit. Lordy, what a day. The nurses are coming!

Sadly, when you wake up in the hospital nowadays, you do not hear a flurry of eager young students as they leave the elevator and swish en masse along the hallway to care for you, their bright young faces bringing hope and healing into your weary limbs and life parts.

Today's uniforms do not make a peep. Polyester and unstarched cotton blends are silent. Now you hear metal. Carts and keys and who knows what all is jangling and clanging. Bright young students go off to colleges to do their learning in classrooms and labs. Some say it makes for a more balanced professional nurse, someone who can think, reason, confront physicians and hospital boards. If I'd been in college instead of trying to live up to Mrs. Vic's impossible standards, I might have made it. Classroom learning would have been a cinch compared to what we endured. As I'd reminded Ole several times in the past weeks, I would have had a career to fall back on. I would not be dependent on Buddy Blight.

On the morning after the knife escapade, the first thing I heard was the telephone. When I picked up the receiver, Mrs. Vic hissed at me. "Where the hell's my self-defense?"

I hissed back. "Your self-defense? You mean that knife? How should I know what happened to it? Frieda-the-Aide or Jackson-the-Guard probably found it. How could you expect to keep something like that hidden?" Now that it was daylight, the entire episode seemed amazingly ridiculous. Not worth lies, but what could I do?

I wanted to remind her that I'd kept her out of some bloody homicide, but instead I hung up. "And good morning to you too, you old witch," I said to myself.

The phone rang again. I had to answer it. It could be Lupe wondering when to come and take me home. Unfortunately, it was Mrs. Vic again, still hissing. "Miranda Smothers, I swear you don't have a brain in your head. You can't lie to me and get away with it. Don't ever try to trick me again."

Then *she* hung up on *me*.

A couple of hours later, Dr. Azadi came in and gave me a long list of dos and don'ts:

- I could walk around my home but not clean a thing.
- I could shower but not bend over to put on my shoes.
- I could eat anything I wanted except fried foods.
- I could go out for a couple of hours but someone would have to drive me. My abdominal muscles would not be strong enough to work an automobile for six weeks.

After I nodded assent, she wrote my discharge order; soon my neighbor Lupe arrived.

I was glad to see Lupe. She wore flip-flops, a lively purple muumuu and a gold pompom in her upswept hair. Lupe and I had nothing in common, really, except that we lived near one another and she gave me advice. She told me where to have my car serviced, where to buy inexpensive insurance, where to find three jars of Oil of Olay for the price of two. And likewise, I enjoyed regaling Lupe with all of my funny stories. She liked to laugh with me, and we shared a bit of mutual need. I was relieved to see her.

"You don't look all that well, darlin'," she said, picking up my plastic bag and bunches of flowers. "Are you sure you want to go home today?"

"Yes. I need the rest. Take me home, the sooner the better."

When the discharge nurse wheeled me through the lobby, I noticed that security was very visible. Old Mrs. Vic had certainly gotten herself well guarded. I took some pride in the thought that I could have outfoxed them all and done away with her in the night, despite all of their precautions.

On the drive to Heatherton, I shared a little about Ole and Buddy visiting at the same time, which made Lupe chuckle. But once we were home, her mood changed. After I lowered myself onto the couch, she sat next to me and looked concerned. "Miranda, I hate to tell you this, but I have to fly to Florida tonight. My brother . . . with the cancer?"

"Oh Lupe, I'm so sorry. But don't worry about me. I can manage just fine. Darcy is coming next week and I have a freezer full of food. I hope your trip will be all right."

She left reluctantly. We both knew her trip to Florida would be sad and definitely not all right.

Remembering the juvenile burglars who evidently lurked about, I locked the door after she left and then walked from room to room to kiss all the dolls sitting safely on their chairs and side tables. I'd noticed clouds creeping in on the ride home; my house felt chilly, even though it was June. I undressed and donned a comfortable flannel nightgown and the blue robe with the cockroach-shaped bleach stain. By this time, I was dead weary.

"Okay, Miss Clara," I said, retrieving her from my bag, "let's stretch out on this couch and get on with our totally cramp-free lives. No pain, ever again. Imagine!"

Stubbornly, whatever Clara Barton knew about the future, she kept to herself.

— 15 —

Before I could have a truly good nap, Mike the mailman was at my door. "Thought I'd bring this up so you wouldn't have to walk out," he said, passing a bundle of letters from behind the screen.

Mike was adorable. Maybe only twenty-five or so. He'd enchanted me for quite some time, with his rosy red cheeks and Danny-boy eyes, Irish for sure. Big dimples. Lots of golden hair on tanned legs under his uniform shorts. Mike raised the U.S. Postal Service to new heights in mailman appeal.

And there I was, wearing the bleach-stained robe. My hair was akimbo, my coming-home lipstick worn off. "Oh, that's sweet of you, Mike." I grabbed Saturday's mail and pulled shut the screen door, putting a film of wire mesh between his beauty and my disarray. "But I have orders to walk, so don't worry about me. I'll come out Monday and pick it up myself. You have a good day and thanks."

I watched him through the window while he wandered on up the street. Because I no longer had ovaries, Dr. Azadi had prescribed estrogen supplements to prevent hot flashes. Now it seemed that this estrogen was giving me teenaged butterflies where I once had a uterus. I wondered if Dr. Azadi knew that estrogen could make you horny.

While watching Mike turn the corner, I saw Ole come onto his porch. He looked in my direction, then took his clippers and began snipping buds from his rose bush. I figured he'd be on my front porch next, and I was feeling odd about Ole. We had been way too chummy in the hospital. I'd been so out of my head.

I tossed the mail onto my kitchen table and then hurried into the bathroom. I freshened my face and hair, brushed my teeth and put on lipstick. After glancing at my closet, I grabbed a flowing caftan that was full of vivid primary-colored swirls, something to make me feel like a well person. I was just pulling it over my shoulders when the doorbell rang.

Ole lugged a pot of chicken soup in one hand and roses in the other. He plowed right on in and was soon busy in the kitchen. "I saw Lupe leave," was about all he said. He was such a fussy housewife, setting up my tray with a rosebud and bringing it to me while I sat propped up on the couch, my billowing gown a grand disguise over my raw and painful sutures.

He pulled up a footstool, sat nearby and watched me eat. I worried that he might try to feed me. "So how was our infamous Mrs. Vic when you left this morning?"

"Mad as blazes at me."

When he looked up quizzically, I gave in and told him the story. I described the knife, my nightmare of the murdering son-in-law turned lab tech, my escapade down the hallway during the code blue, and my final hiding of the knife with Joanie. I tried to laugh it off. The story was totally bizarre in the light of day, like a dream you try to retell that makes about as much sense as a toddler trying to eat spaghetti.

But Ole was taking me seriously. "Are you sure there wasn't someone in your room looking for her? What about that detective? Could he have been there?"

"No, it was all just nonsense. I was so spaced out with drugs and Mrs. Vic—let's not talk about it now. I need to concentrate on getting well." I wiped my hands with the napkin and handed him the tray. "Your soup was delicious. Thank you." I began to get up, but he told me to stay put while he hurried out to clean the kitchen. I watched his tall lanky form for a moment and then glanced at Clara Barton, who for some reason was lying face down on the coffee table. I stared at her high-top shoe with the tiny pearl buttons. I did not tell Ole about the key hidden on Clara's person. That key was real and I could not poke fun at it.

"Could I bring you some cookies and peppermint tea?" he asked.

"No, but I'm tired. I'm longing for a nap. Would it be terribly rude if I asked you to leave?"

"Not at all. I have to run out to the supermarket anyway. Do you need anything?"

"No thanks. I put in a good supply before I went to the hospital. But could you please hand me my mail on your way out? It's all on the kitchen table."

He brought me a big stack of unsorted mail, gave me a gentle hug and then let himself out.

I quickly set aside grocery store ads and solicitations for life insurance and/or cemetery plots, as well as the utility bills. I went instead for get-well cards from various people I hadn't seen since my move. I loved the three cute cards from Darcy, all of them telling me I'd feel better soon. Two had added descriptions of Percy. She seemed to be falling hard. "Good for you, sweetie. Enjoy those fellows while they're young and romantic."

While I was sorting through it all, there was another knock on my door. Three times fast. "This is ridiculous," I told Clara, while I hauled myself out from under the envelopes and off the couch. "I'm supposed to be resting, aren't I?"

The oddest fellow stood beyond the screen. He was one of those bicycle riders who wears a helmet, a bright orange jersey and tight, shiny black shorts. Goodness, I'd never had a bicycle rider in tight biking shorts at my front door. "Are you Miranda Blight?" he said, panting a little, as if he'd been riding vigorously.

"Yes." I quickly shoved my hair about.

"I'm supposed to give you this package." He jerked open the screen door and thrust a large padded manila envelope at me. It was stapled shut, with my name in big scrawling letters. "The guy said I should tell you to hang on tight until he calls you."

"Hang on tight? I don't understand. Who gave you this?"

"Hey, some guy I ran into on the street last night. He said something came up in a hurry; he needed to leave this somewhere safe. He said Morning Glory number 48. I double-checked your name on the mailbox. He paid me fifty bucks to deliver it, and now I've done that. So that's all I gotta do." With that, he turned, jumped off the porch and onto his bike. Grimacing a little, he made all those adjustments to his feet, gloves and helmet that bicycle riders do. He then raced away. He was all muscle from the back as well as the front.

I locked the door and then stared at the large envelope in my hands. There was no return address. This must be a get-well surprise, but why not mail it? Why spend—surely it was not from Buddy. Buddy would never pay someone fifty bucks to deliver a package.

The lilting voice of Julie Andrews spun into my head . . . *brown paper packages tied up with string, these are a few of my favorite things . . . .* I hummed along while I tugged at the staples. I had an appointment to see Dr. Azadi on Tuesday to have my own staples removed. I hoped they weren't as obstinate as the metal securing this envelope. Industrial strength, I would say.

I went into the kitchen and cut the thing open with my large scissors. A second, medium-sized brown envelope was crammed inside the outer padded envelope. It was thoroughly sealed with strapping tape. "I think it must be from Ole, don't you?" I called over to Clara, who now sat primly on the couch, which was actually not far from my kitchen counter. "It's going to be one of those surprises where you keep unwrapping smaller and smaller packages." Before Clara could agree, a piece of folded white paper dropped onto the counter.

I picked it up and read the unsigned note.

> Do not try to open this. Put it in the back of your closet. Don't tell anyone about it. This is a matter of life and death. Maybe yours.

I dropped the package onto the floor and stared at it. "Holy shi—!" This was no surprise from Ole. And I should not have dropped it. I suddenly thought it could be a bomb. Bombs came this way, didn't they? In mysterious brown envelopes delivered to your door by strange men on bicycles who were paid fifty bucks? The Unabomber sent packages through the mail all the time.

"Good heavens, what am I supposed to do now?" I asked my doll.

Although bending was not on Dr. Azadi's list of permitted activities, I stood with my feet apart, braced myself with one hand on my thigh and scrunched down, bending my knees. I picked up the corner of the inner envelope between my thumb and index finger and then laid it carefully in the sink. I put the underlined note and the outer packaging on top of that.

Wondering how to pad the explosion a little, I pulled out all of my kitchen towels and spread them over the top. Spying Grandma's iron skillet on the back of the stove, I clutched it with two hands and placed it upside down over the tea towels, the handle jutting over the counter.

I stepped backwards and braced myself under the doorway, which was supposed to be the safest part of your house for an earthquake. Did that theory apply to bombs?

I debated calling the bomb squad. But how did a person locate the bomb squad in the phonebook? Where *was* my phonebook? Maybe I should call 911. Maybe they'd give me the number for the bomb squad. While I was reaching for the telephone on my coffee table, the phone rang. Maybe this *was* the bomb squad calling right now. It seemed as if they should already know about such a grave and perilous danger.

"Hello?"

"Is this Miranda Blight?" It was a man's voice.

"Yes."

"Mrs. Blight, this is Loving Memorial Hospital calling."

During a brief pause, I came to my senses. A bomb? A bomb? How could I be so ridiculous? The package was not even ticking. Or was it?

"Yes?" My voice was shaky but I was determined to get a grip. Thank heavens this person phoned before I went completely off the deep end.

"We like to call when our patients go home. See if everything was satisfactory. Would you mind answering a few questions?"

"But I just came home. And it's Saturday. You do this on a Saturday?"

"Yes. I'm a college student. I work weekends. If it's inconvenient, I can call back."

I sat on the arm of my couch. "No, it's not inconvenient. It's nice of the hospital to check on me, although—well, I did have good care. The nurses were okay and my doctor was—but I did not appreciate being admitted at midnight. That was just too spooky. And they gave me too many drugs, made me throw up for hours. I'm still having strange reactions."

I stopped. Here I was rambling on to a total stranger, and he hadn't asked one question. "What did you need to know?"

"What else weren't you happy with? Did you have a roommate?"

"Did I ever. But they finally moved her. It wasn't really the hospital's fault. They can't always tell when patients are going to be crazy."

"You had a crazy roommate? Let me see, was that a Mrs. Vickerstromm?"

"Oh dear, I sound like the crazy one, don't I? Please, I should not say all of this over the phone." My eye was on the bomb container in the kitchen sink. I moved as close as the phone cord would allow; nothing was ticking.

The college student said he should not have called me so soon. He'd send me a survey to fill out. What was my address? Morning Glory number 48?

"Yes, yes, that will be fine," I said, then slammed the receiver in his ear. It was a perfectly friendly call, but something felt odd. I looked out the window for Ole, but he was gone.

I really did not think the package was ticking, but as I paced around my furniture, I wondered what would become of my orange and vanilla kitchen if the bomb blew up. Ice cream exploding! The stress of that image jabbed needle-like pain to the far reaches of my hips. It was time for medication; I debated between plain Tylenol and Darvocet, which had an added narcotic. The Tylenol would not make me so crazy, but narcotics would surely work better. I chose the narcotics but hoped to get by with just one.

While I was swallowing, there was yet another knock on the door. "Goodness, what have we become, a community concourse?" I hobbled to the front window and peeked out. "Oh my, it's the Reverend Bob!"

I scooped up the heap of mail from the coffee table into my caftan, then waddled into the bedroom and dumped it on the bed. He knocked again; I had no time to do anything with the bag of explosives in the sink.

Although I liked watching the Reverend Bob preach, I felt he was just too good looking to take seriously as a spiritual comforter, with his halo-golden hair. Because of his effect on me, I hadn't notified the church office before my surgery, although the newsletter suggested we do so. Mama had warned me about preachers and bartenders being dangerous. "They may be intriguing and they can rope you in, but they're always married. Trust me, you don't want to lose your heart to a married man."

"I went by the hospital to see Charlie Granger this morning," he said, after I got him seated on the edge of my whiff-of-coffee Barcalounger, and I slumped into the cream and gold couch. "I just happened to see your name on the patient list. I tried to catch you before you came home. Are you all right?"

I wondered if I should offer him coffee. Grandma always offered coffee to the preachers when they stopped by. Cake too. But I'd never actually had a minister call on me. I figured Buddy was far too intimidating.

"Would you care for some coffee?" I asked. Making coffee would give me a chance to get the bomb rigmarole out of the kitchen sink before he wandered out there and spied it himself. And then it came to me. The oven! I should have put the bomb in the oven. The hefty oven metal would be far more explosion-proof than an open sink. Grandma's skillet would shoot right into my head if I left it where it was. I tried to stand up.

"No, no, stay where you are. I just wanted to see how you're doing. You should tell us when you or your family are sick or in need."

"I'm sorry. I didn't want to bother you. I prayed here at home and read my Bible before I went in. I even wrote out my funeral service in case I didn't make it. By the way, would you like to see my funeral service since you're here?"

Now this did seem like a good idea. After a most ungraceful ascent from the couch in my billowing caftan, I retrieved my white leather Bible with crinkly pages and gold leaf—Holy, it was—a gift from Mama on my fourteenth birthday. We were serving at a Lutheran church that year and I got myself confirmed.

"I keep this by my bed," I advised the Reverend. "And if something happens to me, I have the service on these lilac sheets of stationary. I mean, you never know, do you? A person could be in a car accident or someone could come in the window—anyway, could you arrange the service like this? And *Beautiful Savior*. I know it's not a funeral hymn, but it's my favorite. It's in the Lutheran hymnbook, if you don't have it in yours."

The Reverend Bob stood up, took the Bible from my hand, then steered me back to the couch and tucked me into my makeshift bed. He sat down next to me, folded the lilac funeral service and placed it back in the Bible. He looked at me for an uncomfortably long time.

"Miranda, I'm glad I came by. You've had a rough time, haven't you?" His brown eyes reminded me of the polished stop knobs on a quaint pump organ Mama had once played. Without warning, I began to cry. I was terribly embarrassed but could not stop.

He let me cry. He handed me a tissue and held my hand with his long graceful fingers. When my sputtering wound down, he picked up the Bible, opened it and began reading, his voice low and resonant, very comforting. "The Lord is my shepherd, I shall not want. He makes me to lie down in green pastures." I closed my eyes and saw Ole's meadow. "He leads me beside still waters." I was a wounded sheep. A strong power was holding me. "He restores my soul." When the Reverend Bob finished reading, he said a prayer. I swiped at the last tear with the back of my hand.

"Miranda, you've had a lot of stress with this surgery, along with a host of drugs you're not accustomed to. All of those things can do strange things to your mind. Please, try to quit worrying about dying and your funeral. You're going to feel a bit better each day, and soon you won't even remember much of this. I have a full schedule tomorrow and an out-of-town meeting on Monday. But here's my card with my home phone. Call if you start to feel too worried or panicky. My wife will know whom to call. And I'll be back on Tuesday. Okay?"

"Okay. Thank you so much."

I wondered if I should tell him about Mrs. Vic and the package. Maybe he could make sense of it and tell me what to do. But he was rising to his feet. He obviously had things to do. People to see. Maybe some sweet young couple to marry. Or someone to bury on a Saturday afternoon. Pulling myself up as straight as possible, I saw the lovely man to the door; then I locked us in, safe and sound. Me, the dolls and the bomb.

A moment later, the shrill alarm of the phone jolted me. Again.

– 16 –

"Mrs. Blight? This is Mr. Surrey, an assistant administrator at Loving Memorial. I'm sorry to bother you, but I've had a report from our student worker that you aren't too happy with the care you received."

"No, that's not accurate at all. Loving Memorial is the best hospital in Centerville, everyone knows that. It's just that—"

"Your roommate? Mrs. Vickerstromm?"

"Well . . ."

"Yes. We understand. Ah, Mrs. Blight, perhaps you realize by now that Mrs. Vickerstromm has some . . . ah . . . problems. And we know you are distressed. We're wondering if she did or said anything—in other words, we have reason to believe that she may have asked something of you. Given you something. Or asked you to run some little errand for her?"

I thought of the butcher knife, the explosive package and the strange phone calls. This was all too weird. "Someone's at my door," I said in a panic and hung up, not bothering with a polite goodbye.

Shivering, I went into the kitchen, stood before the sink and inched that hefty skillet off the bomb and back onto the stove. I reached in a drawer, retrieved a pair of meat tongs and carefully lifted each tea towel onto the counter. I was afraid to touch any of it. I transferred the odd note and the outer mailing bag in the same fashion. Taking a step back, I stared and listened carefully for ticking. Hearing nothing, I moved in, bent near and cocked my head . . . not a sound.

How loudly would a bomb tick anyway? Using the tongs, I picked up the sealed package, brought it toward my face and sniffed. What would a bomb smell like? This smelled like mailing paper. A little musty, maybe. Laying aside the tongs, I held the package carefully and passed it back and forth between my hands. How much would a bomb weigh? This package did not weigh much.

So what the heck was it? And who sent that hunky biker over here with it? Holding my breath, I stuffed the sealed package and the underlined note back into the larger mailing bag.

Suddenly, the idea of the Unabomber sending an explosive device seemed silly. Still, I held the bag gingerly when I carried it to the linen closet, exactly as the mysterious note writer had directed me. Groaning a good bit, I bent low and hid the entire business under the bath towels on the bottom shelf.

Along the way, I prayed this was a silly joke sent by Ole, but I did not think so. I also decided to avoid any more Darvocet today. Only Tylenol. I'd wait until my head cleared to unwrap that package. That was final. I'd wait until tomorrow for my head to clear.

Returning to the couch, I clung to Clara Barton, stared at the phone and wondered if that call was really from the hospital. Maybe it was Mrs. Vic's guard, checking up on me. Or the gubernatorial hopeful, one of his men. I wanted to call Darcy but she might be out with Percy. Or in with Percy, in which case I'd die of embarrassment. It was hard to know just when to call an unmarried daughter in these new-fangled, living-together days.

Bulldozed by my own inadequacy, I thought of all the people who'd seen or heard me acting like a lunatic in the past few days. I began to blush, even though Clara Barton was the only one around. I picked her up, unbuttoned her shoe and pulled it off. Yes, the key was real. That mysterious little key was not a hallucination. I quickly put the shoe back on and buttoned it up, then attempted to lie back against my couch cushions and rethink. Rethink!

But my belly was throbbing. Would the pain never go away?

Groaning again, I pulled myself up and went to the bathroom, where I replaced the billowy caftan with my snuggly flannel gown and bleach-stained robe. I returned to the kitchen and swallowed three 500-mg. Tylenol tablets. "Okay! That ought to do it."

Squinting at my prescription bag, I called the pharmacy number. When someone answered, I asked for the hospital's main switchboard. After a bit of ho-humming, they transferred me. When the operator answered, I asked if assistant administrator Surrey was in his office. She said no, all the administrators were off on the weekends. I explained a little about myself and that I'd been receiving strange phone calls. She asked if I wished to speak with the RN who was supervising the house this afternoon.

I said yes, surprised that they still used expressions such as *house* instead of *hospital.*

She told me to hang on, she'd page. The phone receiver steamed in my nervous hand.

After several minutes, the house supervisor answered. "This is Janice Groplen; can I help you?" I imagined her in business clothes, with a long string of graduate letters behind her name. Melvin told me that nurses could earn a nursing doctorate these days. What would that be? R.N., M.S.N., D. N.?

"Hello? Are you still there?"

"Ah, yes, Ms. Groplen, I'm Miranda Blight. I was discharged this morning. I shared a room with Mrs. Vic . . . ah . . . Mrs. Vickerstromm."

"Yes, I know who you are."

I imagined she did. "Umm, I know this probably sounds weird, but I've been receiving strange phone calls today. Is she all right? Did Mrs. Vic die or anything?"

"No, she's fine. What kind of calls? Has she called you?"

"No, but the student worker did. I think I said too much because Mr. Surrey called me. It was really strange—would he be there, making calls? Or would a student call him at home?"

"Let me see if I understand, Mrs. Blight. You're telling me that two men have called you from the hospital today? And you've discussed Mrs. Vic with them?"

"Yes, was that wrong do you think?"

"I'm not sure what to think. But I'll find out. Please don't worry about it. She's fine and you're—how are you, by the way?"

"I'm fine. Well, maybe a little woozy from the medicine, but I'm switching to plain Tylenol. Right now. I just took three."

"Yes, that's a sound decision. Please, try not to worry. And thanks for calling. We'll get back to you." She attempted to sound cool, but the voice of Doctor Nurse had taken on a higher, alarmed tone. I did not believe those calls were from the hospital staff, and neither did she.

If only Ole would come home. I glanced across the lane, but his driveway remained a haunting blank rectangle. I went into my bedroom, a bump-out on the side of my doublewide. After my separation from Buddy, I yearned for a splash of color to get me up in the morning. So I decorated my new bedroom like a box of Fruit Loops, with bedding that rejoiced in cheerful fruit colors: lemon, lime, grape, cherry. The curtains matched the perky sheet set.

Now I lay carefully on my yellow-and-white-striped comforter and studied a cobweb on the ceiling. Whenever I rotated my eyes, I could see the linen cupboard in the hall where I'd stashed the package under the towels on the bottom shelf. What was I going to do about that? Perhaps Ole would come bounding in and tell me to open his great surprise.

Instead, Buddy called. I had to hobble to the living room to answer the phone; it was a real effort, all of this getting up and down. "Hey babe, it's Saturday. You want to go to Arby's?"

"Are you crazy? I just got out of the hospital. I haven't had a moment's rest." The call would have been funny if Buddy had not been so serious. He thought women should be made of steel. Did he really think I was going to buck up and go to Arby's for one of life's great prizes? "No! I'm staying home in bed. By the way, did you send me a package?"

"I thought my mom took care of that. A big box of stuff from the boutique. And I brought you flowers. Wasn't that enough?"

"Yes, Buddy, thanks. That was certainly enough."

"Anyway, I'll come over and sit with you awhile, okay?"

I tried to say no again, but he'd already hung up. I debated barring the door. I doubted if he just wanted to sit, but he knew I could not have sex for at least six weeks.

Sighing, I changed back into my alluring caftan, rewashed my face, brushed my teeth, combed my hair and even slipped delicate jade earrings into my ears. Buddy had a key and let himself in.

He came with pizza and beer. Leaving it on the kitchen counter, he flipped on my television and paced around a little before he spread himself out in the Barcalounger. In the meantime, I hobbled to the counter, pulled down a tray, filled it with Budweiser and pepperoni, and carried it to him. "Here, your highness." He ignored my sarcasm and took a swig of beer.

Making enough noise to irk him, I grunted my way back into the sofa and pulled Grandma's afghan over me for protection, as if a blanket could protect me from Buddy Blight.

"Aren't you going to eat?" He nibbled around the edges rather than taking his usual half-piece bites. His eyes were darting. He was nervous about something.

"Not that stuff. Ole brought me barley soup. I'll have some later."

"Ole? That pansy neighbor?"

"He's kind. And thoughtful."

Buddy watched the news and chomped. He did not ask how I was doing. Sitting by my sickbed was evidently enough. Suddenly, a segment about Mrs. Vic's son-in-law appeared. When Mr. Grenadier answered a reporter's question, he sounded like Mr. Surrey, the assistant administrator. He also sounded like the phantom lab tech.

"Aaack!" I screamed. It was not a full-blown, terror-ridden screech, as with Poppy the pig, but the murdering son-in-law's tone shot all of my pain and frustration from my mouth. I grabbed my head, shook myself and yelled at the voices dueling across the television and into my brain. "Stop it, stop it, stop it!"

"For God's sake, Miranda, why the hell are you screaming?" Buddy hauled himself out of the Barcalounger. "I came over here to tell you in a calm, kind way that I want a divorce, and before the words are out of my mouth, you're screaming like a banshee."

I stopped cold. "A what? You want a what? I thought you wanted—"

"A divorce. I can't stand all these fits and hysterics any more. What the hell were you screeching about?"

"None of your bloody business!"

"Ah ha! See? That's just what I mean. You go ballistic in the middle of a bland television interview, and when I ask what's wrong, you shout 'none of your bloody business.' God, Miranda, if I'm ever going to be in a relationship again, I need a woman who's not hysterical every moment. A woman with a head on her shoulders."

"Do you have someone in mind?"

"Yes, I think I do. There's this girl works in the quarry where I buy my granite. She really has it all together. Body and brains. It's cool between us, you know?"

The quarry? Who were they, *Pebbles and Bamm-Bamm?* Without warning, just as with the kind preacher earlier, my eyes slopped over with tears, which of course Buddy could not stand. He belched and turned away.

"How can you be so cruel? To say that to me today? Of all days?" I could barely choke out the words through my sobs.

He stomped into the kitchen and threw a burned pizza crust into the garbage, then stomped back to the couch. Standing like a hulking caveman, he glared down at me for a long time. Suddenly he relaxed, for no seeable reason. He sat down on the floor by me and put his head against my knees.

I ran my fingers through his hair, which was a little gray, a bit receding. He could be so comforting at times. "Oh, sweetheart, I'm sorry. You have no idea what I've been going through here. Can you just hold me a little while? Please? I'm absolutely goofy from this medicine. I don't know what's real and what isn't."

He came up onto the couch beside me, pulled me into his arms and pressed my head against his chest. He put my face in his hands and kissed my forehead. This was so typical of us. I would choke and sob about life being so scary without him, and Buddy would masterfully kiss me and make it all better.

Lordy, the games we played. I figured he'd been using that Pebbles nonsense to scare me into this. His arms felt so familiar, strong and protective. I was so relieved.

"Can we go lie on the bed?" I asked. "My incision hurts when I sit up like this. Could you maybe take care of me tonight? These past few days have been truly horrible, Buddy."

He kissed my hair and helped me up. Holding onto each other, we hobbled into the bedroom. "We'll just stay on top of the covers," I said; but it felt so much better to slide between the cool, fruit-loopy sheets. So refreshing.

We lay spooning on our sides, him behind me. The sturdiness and warmth of his body sucked me in. His hand came around and rested on my left breast. If I moved back in with him, I could fall asleep like this every night. I'd have no more cramps to drive him nuts. He was still my husband after all. I loved his warm hand touching me.

What happened next is too embarrassing to tell, but it happened. I can't pretend it didn't. Buddy had strong needs and he always appreciated my sexiness. It was such a relief to have him there, petting me, murmuring to me, all my fears washed away.

It had to be hands only, of course, but soon estrogen no longer ran amok. Sighing, I fell into the deepest peace I'd known in a month. Dr. Azadi would not have approved of what we did, but she was not in my befuddled state of body or mind.

After a while, Buddy woke me with his complaining. He had a crick in his back and a spasm in his leg. I wanted him to stay put, but he wandered off to the bathroom and then the kitchen. I could hear him polishing off the pizza and beer. After a few minutes of calm, he hollered from the living room, "Can you come out here, Miranda?"

I groaned but got up, used the bathroom and then felt a stab of hunger. When I came into the living room, I saw Buddy pull a Tums bottle from his pocket and swallow a fistful.

"I wish you hadn't eaten all the pizza," I said. "It sounds good now."

"Don't you have your soup?"

"I need more than soup." I took a Hungry-Man turkey TV dinner from the freezer and put it into the microwave. No point in asking for help.

Buddy pushed the Barcalounger into full recline and turned on a wrestling match. His dark brows pinched into a nervous worry, probably because he knew I hated those wrestling matches. "Please don't watch that in my house," I said and then regretted it.

"Your house? Whose paying for this house, I wonder?"

I turned and stared at him. "Well, you're not. Remember the sale of our house?"

"A house I paid for. By working my ass off while you stayed home with your nursy dolls."

"I was keeping a decent home and raising our child!" The buzzer rang. I turned to the microwave, retrieved my dinner and carried it to the couch. I was hungry, but after just a few bites, I felt too weary to eat.

"Buddy, didn't I just prove I still love you?"

He switched off the TV volume and sat up halfway. His eyes were sparking. "You didn't prove a damn thing—just that we have a strange habit here. I was serious before. I want a divorce."

The word *divorce* whipped my gut into fresh upheaval. My lip quivered and I shoved away the Hungry-Man.

"Damn, don't start crying again. You're going to have to face up to this, Miranda. What we have here—this situation—isn't normal. We need to move on with our lives."

"Is she pretty?"

"Who?"

"Pebbles. The quarry girl."

"I'm not talking about her."

"You must be. Why else would you want a divorce?"

"Because I don't want this damned relationship any more. I'm tired of servicing you, Miranda." He got up to leave without putting the chair in an upright position; the footrest was protruding, waiting to snag me.

I struggled to my feet and shoved both hands into my armpits, forming a shield across my chest. "*Servicing me?* Like a gas station? What do you mean by servicing, Buddy?"

"Filling your sexual needs. What happened a little bit ago."

"We did that for you!"

"Like hell we did. I was with Lou Ellen yesterday. I certainly did not need you whining and crying, getting all turned on when I kissed you."

"Buddy!" My hands flew from my armpits. I clutched my abdomen but it cramped up anyway. "Why are you doing this to me? I've just come home from the hospital. I'm tired and sick." Without thought, I went to the kitchen, picked up the pharmacy bottle, poured out two Darvocets and swallowed.

"Sick and tired. That's you, babe. You just want to be cuddled and taken care of, made love to all the time. We have to stop all this bullshit."

"Buddy, I don't understand. You think I want too much sex?"

"Let's face it, Randy, you're horny half the time. You were always grabbing at me. Wore me out. I did my best to keep you happy."

"But I did it for you! To keep you home, to keep you from straying. And you—"

"You're fooling yourself with that notion. No, you have hot juices, babe. You'll lose them soon enough now. You'll spread out in the middle and be too embarrassed to go showing off in front of men. And you'll have to get a job. It's about time. Don't worry about the divorce, Miranda. I'll have my lawyer take care of everything."

Buddy did not look back or say goodnight on his way out.

As soon as I locked the door, the phone rang. It was Darcy calling from an emergency room. She'd fallen off Percival's motorcycle and broken her lower leg. She was in a cast and could not come home. I reassured her that I could get along just fine.

So there it was. I was on my own. Buddy, Lupe and even my lovely daughter had deserted me. And despite the Reverend Bob's comfort, I had no idea where God was in this mess.

Soon after, I fell into a narcotic wooziness and cried myself to sleep.

— 17 —

Instead of getting out of bed in the morning, I curled in a ball and decided to die—but only for ten minutes. The fetal position was painful and I had to pee. So up I got and did my business, washed my face and put on my cockroach robe. Life was useless, but I hobbled out to the porch, bent from the knees and scooped up the Sunday paper. Peeing and the paper were essential, whether you were dying or not.

Maybe Buddy was right. Maybe it was time to start acting like a competent person. "Do you think I should let my hair grow out?" I asked Clara on my way to the kitchen table. "Dark and long?" I could apply dusky-mink eye shadow and don hoop earrings, wear leather jackets and mercurial-red skirts.

Clara looked askance and sighed.

Shrugging, I poured myself a bowl of Cheerios and milk and sat at the kitchen table. My eye settled on an article about Sonny Bono and his Palm Springs politics.

"Weren't they something? Sonny and Cher? Was there anything like her getups? Her pizzazz?" Clara remained upright on the couch in the manner of a totally composed New England lady. She'd never approved of Cher, but I kept trying to convince her. "That's it, Clara! *Cher!* She's my perfect role model, don't you think?"

Clara reminded me that I was five feet four with streaky blond hair and flat cheekbones. Cher was as statuesque as a Cherokee goddess, with an abundance of dark hair to match her energetic, thrill-seeking spirit.

Cher had more guts than I did, even when she was Loretta in *Moonstruck*. And standing on that stage at the Academy Awards, accepting that Oscar. Wow!

Pulling myself back to practical, I put the bulk of the paper on the chair and spread out the want ad section across the table. I grabbed a red marker from a utility drawer to circle job possibilities for a forty-something woman. The pickings were bleak; my best chance was maybe as a nursing aide. The hospitals were running long columns of ads. They needed help. But *hospitals?* I wanted no part of hospitals.

What I secretly wanted to do—and this had nothing to do with glamour, although I could see Cher in the role—was to buy myself a pair of dungarees, climb up in one of those big hefty cabs and be an interstate trucker. I'd have a cute code name, maybe *Randy Eleven*. I'd have safe brakes and be sweet to the police. I could eat in the truck stops. Sit back and watch the men cruise by.

The idea had come to me when I was a kid traveling the highways. It grew when I hit my teen years, and Grandpa let me chug across his broad fields on his humongous John Deere. I loved driving Buddy's trucks, too, but he seldom gave me the keys. He dragged me to a lot of trucker movies, however, and suddenly Burt Reynolds, Chuck Norris, Kris Kristofferson all came to mind—*Breakers, Smokeys, Convoys*. I even thought of Willie Nelson, who was cool, if not gorgeous. I figured Willie had driven his bus down the interstate a time or two.

There were no truck driver ads in the paper today. It must be an inside thing, handed out to people with the right connections. But there was a truck stop on the outskirts of Centerville. Maybe I could wait tables and experience the glamour around the edges. Maybe Burt Reynolds would stroll in and order a java or two. At this point, I got up and headed for my Mr. Coffee automatic-drip.

While I measured and poured, I figured that every woman in the world, deep down in her heart, would like to perch herself up in the cab of one of those eighteen-wheelers and blast that air horn up the bumpers of all the men she passed by. I wanted to blast something up Buddy's bumper, that was for sure.

Waiting for the coffee, I poured myself a cold Diet Pepsi, although it was not yet noon. I swallowed two Tylenol with the first gulp. Scowling at the Darvocet, I hid the bottle from myself in a bag of Gold Medal flour.

I still wasn't convinced Buddy wanted an actual divorce; but if he did, would he stop giving me money? I'd have to sue him for alimony. The thought of meeting Buddy in front of a judge gave me the willies. I poured myself a cup of coffee, took a sip and then took a big swallow of Pepsi. I left the paper strewn across the table, went to the desk in my sewing room and rummaged about for my savings account book. I'd been squirreling away a couple of twenties a month for years; my total was now $4,988. It would grow to over $5,000 with this quarter's interest. Maybe it would be enough to live on until I learned how to be a nurses' aide. I'd likely need a refresher course, at the least.

I stepped into the bathroom and smiled at myself in the mirror. I was surviving this Sunday morning with Cher, Burt and Willie, after all. Maybe I'd kick back in the Barcalounger and read the rest of the paper.

Oh silly me. I could not straddle a Barcalounger. Buddy had intentionally left that thing open. If I got tangled in it and died, he could chase after Pebbles scot-free.

Back in the kitchen, I swallowed most of my coffee and then took my Pepsi and the local section of the newspaper to the couch. I picked up my soda, looked at the paper and stared.

There it was—the Private Eye! His photo. Sebastian Cross. The headlines said the man was dead. Dee-aad for real! Rigor-mortissed! Mrs. Vic's photo was lower on the page.

The Pepsi sloshed in my glass and splattered across the paper.

Reading through the dampness, I saw that he'd died suddenly of a heart attack Friday night while watching a Little League game. A reporter had discovered that he was the same investigator hired by Mrs. Vic to gather evidence in her daughter's tragic death on Precipice Point Road.

Mrs. Vic had issued a statement from her hospital room, saying she was very grieved upon hearing of the man's death. She also said no one should believe it was a heart attack. She was certain he was murdered, just as her daughter had been murdered. Obviously, the man had uncovered evidence that would prove her son-in-law was a killer. Mrs. Vic even speculated that poor Mr. Cross was injected with a lethal dose of some toxic chemical while the baseball parents were in the middle of a wild cheer.

When the reporter asked where and what this evidence was, Mrs. Vic said it was in safekeeping and would be produced at the right time. She was not going to turn it over to the police, because the police were all crooks, everybody knew that.

The story also said that Tom Grenadier was now retaliating, stating that Mrs. Vic was no longer in control of her senses. As much as he hated doing it, Grenadier might go to court and have her declared incompetent.

While I read, I wondered if the package hiding on the bottom shelf of my linen cupboard was the evidence Mrs. Vic alluded to in the newspaper. Could my secret package have gotten a man killed? I could picture her words, exactly as she described it.

Sebastian Cross went to the cemetery and actually found a diary to match the key in Clara's shoe. Maybe it was in the flower vase on Ed Vichy-whatever's vault, as I'd suggested. Cross took it home and secured it in the stapled package—he even put in a note to me—just in case.

He called Mrs. Vic and then realized he was being followed. He tried to run with the package to some safe place, but the gangsters closed in. He grabbed the biker, remembered my house number, threw the package at him and sneaked into the ball field. But the criminals were clever. They followed him. Shot the lethal injection of toxic chemicals into his neck with a poisoned blow dart during the wild rallying cheer for the home team.

This was all too, too bizarre. I would never have a role in such a weird James Bond-type scenario. I realized how silly my thoughts were and smiled a fraction of an inch. Then, despite the serious business in my newspaper, I fantasized for a moment about Sean Connery. A terrible hot flash ensued. My entire head filled with heat generated by the sexual energy of James Bond.

After I calmed down, I decided to go have a closer look at that package. I hoisted myself off the couch and dropped the wet newspaper on the coffee table. I was dizzy again, although I'd had only the Tylenol. "Just take it easy and think," I said aloud, groping the wall to steady myself. "Get rid of that thing and all this ridiculous supposing."

At the linen closet, I was able to squat carefully, retrieve the brown package and carry it to my bed. Using a scissors from my bedside table—my weapon of choice in case of an intruder—I slit through the tape and seal of the inner bag, then turned it sideways and put my hand around a small book. When I pulled it out, I wondered if something else had dropped out, but I could not spot anything on the bed or floor.

The object I held in my hand was a small diary with a gold lock, which probably matched the gold key in Clara's shoe. Both the front and back covers were padded in a gaudy print fabric; gold lamé eighth notes danced helter-skelter across a black background. I could not imagine a sophisticated pianist carrying this thing about. She might carry a proper, leather-bound journal in her briefcase. But this?

I checked the bag for other contents and found a note written on soft ivory stationary with her name, *Margo L. Grenadier*, embossed on top. She'd written with indigo-blue ink in a graceful style; oddly, the note was dated ten years ago.

> *Mother: T-bills and CDs worth half a mil. are in our mutual name, Margaret Vickerstromm, so either of us can sign, we have such similar handwriting. I don't think he realizes that your maiden name was Nora Margaret Greene, not Nora Peg as Grandma always called you. I think he's forgotten my name is Margaret at all! Anyhow, the money is all from concerts and Daddy's estate. Obviously, in ten years this is going to grow considerably. Probably double to a million!!*
>
> *Things with Tom aren't right. I don't want him to have this money to finance his political campaigns or pay off his gambling debts. In the meantime, I'll try to get him into some kind of therapy or counseling, maybe Gambler's Anonymous. You know I love him, even tho'—Anyway, if anything happens to me, everything will mature in June 1989. I'll put this note in my locked diary for a while and keep it in my old bedroom at your house until I figure out what is happening to Tom. Love you, Margo*

I stared. I stared and stared. Why would Margo Grenadier write this important note, hide it in a diary, and then move the diary from her mother's house to a cemetery just before she fell off a cliff?

Totally confused, I paced from living room to bedroom in my nightgown and robe. Each time I passed Clara Barton, I asked her the questions that were puzzling me.

"Did that gambler son-in-law find out about his wife's secret assets and kill her, so he could get his hands on the money?

"Or did Margo realize her mother was going bonkers and she had to get the diary out of the woman's house?

"Or was Margo the crazy one? Maybe she jumped off the cliff because she was sick and tired of practicing her piano."

I picked up my doll, stroked her hair and gave her a tender kiss, as if she were about to go into battle and die. I checked the calendar in the kitchen. "A half million dollars worth of CDs and T-bills will roll over or need to be withdrawn—whatever you do with such things, I'm not certain—but this month! Does Mrs. Vic know about this? Could T-bills and CDs be stashed in that gaudy diary right now?"

Before I could get the key from Clara's shoe, I spied Ole crossing the street. I hurried to the bedroom and crammed the packaging and contents under my pillow, then answered his knock on the door. I hadn't fixed myself up but did not care.

He came with the newspaper section, waving the photo of the dead man in my face. "Did you see this story?"

"Yeah, I did. Can I get you some coffee?"

He glanced in the kitchen to see if I had actually made coffee. "What do you think? Do you think there's some sort of evidence that's come to light?"

I kept my mouth shut and made a beeline for Mr. Coffee. I'd looked like a fool long enough. I'd blabbed, spouted, cried and had hysterics. What would people say if I claimed to have a million dollars under my pillow right this very minute?

"Did she say anything to you?" he asked, taking down a cup from the cupboard so I would not have to reach.

I pointed to the kitchen table. "Look Ole, I was reading the want ads this morning. Looking for a job. Isn't that great?"

Ole stared at the paper where I'd drawn red loopy circles around nursing aides' notices. The phone rang before we could launch into a discussion of my job qualifications. I located the receiver under the newspaper on the coffee table. I answered with a bright hello. Maybe it was Darcy calling to say her broken leg was a big joke.

But no, it was Mrs. Vic. I should have expected it. "Miranda, how are you today?"

"Fine, I'm fine, Mrs. Vic."

Ole heard her name, turned around and watched me.

"Are you keeping your door locked?"

"What?"

"Your door. Is it locked?"

"Of course my door is locked. Why would you care?"

"Well, it's perfectly clear to anyone with eyes in their head that you're a little scatterbrained. And there are strange people running around. So what's this about the hospital calling you yesterday, wanting to know about me?"

"Oh gosh, why did they tell you that? There were a couple of calls. I didn't understand them. No one has ever called back with an explanation."

"Don't try to understand. Just do the right thing. Did you see the story in the paper? My friend was careless and now he's dead. Pay attention, Miranda. You need to follow every order specifically so there are no dire consequences. It would be a shame to see your—do you understand me?"

"Yes ma'am." I had no idea what she was referring to, but her voice was too spooky to stand up under. I sank onto the arm of the couch.

"Goodbye then. I'll call you tomorrow. Stay home and lock your door."

Ole asked what was going on, and I wanted to blab it all to him. Instead, I changed the subject again. "Buddy was here last night. He wants a divorce. I *have* to find a job."

"What?" Ole's eyes popped wide open. He stared at me perched on the arm of the couch, garbed in my yucky bathrobe and slippers, holding my belly, rocking to and fro. "Is this something new?" he asked.

"I guess. He told me last night. He came to pay a sick call."

"Your husband came over here on the day you came home from the hospital and told you he wanted a divorce?"

I nodded. "And he says I should find a job. Get on with my life. Don't look so shocked, Ole. You told me the same thing."

"Not like that. Good heavens, what kind of a monster is he?"

"He's not a monster, he's just . . . Buddy Blight. That's the way he is. Direct."

I watched Ole think. His eyes were sometimes transparent; you could see his brain working in the background. He finally said, "You know what I think? I think you've had just about enough for one week." He paced the room, rubbed his head, leaned toward me and picked up my hands. "Listen, I have to drive to Stony Ridge and take some measurements this afternoon. Why don't you ride along? My car is comfortable and you could use the fresh air. It will help you relax. You're as tight as a drum, Miranda. Look at you!"

Ole moved behind me and rubbed my shoulders. For a moment, I leaned back into his grasp and let those big bony fingers work at the tension in my neck.

"I know, but I don't think I could . . . these staples . . . and the sutures under them. There are muscles, nerves, blood vessels, skin . . . and fat . . . that all need to hook up again."

"Oh, sweetie, you're hooking up just fine." Ole grabbed my hands and pulled me to my feet. "Come on, put on some clothes. I'll drive slowly. You need to get away from that phone, if nothing else."

Sweetie? Ole called me *sweetie*. I got a little tickle from hearing that. I decided to go for it. "Okay. Give me a few minutes to get dressed."

While he sprinted home to pack a basket of goodies, I pulled on a bra and panties, both a bit dingy, a kind of arctic-fog-gray but with loose, comfortable elastic. This under equally old and non-binding tan sweats and my Reeboks. I quickly washed, combed my hair and dabbed on a little lipstick. Before leaving the bedroom, I stared at my pillow that hid the diary, the note about the money and maybe the banknotes themselves.

Really, it was too much. I wanted no more of this. Tossing the pillow aside, I shoved everything into the large mailing bag and headed for my trashcan. I threw away the whole confusing mess. Let the FBI come searching for it, if someone wanted it so badly, which I now seriously doubted.

But in the living room, Clara raised an eyebrow. I took the key from her shoe and retrieved the mailer from the trash. After emptying it over the kitchen counter, I tried the key in the diary lock; it was a perfect fit. I opened it quickly and shook. No bank notes. No money. And I doubted there'd be one shred of evidence about Tom Grenadier. Still, I would read this thing while Ole was taking his measurements. I should have done it the minute the package arrived. Leaving the wrappings on the counter, I put Margo's note inside the diary, then wrapped it in one of my explosion-proof towels, a thin old tea towel upon which Grandma had embroidered a row of clucking chickens. I slipped this package into my cable-car shoulder bag and tucked the key back into Clara's leather shoe. I liked it there now. It gave her an aura of mystery. I kissed her goodbye.

As I left, I was determined to pump myself up with a positive message. "Try and enjoy this Miranda. It's all just Mrs. Vic's foolishness. Have the courage of Cher or James Bond. Mr. Cross had a heart attack. That's all that went wrong with Mr. Sebastian Cross."

There was absolutely nothing to be so jumpy about.

— 18 —

On the drive up to Stony Ridge, Ole and I began to reminisce about teachers. His craziest was his Latin teacher, who'd lugged invisible verb roots around the room.

"He'd write the Latin infinitive on the blackboard," Ole said, "and then pretend to lift it off, carry it around the room between his two empty hands, and then plop it on another blackboard as if it were a real object. When he let go of it, he'd slam his fist against the board hard enough to make us jump in our seats, as if the would-be infinitive were the Romans fighting the Gauls. His favorite verb was *amare*. He'd write *amare* on the board, whack it a couple of times, then *amo, amas, amat, amamus, amatis, amant*. You know what that means?"

"We had to take Latin for nurses training, but I can't—"

"*Amo*, I love. Present tense. *Amas*, you love. *Amat*, he loves. Love, love, love, in all its forms—present, past, future. He'd sling love all over the room and we'd snicker through it all. I guess any idea of love and this weird little fellow made us laugh."

I leaned back into the upholstery and chuckled myself, my first laugh of the day. "Well, you still remember how to do love."

He gave me an amazed look. When I realized what I'd said, we both laughed.

He also told me about his fifth grade music teacher who threw a blackboard eraser at some poor monotone because he was off key. Ole's story made me think of that surgery rotation when the doctor threw the stainless steel forceps at my head. "He almost killed me," I told him, recounting the dreadful day.

"Why would a doctor do such a crazy thing?"

"I passed him the wrong suture. I'd just jabbed a needle through my sterile glove, and I was sweating bullets about whether to report it or not. That would have meant stopping the surgery and getting me completely rescrubbed for ten minutes. You know, the hand washing, getting into all the sterile garments . . ."

"You're right, he could have killed you."

"I know. But instead of someone yelling at him, Mrs. Vic grabbed me when I left the OR. She stood me up against the wall, put her face right up next to mine and said, 'How dare you insult a doctor like that.'"

"Did you insult him?"

"Well, yeah. I mean, he shocked me, throwing sharp steel at my temple, the most vulnerable part of the body. The words blurted out of me: 'Why for the love of might are you throwing things at me? At my temple, the most vulnerable part of my body?'"

"Is that why you didn't finish nurses training?"

"No, it wasn't that."

"So when did you leave?"

"Surgery was the last rotation of my second year. I thought I'd be home free if I could survive surgery. Then it all fell apart."

"What happened?"

"I never talk about it."

"That's not healthy. Come on, tell me. Confession is good for the soul."

"I doubt you'd want to hear this one. It makes me sick to think about it. Even worse than lighting a cigarette for a comatose woman or yelling at a doctor."

"I've got strong innards, Miranda."

"I know but . . ."

Ole waited silently.

I squirmed. "Okay . . . I . . . well . . . actually . . . I did kill one of my patients."

"Who? The surgeon? Nah, I can't picture you as an avenging lady murderer."

"No, it was not the surgeon. It was an old man. I murdered a poor old asthmatic man who thought he'd be kept alive by my loving care."

"On purpose? A mercy killing?"

"No, goodness no, but—"

And so I told him about my last medical floor rotation five months before graduation, about missing curfew with Buddy and being so tired the next morning I couldn't think straight. I'd been assigned a four-bed men's ward and not one of them was ambulatory. They all needed urinals, bed baths and linen changes. It was a lot to accomplish between 7:00 and 11:00 a.m., when I had a class in epidemiology.

"Man, I ran my buns off. We were in the old tower with no patient bathrooms. I had to sprint back and forth to the utility room a zillion times. Today those men would all be ambulatory and made to move around, take showers—"

"Goodness, Ole, I can't tell you about this."

"It's okay. Spit it out."

"Well . . . I ran around and did up the first three because they were, for the most part, routine. Then I turned to Mr. Ninke. He was an old codger who'd been shipped in from a nursing home. He was an asthmatic who'd kept everyone awake all night with his wheezing and rattling. He also had a huge bedsore on his buttock. By the time I was ready to give him his bath, his respirations were . . . well . . . tortured, to say the least. His face was this creepy, eerie blue-gray color. I reported him to Mrs. Vic, but she said a resident doctor had checked him the night before. 'Just bump up the oxygen,' was all she advised.

"So like a good girl, I went back to Mr. Ninke's bed and found his plastic oxygen cannula under his head. I stuck it in his nose and turned up the O_2. But before I could change the sheets, I had to change the dressing on his rear end. Trust me, I took it seriously. I cranked down his bed and prodded him onto his side. I had to prop him with my shoulder to keep him from rolling back onto my sterile dressing tray. He had a horrible wound on his rump, as big as my fist and oozing with goop. It almost made me throw up to look at it. But I braced him up and cleaned off the green pus with big cotton swabs dipped in hydrogen peroxide. Eventually his buttock was so clean it shone. Of course it was still red and raw, but nonetheless—"

"But you weren't checking his breathing or his color?"

"Well, no, but I was really impressed with the great job I was doing on his rear end. That's when I heard Dr. Grubenholz come in on rounds, with a flock of interns trailing along. I popped out from behind the curtain and asked him if he'd like to inspect Mr. Ninke's clean decubitus ulcer before

I rebandaged it. 'Ya sure,' he said in a thick German accent. Half our residents were from other countries. We could barely understand them at all. Anyhow, when he and his troop of underlings came around the curtain, Dr. G. did not look at the buttock, oh no, he went straight for the guy's head, which was completely blue. The oxygen had fallen off; it was twisted up in the sheet under his ear. Dr. Grubenholz kept yelling, 'Vas ist kaput mit dis patient?' All the other doctors tried to untangle Mr. Ninke from the dirty linens and sit him up so he could breathe.

"Oh Lordy." I put my head in my hands, remembering.

Ole let out a huge roar. He nearly lost control of the car.

"What are you laughing about? It was horrible. I was so ashamed. I tore out of that room and raced down the hall until I found Mrs. Vic and another instructor in a conference room, drinking coffee, not a care in the world. I burst in on them with my cap half off, my cheeks flaming red. 'I just killed my patient!' I screamed at them."

Ole pulled the car to the side of the road so he could wipe his eyes and blow his nose.

"What? What are you laughing at? The next day poor Mr. Ninke died! Deeaad! Rigor Mortis!" I hurled those last two descriptions right into Ole's ridiculing face.

He blew again, then leaned back, gulped for air and shook his head. "I'm sorry, but you crack me up, Miranda. The picture of you in your cap and starched uniform bent over this guy's ugly rump—you were so intent, so serious, and all the while—can't you see the humor in it?"

"No! Mrs. Vic kicked me out because of it. She called me into her office two weeks later and told me I was no longer qualified to be a nurse. She sent me packing without another word. She'd already called Grandpa. I had to leave that very evening. It was so humiliating. I did not even make it to my maternity rotation, the prize I'd been working so hard for. We all longed to take care of the sweet little newborn babies."

"So you married Buddy?" he asked, trying to sound serious.

"It was a handy excuse for what had happened."

When Ole spoke next, it was with a serious tone. "So how come she waited two weeks?"

"Who?"

"Mrs. Vic. To kick you out. Why two weeks? Did she tell you why she was expelling you?"

"Just that I wasn't qualified."

"Did she mention this Ninke guy?"

"Well, Ole, everyone in the hospital was laughing about it. Everyone was saying, 'Hey, Miss Smothers, bump up the oxygen!'"

"Of course they were laughing. But they weren't laughing at you, sweetie, they were laughing because it's a funny scene."

"But he *died*, Ole!"

"He would have died anyway. The guy was blue when you came on duty, an old codger with emphysema. His lungs were probably shot. That wasn't your fault. You did bump up the oxygen."

Ole turned on the ignition and pulled back onto the highway. "That's not why she dismissed you. There was another reason. I'd bet my life on it."

"Well, if you're right, it's because she was protecting her own backside. She should have called a doctor in the first place . . . I did report that old man's condition."

Before we could speculate further, Ole turned the steering wheel quickly and swerved a little. A black car—actually, it was a car for gangsters or the FBI—suddenly sped up and passed us, despite the double yellow line. For a moment or two, I could not breathe. Regaining control, he mumbled, "Good. That idiot's been tailgating me all the way up this mountain."

"But we only just drove back onto the road."

"I know. Odd, huh?"

There was no time to worry about something new. Ole turned into his property. "I'm sorry I laughed so hard. I know you felt badly about Mr. Ninke. But you owed me that."

"I owed you what?"

"A good laugh. You laughed when I was bent out of shape over paying drug addicts to use condoms."

"Yeah, but that was funny."

"Anyhow, if you ever have the chance, you should ask Mrs. Vic why she really kicked you out of training."

"No, I won't have that chance. I don't plan on ever seeing that woman again."

I patted the bag on my shoulder, the one that contained her daughter's diary, snugly entwined in Grandma's chicken-clucking tea towel.

Ole reclined the passenger seat for me, propped my head with a small pillow and draped a red-and-green-plaid car robe over my legs. When he was certain I was comfortable, he pulled a metal tape measure from his pocket and picked up a clipboard from the back seat, then headed off to the far side of his lakebed. As soon as he was out of sight, I tossed off the car robe, screwed up the back of the seat and pulled the diary from my bag. I flipped to the last page. If Margo Grenadier's life were so screwed up she'd have to die for it, it seemed logical that the evidence would be at the end of the diary, not the beginning.

But the final page contained only a description of a concert with the Berlin Philharmonic that brought standing applause, followed by a short trip into East Berlin. "Such a sad experience, everything so gray and depressed." Those were Margo's last words, written in February. She died in March. Now it was June. No time at all for Mrs. Vic to heal. Maybe I should be kinder.

I worked toward the beginning and saw that most entries described concerts and travels. This concert was great, that one was horrible. She must have retrieved the diary from her mother's house when her career took off. There were a couple of references to her husband's gambling, but she coerced him into treatment. He was getting better. There were comments about other women, but it seemed more in jest than real worry. Tom Grenadier traveled with her a lot. They took marvelous ski trips to the Alps. In Zurich, she bought herself a purple ski outfit, a red one for him.

I closed my eyes for a moment and imagined them darting down the hills, a streak of red, a whisk of purple against the pure white snow. Goodness, it was romantic. On the other hand, she did seem to be accident-prone; she took some terrible spills. She split her lip on one trip, banged up her eye on another. After that she wrote, "I must get control of this!"

I read most of her entries and decided for the umpteenth time this weekend that, due to extreme grief, Mrs. Vic was imagining all the sinister activity. I ran my index finger over Margo's handwriting on the final page. And then I bent my head, looked more closely and discovered a raw edge under my touch.

The last page had been torn away. Raising the book to catch more light, I turned it for better inspection and noticed an indent inside the back cover, as if a hard ballpoint pen had been pressed into that absent page. I scrunched up my eyes until I could read the words: *The girls!*

"Are you keeping a diary of all this?"

I jumped and slammed shut the book. Ole laughed and opened my door. "Come on, you need to stand up and stretch."

"It's not my diary," I blurted out, staying put. "This is Mrs. Vic's evidence. She thinks this book caused Mr. Cross to be zapped with a lethal injection."

"You mean this little thing is the so-called evidence mentioned in the paper this morning? How'd you get it? And why are you carrying it around with you?"

"It's a complicated story. I can tell you on the way back. But I can't keep this any longer. Could I stash it in the cabin fireplace? Until we can sort it all out? Maybe next week I'll go to the police, but I want a clear head."

I placed the original note about the T-bills inside the diary and handed it to Ole.

"Okay, but this is really bizarre. What's in here anyway? It's so garish."

He flipped to the back the way I had and immediately spotted the raw edge and the imprint inside the cover. He also noticed that the lining was loose. He tugged on the cloth, reached his finger in and pulled out what must be the missing page. He read the words aloud:

> *These are the girls. Oh my God, who can I trust with this*
> *information?*
> *Juanita Sanchez*
> *Reiko Ishihara*
> *Ute Braün*
> *Isabella Tosca*
> *Heide Domingo*

"So there really were other women in his life?" Ole wondered.

"They sound foreign," I added. "Did he meet them while they were traveling, do you suppose? Were they opera singers he had affairs with? Or her maids, or what?" I began shivering again. "Come on Ole, please go hide that thing. Snooping into their private lives gives me the creeps. Let's get out of here." I pulled the tea towel from my bag and gave it to him. "Wrap it up in this. It will keep a little dirt off."

Ole smiled at the row of chicken cluckers embroidered on the towel, then took it all and headed for the woods. While he was gone, I eased myself from the car and stretched my arms and legs. He'd brought a snack;

133

although I was not hungry, I nibbled on a blueberry muffin and swallowed a Tylenol with a can of root beer.

A few minutes later, we drove down that long, curving Panic Place highway. I finally explained about Mrs. Vic giving me the key and hiding it in Clara Barton's shoe. "It all seems so silly because anyone can break a diary lock. And how did Margo keep that thing hidden from her husband?"

Ole listened and thought. I described the way the biker delivered the package, and he listened and thought some more. Finally, I confessed to him my bomb scare, described the sink and the towels stuffed around the package; also the Reverend Bob arriving. Ole relaxed and chuckled.

We came to the intersection with Precipice Point Road. I asked him to turn. "I want to drive out there and see that place."

"You sure you're up to it?"

"One way or another, I am. I've gotten involved in this and I'd like to see where Margo—somehow, I feel I owe it to her."

We drove for a mile or so along a treacherous, cliff-side road and then came to a rest area. There was a cement picnic table, a garbage can and an overlook on the left, with a guardrail protecting the viewpoint from the canyon below. I got out of the car and walked across to the edge. It was a lover's leap kind of place, an amazing pinpoint of land on which to stand and survey the view. The tiny rooftops of Heatherton, the parking structure at the Pine Woods Mall, the rooftop garden at Loving Memorial—all were sugar cubes in the distance.

We peered over the cliff and stared down onto boulders balanced on more boulders. I envisioned Margo Grenadier tumbling and screaming, her lovely pianist hands bashing onto the hard rocks, strong pianist fingers shattering. I felt sick and disoriented although I was behind the guardrail.

When I stiffened my legs for support, another image emerged, as if her broken body had morphed into a vapory substance and now swirled upward like wood smoke; the wisps melded together and sprouted long arms that reached out and squeezed me; her fingers slithered along my spine. My nerves buzzed and prickled. I felt rather than heard piano music, something Mama might have played for a funeral. I tried to brush the ghostly vision away, but I could not shake free.

"Miranda, are you okay?" Ole grabbed me and turned me toward the car. "You look as if you're about to fall."

"Or maybe be pushed," I whispered.

Before Ole could climb into the Reliant, another car sped along too rapidly and too close for that road. Ole slammed his door and flattened himself against the side of the car until it whizzed on past us. "My God, what's wrong with these people today?" He lowered himself into the driver's seat and looked as shaken as I felt. I pressed myself into the upholstery and could not answer him.

He started the engine and backed carefully, maneuvering this way and that to turn in the tight space. I wondered how many days it would take for our wrecked remains to be spotted at the bottom of the chasm. "How could she have slipped, with the guardrail there?" is the question I finally asked.

"If I remember correctly, the rail wasn't there at the time. They put it up afterwards. But still, it's been an odd experience today. Where do you think Margo bought that kitschy diary?"

"Maybe in Europe. Or maybe Mrs. Vic gave it to her. I suppose she carried it around because it had no set dates on the pages and could fit in her purse."

"Hmm . . . maybe. Still, I've gotten more than I bargained for when I brought you to Stony Ridge today." He smiled; I scowled.

— 19 —

Everything from my belly down was aching by the time we turned into Morning Glory. But when I glanced at my porch, I forgot the pain. My pot of plastic geraniums lay on its side. I was sure we hadn't done that on the way out. "Ole, why isn't the curtain hanging properly over the window? It's all askew. There's something wrong with my house."

He leaned forward and looked, then pulled in behind the Glitz.

Ole turned off the motor but left the key in the ignition, opened the door just a little and eased out. Standing, he used the car as a shield and looked around. I rolled down my window, but the lack of glass did not bring anything into focus.

When Ole was satisfied, he moved from the car, shut the door and came around to help me out. As soon as he opened the screen door, we saw that the metal around my doorknob was dented. Ole held me back with one hand and tried the knob with the other. It turned. "Did you lock this door?"

"I always lock the door."

"Wait here," he said. He stepped in cautiously and I followed.

"My God, Ole, I've been robbed!"

Viciously. We stared in disbelief. I shook with fear and could not speak or even cry out. Pictures and torn couch cushions lay in heaps on the floor. Broken dishes and tea towels were scattered from one end of the kitchen to the other.

"Don't touch anything," Ole cautioned me. "We'll go to my place and call the police. Is anything missing?"

I pointed. My television was gone. Grandma's heirloom silver tea pitcher was missing. Then something sharp, hot and smashing beat against me. I'd known it from the second I'd walked in, but I hadn't let myself see it. Clara Barton was missing. Florence Nightingale was gone. Even the sewing room and bedroom had been ransacked. The original Bennet sisters were nowhere to be found. All of my dolls had disappeared!

Running out to the porch, I heaved root beer and blueberry muffin into the bushes.

Ole's big hands held me. "Come on, sweetie, let's get away from here," he said while I tried to catch my breath. "We shouldn't have gone in anyway." He helped me across the lane to his kitchen, offered me a swig of mouthwash and then placed me in his black recliner. He tenderly snugged me in with a maroon blanket. "I'll call the police." He brushed his hand across my forehead and hurried to the phone.

During the next hours, enormous uniformed policemen stomped in and out while clusters of neighbors peered around corners and asked questions. The police officers were handsome fellows in halt-or-I'll-shoot-blue uniforms, very courteous and kind, but they had to drag me back to my house so we could itemize all that was missing. We could not clean anything; I could only look. "Don't touch," they said.

Morning Glory number 48 was heartbreaking to look at, but nothing was missing except the television, my dear dolls, the teapot and a little cash I kept for emergencies in a cup at the back of a kitchen shelf. The robbers had dumped out my desk drawers but left my savings account book in the heap. Those thugs had almost dismembered my new zigzag sewing machine—apparently just for the pure hell of it.

When the police were ready to dust for fingerprints, Ole led me back to his house, through his living room and past the Marlite gardening boards. He helped me lie down on his bed, covered me with the maroon blanket and patted my shoulder. "Stay very still. I'll be back after I speak with the officers one more time."

"Ole, what about the other stuff? About Mrs. Vic's evidence? Are you going to tell them?"

"Do you want me to?"

"It might be too confusing."

"I agree. Let's wait until morning."

It was growing dark when he returned. He switched on a small bedroom lamp and said the police were certain that juveniles had done this. They lived nearby and kept track of people's comings and goings. They hid in the woods and darted in and out of Morning Glory the way football players sprinted for the goal line. The police had also checked Lupe's place, but she'd escaped the carnage.

Groups of neighbors hovered around like ghouls. They were flat out amazed that someone could go into my house on a Sunday afternoon, destroy the place, rip off my most valuable possessions and not be seen. Someone said I was in shock and another said I should return to the hospital, and so I called for Ole and told him he'd only take me back to that hospital over my dead body. "J-J-J-Just get r-r-r-rid of everybody and give me some ch-ch-chicken soup," I begged. "And my pain pills. The Darvocet . . . in the Gold Medal flour bag . . . in my kitchen. I've got major cramps now. Did the kids find those drugs? Is that what they were after?" I clutched my abdomen and rocked myself as best I could.

Ole shooed away the neighbors and called Dr. Azadi. I heard him speaking softly. A few minutes later, he came with hot soup and two of my pain pills. "The kids didn't find your meds, but they sure were looking." His shirt contained smudges of black fingerprint dust, overlaid with white baking flour.

"Ole, you're a holy mess," I mumbled.

My spoon shook in my trembling hand. He tucked another blanket around me and slipped a hot water bottle under my feet. He jogged back and forth across our lanes to check on the police. He said they'd dumped fingerprint dust on nearly every surface. "You can stay here tonight, sweetie. Let me take care of you. God, I wish it had been my house instead of yours."

I looked up at Ole and realized that he was almost in as much shock as I was. His fair skin seemed drained of all color. I told him to have some broth and sit down for a while.

He brought in his soup on a tray and sat in a blue-and-maroon-tweed armchair.

I looked around and realized that Ole had put color in his bedroom. I closed my eyes and visualized the mess in my own house. I wondered where the dolls were. That was the heart of my true pain. Where were my dolls?

"Ole," I said, "I can't stop shaking."

He hurried to the bed, pulled off his shoes and lay down beside me. He gently nudged me onto my side, curled up behind me and wrapped my blanket and me in his long arms. I could feel him breathing on my neck. This was the exact opposite of Margo's ghost hug along Precipice Point Road.

We lay quietly until the pills began to lull me and the trembling stopped. Night crept in and darkened the room, except for a slant of light from the bathroom door. I closed my eyes and willed my mind to sleep. But from somewhere in my fog, I realized something more. I had not seen the big padded envelopes I'd left on my kitchen counter.

"Ole?"

"Hmm?"

"The police are wrong. We're all wrong. It wasn't juveniles at all. It was a hired job, paid for by Mrs. Vic or her murdering son-in-law. They were searching for that diary. Goofy as it sounds, I know I'm right. One of those two people kidnapped my dolls."

Daylight snuck between the slatted blinds and created an eerie grid on the wall. For a moment, I could not place myself—who or where I was. I felt like dead weight, too paralyzed to move or find out. But while the dim light filtered into my eyes, I began to realize that I was in bed. With Ole!

I could hear him breathing behind me and feel the warmth and pressure of his arm resting against my shoulder. It was a mighty strange sensation. Until now, I'd never been in bed with any man who wasn't Buddy Blight.

But yes, I'd been in this bed with Ole last night. I'd been terribly upset. I'd wanted to call Buddy and tell him what had happened. But Ole said no. I must overcome my dependence on Buddy. Ole said it with a definite thud, a slamming of the door on Dwight Blight.

Coming more awake, I remembered my house. A zap of anxiety demanded that I jump up and run across the lane, clutch and cling to my abode, protect it like a fallen child. More than the house, I had to find the dolls. But when I tried to sit up, I felt the dizziness in my head and pain in my gut. No, I was not jumping or running anywhere. Instead, I slumped back onto the sheet. It was easier to stay in this snug warm bed with Ole and ignore every ugly thing in the world. I listened to the sound of his easy breathing. No snoring like Buddy's.

Wriggling a little, I turned on my back so I could see his sleeping face near my left shoulder. Little sprigs of red hair curled over his forehead. His features were relaxed in slumber—men are so gentle when they sleep.

When Ole lay down beside me last night, he was wearing khaki pants and a plaid shirt. Now he was in purple cotton pajamas that looked and smelled brand new, the kind you save for company. I could still see creases from the packaging.

We'd been under a casual blanket on top of the covers last night. Now we were between the sheets. I was somehow in blue pajamas, which were velvety and soft against my back and legs. I stretched out my arm and thought of the Blue Boy painting. Where did Ole find these things, and how did he get me into them? What had this strange man been doing here?

The clock on the bedside table read 6:30 a.m. It must be Monday morning. The end of a week since my surgery, but it felt as if my ordeal had been going on for many years. The cramps had certainly not subsided; they'd simply moved from my uterus to my gut, and now to my brain. I wondered if a person's brain could spasm. Could that be a medical diagnosis? Cramps of the brain? Yes, that was my disease. A grown woman who could not live without her dolls.

Giving in to it, I closed my eyes and begged. *Dear God, let the police find my dolls today. Please. I don't care about divorcing Buddy; I don't care about Mrs. Vic and her crazy evidence. I just want my dolls.*

Of course, the Heatherton police did not have enough manpower to do that sort of thing, to send out detectives to look for kidnapped dolls. And Ole probably had to work. He would certainly not have time to take me out on a doll hunt.

Growing more restless, I scanned the room. The linens and other effects were maroon, with bits of blue thrown in. A photo hung on the wall over the built-in dresser, a younger version of Ole next to a pretty woman with light hair and gentle eyes. She looked up at him with an adoring smile. The photo could be of his mother and father, or maybe Ole and a younger sister.

The bed jiggled behind me; his hand fell away from my shoulder. He rolled onto his back and woke up.

"Hi," I said, turning a bit toward him, looking at him full in his face now, wanting to reassure him that it was okay he'd slept with me. Or at least I assumed it was.

"Hi." He rubbed his eyes and then a sheepish look crossed his face.

We looked and smiled at one another like two silly kids, but we were careful not to move too much or bump the other too closely. I told myself to relax and sink into the peace of this cozy bedroom, hold off the day a little longer. But Ole was beginning to see what he'd gotten himself into. His face changed without moving a muscle, in the same way a good actor can manipulate his countenance by simply willing it inside his head. That is something that always amazes me when I see it in a movie. Robert Redford, for example.

A second later, Ole made a move to get up.

I put my hand on his arm and stopped him. "Wait. Before we wake up to whatever comes next, I need to thank you. You've been the best friend I've ever had. Thank you, Ole."

He brushed hair from my eyes. "I was happy to do it for you, Miranda." He slid his finger along my cheek and then pulled up abruptly. "Stay where you are," he said, straightening his pjs and putting on a robe. "I'll make some coffee and toast. We'll eat in here. The sun comes up through this back window. Then we'll face this day."

"I can help," I said, rolling onto my side, coaxing my legs over the edge of the bed and then slowly putting my feet on the floor. Yet again, I was off balance, weak and woozy, trying to stand.

"You have more pain now, don't you? Yesterday was too much. You are not to lift a finger today, Miranda."

"Can I at least go to the bathroom?"

"I suppose. If you must. By the way, there's a clean washcloth and towel and a new toothbrush on that shelf over the toilet. Also, I washed your clothes. One of the neighbor women brought over those pajamas and got you into them last night." He pointed to the chair with my old tan sweats and the arctic-fog underwear on top. Everything was neatly folded. I felt myself blush with embarrassment.

His bathroom shone. He had set out the company things—maroon and white—obviously newly purchased. He must have arranged lilac-scented guest soaps and the new toothbrush before he lay down beside me last night.

By the time I'd washed and dressed, Ole was carrying in a breakfast tray prepared with powder-blue napkins and a pink rose in a small crystal bud vase. There was steaming coffee and toast with peach jam. A small omelet with cheese, black olives and spinach.

When he opened the blinds, the window danced with a dazzling array of blossoming plants in crayon reds, acrylic yellows, watercolor blues and pinks in oil. Flowers grew in the window box, hung from baskets and climbed trellises across his garden. I could imagine the entire lakebed at Stony Ridge bursting into similar vibrant colors when he brought it to life. He propped pillows against the headboard and we reclined on top of the covers. With the breakfast tray between us, we looked out over the garden. A few clouds created interesting shadows.

Lordy. Buddy Blight had never served me an elegant breakfast in bed—not so much as a Pop-Tart.

"The coffee is good," I said, filling the blank space of our unsure silence.

"Thanks." He took a long swallow.

"So are the eggs and toast." I dabbed my lips with the dainty napkin.

"Do you like the peach jam?" He used his napkin for fidgeting.

"It's delicious. You have a peach tree, don't you? Did you make this yourself?"

He sipped his coffee. "I suppose your husband would not be caught dead making jam."

"He's not my husband anymore. I don't want to talk about him. Ever again. That door has been slammed shut!"

"I wish I could believe you."

"I think you can, Ole." I looked directly into his eyes. "You're showing me what the difference is."

"Hmm, that's the best news I've heard in a long time." He wiped a smudge from my chin.

I dabbed again with the napkin. "You'll have to wash these."

"I don't mind." He took my napkin from me, then put his left hand over mine, held it and took a final long swallow of his coffee, draining the cup. He picked up the tray and placed it on the floor; he then sat upright and propped himself against the headboard.

"Don't you have to get ready for work?"

Casually, as if we did this every morning, he put his arm around me and pulled my head to his chest. "I'm not going to the office today. I'll stay here and take care of you. You deserve some TLC."

Something about the way he whispered TLC into my hair made me look up at him. "Ole?"

His eyes turned down and latched onto my mine.

Now there's a scene in *Butch Cassidy and the Sundance Kid* when Katharine Ross the schoolteacher comes into her cabin and begins—slowly—to remove her starched white blouse; she's totally unaware that someone is watching her. But as she turns, she sees Sundance—Robert Redford, of course—sitting on a chair in the shadows, ready to ambush her. Terror registers in her eyes. Her fingers stop at the top of her undergarment. But the man nods, raises his eyebrows and lets her know he's in control. "Keep goin', teacher lady." Sundance laces his fingers over his chest and eats her up with his eyes. When she hesitates, he picks up his terrifying six-shooter, points it at her and orders her to keep undressing. He watches as if he's about to explode, while she unties a tiny ribbon and then slowly peels off her chemise and exposes herself, little by little. He unhitches his belt buckle, rises to his feet and moves toward her with power, control, possession, and yet—because he finds her so utterly delicious—he is totally at her mercy.

That's what Ole's eyes said to me. They were delightfully blue eyes that sparked and reflected the maleness of his soul. *I have taken possession of you, Miranda, yet I am totally, completely, at your mercy.*

And so we kissed. A kiss that both took possession and gave it away. In my mind, I slowly and deliberately undressed for him—at gunpoint if he wanted it so—while he leaned back in his chair, laced his fingers over his chest and watched each tiny, hesitant, slow movement. I was completely at his mercy.

But only in my mind and in the long exploring kiss. The rest of my body was off limits, freshly tormented by the reality of surgery, not the fantasy of love. Ole had the sensitivity to understand it and pull away. Carefully, he removed my arms from around his shoulders.

"Sweetheart," he said, clearing his throat. He smiled—twinkled, really—and stroked my cheek with his thumb. "You are such a blessing." He continued to look at me for a long while, baptizing me in wedgewinkle blue.

Then he jumped up and spoke in a pre-kiss tone. "Do you want to go out to the couch and watch television? While I go over and begin cleaning your house?"

"No, I'll go with you. I'd rather sit over there. Anyway, I was wondering if we should go look for the dolls."

He was busy pulling clothes from his closet and did not answer.

"Do you think we could? Look for the dolls? If you really want to help me, that's what I need."

He looked a bit confused. "Miranda, where would we even begin? I have no idea where to begin."

I needed to leave his bedroom so he could dress, but while I dangled on the edge of the bed, I glanced at the photo on the wall. "Ole, who's the lady in the picture?"

"What picture?"

"The one on the wall. She's pretty. Is she your sister?"

"No . . . my wife."

I'd known all along she wasn't his sister, but his words shocked me. I'd never, ever imagined Ole with a wife. He saw my confusion and hurried to explain. "I still think of her that way. Actually, she's dead. She was killed in a car accident. Eight years ago."

I stared at the happy couple in the photo and then looked up at him. "Oh goodness, Ole, what a dreadful thing. I'm so sorry."

"Well, it's been awhile. I should be adjusted by now."

"What was her name?"

"Elaine."

"That's pretty. A wife. Gosh, I never realized you'd been married."

"You never thought I could, did you?"

I tried to hide my embarrassment. "I don't know what I thought. You're not like Buddy or any of the men I've ever known."

He sat beside me on the edge of the bed, took my hand and smiled at me. "Not every man can be a good-looking macho stud, Miranda."

"Oh, but you are, Ole! I'm sorry if I made you feel that you weren't. But why didn't you tell me about her?"

"I'm sorry, it's difficult. I still never really believe she's gone."

"Hmm. Relationships dig deep. Send roots way down, don't they? What happened? Can you tell me about it?"

"There's not much to tell. We'd only been married a year. We were living in upstate New York. I'd just finished grad school at Cornell. We were out for a Sunday drive, to see the colors in the trees. It was a gorgeous fall day . . . and then . . . some idiot pulled onto the highway from the right. He was drunk, going about ninety miles an hour. Slammed into the passenger side of the car.

"She was in a coma for two weeks with a massive brain injury. I sat in the hospital day and night and watched her slip away from me." He stood and wandered to the window, where he gazed out at his flowers.

"Is that why you have so much black in your house?" I asked.

He jerked, as if the idea were completely new to him. "Yes, perhaps it is. I've never thought about it."

"That's how my mother died, too."

"In a car accident?"

"No, but she had brain death. A ruptured aneurysm, the summer I turned sixteen. One day she stood up from the lunch table at Grandpa's house and said she had the most terrible headache. Then she collapsed on the floor. By the time we took her to the hospital, she was in a coma. She died two days later. I never left her room."

Ole looked forlorn. How quickly our passion had turned from pleasure to gloom. When the phone rang, I braced myself for more bad news. I made my way to the living room while Ole answered. Then I heard him say, "Okay, yes. Okay. I'll come down, if that's all right."

When he hung up, he took my elbow and led me to the couch.

"What is it? Is this bad news?"

He ran his fingers across the top of his head and paced. "Well, it's not good."

"About the dolls?"

"Ah . . . yes."

I could scarcely breathe. "What's happened to them?"

He turned on the kitchen faucet and poured himself a drink of water. "They were behind the A&P supermarket, the one on Rosemary."

"But isn't that good? Can't we go get them?"

"They're a . . . they're broken, Miranda. The police took most of the . . . ah . . . parts . . . back to the station to hold for evidence."

"I don't understand. My dolls are broken?"

He sat on the arm of the couch next to me and patted my shoulder. "I'm afraid so."

Of course, I realized they were dolls and not real people like his wife Elaine or Mama or Sebastian Cross, who were all dead. The dolls were ceramic and cloth, but they were a family to me. They shared their stories with me. I had painted every smile on their faces. I'd put every tiny stitch into their clothing. Tears rushed to my eyes but I tried to hold steady. "Do the police still think it was vandals? Teenagers?" I asked in a feeble voice.

"Yes. Your other possessions weren't with them. Things kids would want to keep or sell. Like the television."

The tears overflowed while I tried to force logic from my mouth. "Then why didn't they just leave the dolls somewhere? Why hurt them?"

Ole slid onto the sofa beside me and clasped both of my hands. "Miranda, it looks as if they were . . . shot at . . . with BB guns. Propped up on one of those concrete walls behind the shopping center. The kids used the dolls for target practice."

"My babies were shot at? Oh God, Ole, they were shot at? *For the fun of it?*"

He squeezed my hands. "They're just dolls, sweetheart. I know you love them. I know you've worked hard on them, but let's keep this in perspective. They're just dolls."

"No, they're so much . . . oh God. Oh my holy God." I jerked my hands away from his and clutched my abdomen. My thoughts burned. "If Clara is gone, that means the key . . . from the shoe . . . it's gone too. And the mailing bags—was it for the diary, Ole? All of this, to find that damn, stupid little diary?"

"Listen to me. I know your situation with Mrs. Vic is weird, but this really sounds like teenagers were just out on a spree."

"No! It was *them*! Whoever *them* are. They were looking for the key. And the diary. Mrs. Vic's evidence. Don't you see it? I told you. The mailing bag is gone."

I thrust my face into my hands to stifle my sobs and absorb my tears.

Ole stood up slowly. "Miranda, I lay awake for a long time last night. Perhaps you've been right all along. Mrs. Vic probably does have mental problems. She's paranoid, I imagine. That diary is nothing, really. An old stereotype kind of sinister evidence at best. But if we could find Clara, and the key has actually disappeared, then maybe. Maybe we'd have reason to pursue this further. With the police, I think."

"Yes, but you said the dolls were broken."

"Well, maybe there's—I'll tell you what. I'll go look. I'll check at the police station and run out to the A&P."

"I want to go with you." I tried to stand up but he nudged me back into place.

"No. You stay right here. You're too exhausted. I won't be gone long."

I'd been maintaining some sort of control over my voice, but suddenly hiccups, hisses, snorts and snot all tumbled out of me. Ole looked as if he'd like to help and then thought better of it. Instead, he dressed quickly, picked up his car keys and locked me into his black-black-black-black house.

"Why is God doing this to me?" I asked through the sobbing, while everything that had gone wrong in the last three years sputtered to the surface—Darcy's leaving, the marriage collapse, the stupid surgery, even Buddy's predictions about my stomach spreading into an ugly, old-age blob.

The cramps in my brain spewed out unholy noises for a long while. I'd stop occasionally, blow my nose and try to get up, sit back down and begin sobbing all over again. I was still planted firmly on my pot of self-pity when I heard Ole's car on the gravel drive. I dabbed at my eyes, inhaled deeply and braced myself for more horrific news.

Instead, Ole bounced through the door with an enormous smile on his face. He whipped his hand from behind his back and held Clara aloft.

"Clara Barton!" I lurched from the couch, grabbed her and kissed her lips, even though she tasted like garbage. I pulled something crumbly from her hair and stroked the red cross I'd stitched so carefully onto her bodice. "Where was she?"

"In the bottom of the dumpster. They must have tossed her in there and the police missed it."

"How'd you get her out?"

"I climbed in. Stood on the hood of the car so I could reach the top. There were footholds inside to climb up and down. It wasn't too bad."

"Thank you, Ole! Thank you so much." I hugged him and then kissed his mouth. He tasted like garbage, too. I began to pat at Clara's clothing and then I froze. Something was terribly wrong. I lifted her petticoat and stared. Her lower left leg and foot were broken off, with nothing but shards of ceramic and torn pantaloons. The stocking and high-buttoned shoe were gone. The key, of course, was missing. I sat down and was very, very still. Ole and I looked at each other hopelessly, the way Butch looked at Sundance just before the shootout in Bolivia.

When the phone rang, we both jumped. It was Ole's boss, wanting him to come into a meeting for a couple of hours. Some big shot had flown in from out of town. Ole was the only living soul with the information the man needed. Ole tried to protest—but when you're the only living soul—

While he headed for his bedroom to clean up, I stood at the window and stared across the lane at my house. Who was really in there yesterday? And why? What could be so important about that flimsy little key? The diary wasn't even locked.

When Ole was ready to leave, he tucked me into his black couch with the maroon blanket, then turned on the television. "Please don't move from this spot. Watch *Today* or *Regis and Kathy*, whatever. We'll clean up your place when I get back. I shouldn't be gone long." His attempt at nonchalance was as transparent as the veiling I used for the dolls' summer hats.

He handed me the remote, kissed my lips sweetly and locked the door on the way out. When I could no longer hear his car, I turned off the television, tucked Clara and my narcotics safely into my cable-car bag and headed home. I had to face whatever disaster had laid waste to Morning Glory number 48.

And I was going to have to tackle it alone.

— 20 —

The nastiest place in my house was the bathroom. No matter how weak I felt, I could not ignore the bathroom. Oily black fingerprint dust covered the sink, the faucet and the gold Formica countertop. I wiped up the gruesome slick with paper towels and bathroom cleaner, but black smudges left permanent stains. The toilet was clean, but I scrubbed the seat and handle anyway. I shoved an old towel around the floor with my foot to wipe up shoe marks.

With that done, I stepped into my fruit-loopy bedroom.

That scene wasn't much better. The burglars had scattered the unopened mail hither and yon. They'd emptied drawers, pawed through my personal things, and flung my shirts, shorts and underwear across the floor. The police had then come in and stomped through my panties and bras. I felt raped.

Ignoring the doctor's orders, I bent from my waist, gathered the defiled clothing and staggered out to my washer/dryer behind the kitchen. Not everything fit, but I stuffed the load in anyway. I poured in the soap and set the water to hot, which I never did to my good clothing. But I had to sterilize these things. While the washer filled, I returned to the bedroom, pulled the black-smudged comforter and sheets off my bed, threw them into the corner and collapsed on the bare pillows and mattress cover. I was extremely thankful that my lingerie would be cleaned up before Ole returned. I did not want the lovely Olafson to fuss with my underwear, ever again.

Closing my eyes, I saw the doll massacre on the cement wall. The bullets zipped and the ladies cried out. Their screams made me think of the Czar of Russia and his little children, shot to death and tossed into icy cold graves. My eyes popped right back open and I looked around. My holy, gold-leafed Bible lay open on the floor. My lovely lilac funeral arrangements were crumpled and scattered. I could not even die in peace.

Rolling onto my side, I let my head droop over the edge of the bed; I stared at the mess in my gossamer-wings carpet. The burglars had dumped out a special shoebox of Mama's things that I normally stashed in the bedside table. I turned onto my abdomen and slid down onto my hands and knees, then leaned against the bed and began to reexamine all the bits and pieces of Mama's life.

I found a letter from my father telling my mother how much he loved her and the baby she was carrying. He included several paragraphs about the frightening conditions of war—more tragedy I did not want to think about. I put the letter in the bottom of the shoebox and began to pile everything else on top of it: her corsage for Homecoming, her diploma for graduation, the photo of her parents, who were very dark and swarthy indeed. They could have been gypsies from the looks of them, despite their Christian preaching. I also came upon my parents' marriage certificate: Gary Beau Smothers and Evelyn Maureen Bedlo.

I picked up a broken glass frame and removed their photo. Mama was in an early 1940s silk dress, a pillbox hat and veil on her head. My father stood erect in his army uniform. They looked very young and brave. Later, when Mama's brain aneurysm ruptured, she said nothing more than, "I have the most terrible headache." But at the very end—at Loving Memorial when I was asleep in a chair by her bed—something woke me. Mama's eyes were wide open and the most expectant smile shone across her face. She stared at a blank spot on the far wall and said clearly, "Dear Beau, you're silly. Of course I'll be your wife. Forever and ever." And that was it. Mama fluttered away to be with Beau Smothers forever and ever.

I brushed aside the broken frame and placed the photo carefully in the box. Then I spotted a funny little note about the scandal when Mama stole Beau away from the senior girl who had her hooks into him. I smoothed it out and almost relaxed enough to chuckle when I reread this silliness.

I wish you could have seen the look on Peggy Greene's face when I showed up on Beau Smothers' arm Friday night. She's so furious,

demanding that everyone call her Nora Margaret instead of
Peggy. All references to "make-out queen" are strictly forbidden!

Trust me, I was not chuckling by the end of that note. I was seeking answers. Was Peggy Greene actually Nora Margaret Greene? Peggy was a nickname for Margaret. But how could it—*Margaret?* And *Peggy?* Superimposed?

While each half second passed, my brain seized into a larger question. I remembered the long-time head of security at Loving Memorial using the name Nora Margaret. Could Nora Margaret Greene be one and the same as Peggy Greene, the Make-out Queen? Could Nora Margaret Greene actually be Nora Margaret Vickerstromm?

I broke into a cold sweat. Had Mrs. Vic dated my father? Kissed him? My God in the heavens, was Mrs. Vic the scandal?

The image was sheer repulsion. I had to tell myself to breathe or I would have passed out. In my mind, my father was forever a handsome soldier in his army uniform, his arm around my mother. Whereas Mrs. Vic crawled like a creepy, two-headed monster through my brain; one head with a long sharp nose, brown hair in a bun, a board-stiff white uniform; the other with clamshelly, beeswaxy hair—a crone in a lethargic-blue hospital gown.

The repulsive images pushed me to gather up all of Mama's worldly goods, cram them back into the box and put the lid on tightly, with the exception of the scandal note, which I was determined to flush down the toilet.

When I shoved the box to one side, I noticed debris along the crease between the built-in-bed and the wall-to-wall carpet: a couple of bobby pins, more than one paper clip, two pennies and . . . whoa . . . a small white shard of porcelain. Maybe it was part of Clara Barton's amputated leg. My hand moved before my brain could figure it out. I picked up the shard and brought it to my eye. In a nanosecond, I yelped and dropped the disgusting object into the carpet; I flailed my hands as if I'd been holding a scorpion. I tried to spring away, but when my body could not spring, I turned onto my hands and knees and tried to escape by crawling through the carpet. I did not get far before my curiosity made me glance back.

The hard, white object was not wriggling, slithering or hissing. I turned slowly and crawled back, leaned in and squinted. It was not a shard of ceramic, nor could it be any part of Clara Barton. I bent closer and touched it gingerly with the top edge of my pinky nail. It looked like an elongated white tooth with a rusty stain on the tip that would anchor into a mouth, probably an eyetooth. But from what kind of mouth? What kind of stain? Was it blood?

For some idiot reason, I felt my own teeth. I pressed every one of them firmly with my fingertips until I was certain they were all in place. In the meantime, I wondered if the teenaged burglars had gotten in a fight and punched each other's faces while ransacking my drawers. If so, this tooth would be a clue. Maybe I should turn it over as evidence.

I squinted at it in wonder. The enamel was neither the fresh white of a juvenile nor the corncob discoloration of an old timer. Instead, its color was a mid-life dull, like mine. The edge was chipped. I sighed and decided that it must have been in my rug all along, wedged deeply between the carpet and bed frame. Maybe with all the burglar-police commotion, it had erupted onto the surface like the bright new tooth of a grinning first grader.

Through all of my fear and speculation, I clung to the scandal note with my left hand. Now I used it to pick up the tooth. I crawled into the bathroom, reached up and dropped the tooth onto the formerly gold counter. Still on my knees, I wadded the abominable note and flushed it down the toilet, as originally planed.

The phone began to ring. Bracing myself against the edge of the bathtub, I pushed up and hobbled out to the living room, not far in a mobile home, even a doublewide. But my muscles cramped and I walked hunched, like a gorilla.

The living room was equally ruined. Black fingerprint dust discolored every shade of gold, mocha and cream. My gossamer-wings carpet looked beyond salvaging. The pearly white phone was now oily gray. I tore off an inside piece of the Sunday paper and used it to grab the receiver. "Please, please be Darcy. I need to talk to Darcy."

"How are you today, Miranda?" Mrs. Vic asked in a snide tone.

I hung up on the evil witch and wiped my mouth on my sleeve. "That bitch! How dare she call me after she kissed my father? I will never speak to her again." I tottered to the kitchen, grabbed a couple of paper towels, came back and wiped off the phone. It looked permanently stained in dead-oyster-gray, just the thing to go with my arctic-fog underwear.

When it rang again, I swore to God I would not answer. But it could be Ole, scared to death about what had happened to me. Or Darcy, desperately needing my help, what with her broken leg in a cast, swollen up and itching. I finally gave in and picked up the receiver.

"Do not hang up on me or you will be dead meat. Do you understand? This is life and death, Miranda. We're not playing games, you ninny."

"Why didn't you tell me about my parents? Did you know who I was all along?"

"What are you talking about?"

"My parents! Beau Smothers and Evelyn Bedlo. She stole him from you, didn't she? Don't try to deny it."

Her voice snarled in response. "And just who is Beau Smothers?"

"Your high school sweetheart. Don't play dumb with me, Nora Margaret Peggy Greene. Oh, there's evidence, all right."

"In high school? Why are you talking about high school? With all that's going on?"

"Because high school is more important than what's going on. Because you robbed the cradle with my father. And you—so high and lofty in your purity as a nurse—you were a tramp!"

"For heaven's sake, that was nearly fifty years ago. We have more important things to discuss. I need to find out if you're taking care of the items you've been given for safekeeping. Are you, Miranda?"

"I don't have a damn thing of yours."

"Yes you do, dear, and I need you to bring it all over here. I want you to come and visit me for a little while."

"Tough! I'm not allowed to drive my car for the next six weeks."

"I know, but it's not far and I need you. It's quite urgent."

"Mrs. Vic, I was robbed yesterday. My entire house was destroyed. Anything of yours that might have been here is long gone."

"You were robbed? Yesterday? Ah ha! I knew it. I knew I could flush him out. Oh, this is wonderful. Now listen, I'll send a cab. You won't have to drive at all. He didn't find the things I told you to guard with your life, did he? I want you to bring them over here at once. At last we're getting somewhere."

"Damn you, you old witch! Just leave me alone! I don't ever want to hear your crazy voice again." I slammed down the receiver and spat at my telephone.

She had me so riled up that I scuttled around and got to work cleaning the living room. I needed to focus. I squirted bathroom spray on every black surface until all the fingerprint dust puddled and pooled in ugly black globs across Morning Glory number 48. I grabbed an old T-shirt and started wiping.

The phone rang. It was Ole, wanting to know why I had not stayed put at his place. He was going to be tied up all day. The big shots were demanding.

"It's okay, I'm cleaning," I answered, wishing he would come back immediately.

"You're what? Miranda, please, don't stay there alone. Go back to my house. Please."

"Forget it. My blood's boiling. Mama had an old photo of her parents and they were dark and swarthy. The woman wore wild clothes. Even if the man was a preacher, they were gypsies and I am too. I've got wild blood in me, Ole. I'm so fired up that I can bend, spray and scrub without shedding a tear. All of this black gunk is coming off my house today. By the time you're home, my underwear will be folded and out of sight. So don't worry about me, I'm fine!"

"I don't understand what—" Someone hollered at him. Another important meeting was about to begin. Poor Ole. I'd never told him about my gypsy blood coming to a boil.

I continued cleaning. Nothing on my body hurt any longer. I was strong. I was invincible. I was ready to dance with a knife in my teeth and a rose in my hair! If I could not look or act like dark, swarthy Cher, I could be blond Helen Reddy. "I am woman," I tried to sing, but in truth, I could not quite roar.

I thought about my gypsy blood and the tooth. I almost laughed. That tooth! I realized now that it must have come from Mama's box. It was an old keepsake, maybe from my gypsy grandmother. I'd have to study the photo again and see if I could spot a gap in Grandmother Bedlo's mouth.

After I sopped up a few pools of grimy fingerprint dust, the phone rang again. I answered it. Why not?

"Miranda, don't argue with me. Get in the cab when it comes. Bring along everything you've been given. Bring your purse and your driver's license."

"Why the hell would I want to come over there? What could possibly entice me?"

There was a long silence. Her voice was softer and less demanding when she spoke again. "Miranda, I have things to tell you about. Ah, you mentioned your father . . . and me. You were right, we were friends . . .

more than friends, in high school. And then your mother intervened. And they were married. But . . . but that wasn't exactly the end of it.

"I loved him and well . . . I was already pregnant when I married Ed Vicker . . . eh, your father was . . . Margo was . . ."

The name Margo sliced through my chest like the blade of her butcher knife. My father, Mrs. Vic and her daughter Margo? No! This had to be the worst lie she'd ever told. She was a raving lunatic.

Still, curiosity drove its own blade. I whispered into the receiver, "I don't have your stuff. I was robbed. Clara was—"

"I want you to come over here anyway. I have things to tell you. I know a certain cabdriver. I'll send him to fetch you. Be nonchalant when you arrive at the hospital. Walk quietly through the lobby; don't call attention to yourself. Don't talk to anyone or act like an idiot. Take the elevator to the third floor and wander down to my room. I assume you remember how to find my room?"

"Yes."

"And Miranda? This is private, between you and me. Don't call your husband or that oddball boyfriend of yours."

I hung up the phone just as the washer stopped. I went through the kitchen and switched the clothes from wash to dry. Hot, hot, hot dry.

I would accept her invitation because I was curious and horrified. I could not sit in my house any longer, with all the crazy thoughts raging through my head. I glanced at myself. The tan jogging suit that Ole had washed was covered in black filth.

I changed into an even older sweat suit from the back of my closet. It had once been a lovely coral but was now a bleached, faded-starfish color—horrible—I never wore the thing out; today it went well with my arctic-fog underwear. In the bathroom, I rubbed bright magenta lipstick on my mouth and slopped black eyeliner over my brows and around my lashes. I found a long, garishly colored, paisley scarf in the back of the cupboard and wound it around my head. I hauled out my biggest, darkest sunglasses.

I spotted the gypsy tooth on the counter and held it up to my own mouth. It looked pretty much the same shape and size as my eyetooth. I held it to the light, squinted at the stain and decided it was definitely blood. So this was the major keepsake from my mother's family? I plunged the sharp little tooth down my dingy bra to ward off evil. The devil himself would not bother me now.

Wearing the colored glasses, I returned to the living room and placed poor crippled Clara in my San Francisco cable-car bag; I promised myself I'd never again leave home without her. When the cab arrived, I locked my door, which was odd. What difference would a locked door make now?

Her cabdriver had brown skin, black wavy hair, round dark eyes and a hefty black mustache. He was probably fresh over USA boarders from a family of drug lords. I wondered if he was missing an eyetooth, but he did not open his mouth. The caption on his license photo said he was Sydney Jones. Ha! This was no Sydney Jones. This was more likely a José, an Ivan or an Abdul.

I felt like a fool. Mrs. Vic wasn't going to talk about my family. This was bound to be another setup in some weirdo scheme against Tomlinson Grenadier.

But then a new thought came to mind. Mrs. Vic must have hated my mother. Could she be using her son-in-law as a decoy to get revenge?

Was this woman actually after *me*?

This entire time?

— 21 —

The supposed Sydney pulled over at the hospital entrance, jumped out and opened the back door of his taxi for me. He grinned for a moment, long enough for me to catch an entire array of teeth blazing in the sun. Nothing missing. He placed a strong grip on my elbow and steered me toward the automatic opener. His foot tapped the mat and the door slid into the walls. He gave me a little shove into the lobby and followed, while I hobbled in my dead-starfish sweat suit, my whoring-magenta lipstick, my humongous sunglasses and the wild scarf wrapped around a scrub brush of hair sprouting from the top of my head. All of this, along with the charming gorilla walk.

The lobby was quiet. It was 10:20 on a Monday morning. All the surgical patients were in surgery; all the families and loved ones waited elsewhere. The hospital lobby had been remodeled since I was a student. Formerly, the administrator's office was housed in a cubbyhole next to the gift shop; now a sign pointed to *Administration* far down a hallway, away from any troublesome visitors. I figured it was one of those places with a mammoth conference table of polished mahogany, surrounded by tall swivel chairs in which white-haired men reclined, scratched their chins and made cozy decisions with small, private medical clinics—buying them up and converting them into new HMO conglomerates owned by the hospitals. It was all paid for from the patients' bills, of course. Lupe had told me how grand the big boys had it in the medical world. They even had kitchens stocked with wines and special gourmet cuisine prepared and served by Food Services. Upstairs, the patients were fed gruel and Jell-O.

What would happen if I trotted down that hall and grabbed the CEO away from his shiny office furniture? What if I screamed and hollered about how Mrs. Vic was tormenting me, how she'd commandeered this hospital and the entire staff, and how she'd even employed people from the underworld!

Instead, I followed orders. I floated along like one of those little steel dogs on a piece of paper; Mrs. Vic was the strong horseshoe magnet underneath, sliding me every which direction. The magnet moved me to the elevators and on up to the third floor. Thankfully, the imposter cabbie remained behind.

Jackson-the-Security-Guard was standing opposite the door when it opened. He was chatting with a young nurse who wore a sassy white uniform above her knees. Stringy yellow hair hung halfway down her back and hoop earrings waited for a mental patient to yank them from her head in a bloody mess. Jackson did not recognize me—the smudgy, disheveled, wanton ape I'd become.

Escaping him, I wandered toward the kitchen, slipped in, took a few cautious steps to the fridge and peered into the empty space. The knife was gone. Somehow, Mrs. Vic must have retrieved it. Maybe it was under her covers and she planned to kill me with it. I should have hidden one of my own knives in my bag, instead of a doll.

Watch her every twitch, I told myself.

Again I trekked down that long corridor. My disguise with the gaudy scarf and sunglasses seemed to be working. No one cared what kind of idiot wandered down these halls. At room 301, I stopped and took a deep breath. There was no security guard in sight. What a dud Jackson had become. Or maybe she'd sent him away so she could whack off my head when I crossed her threshold. No one would hear me scream.

On guard, I shoved open the door and inched through.

"It's about time," she growled from the shadows.

I lurched at the sound of her headless voice and then spotted her sitting in a collapsible, hand-push wheelchair with a tan leather seat and armrests. It was a flimsy thing compared to the battery-operated vehicle that had hidden a butcher knife. That mammoth electric chair was not in sight today. She wore a fuzzy dark green jogging suit with a bright yellow bumblebee appliquéd on the front. She'd smeared red rouge on her lips and cheeks and dark eye shadow across her lids. Together, we looked as if the circus had come to town.

"You scared me," I whispered, clutching my bag to my chest for protection. I could feel the little tooth scratch my breast; I sensed Clara Barton's outline holding firm under my hand.

Mrs. Vic's eyes traveled up my body and down again. "My God, if you aren't a sight. But you'll do. Did you bring along the package? And where is my knife?"

"How would I know? I left it in bed with you."

"Never mind about the knife. Where's the package? It's vital evidence, Miranda. Absolutely the final piece. You were right. Poor Sebastian Cross found it in the silk flowers. He just managed to call me before—"

"Then why haven't you told the police? Why me?"

"I told you why. The police are bought and paid for. Don't you remember how they covered up the Kennedy assassination? Anyway, you're the perfect person to flush him out. I explained all of that. Come on, let's go. Be assured, I will tell the authorities about that butcher knife if you don't comply. I'll say *you* brought it to the hospital and threatened *me* with it. My word is respected in this institution, you ought to realize that."

"Oh no, no, no!" I stiffened myself out of the gorilla hunch and stood up straight. "You're not tricking me into some—look, I came here to find out about my father. I want to know if you hated my mother so much that you're going after me. Are you seeking revenge for him? Is it an eye for an eye and a tooth for a tooth?"

She gave me a long look. In doing so, she lost thirty years. Her nose and earlobes shrunk to normal. Her hair returned to brown and twisted into a bun at the back of her head. Her eyes became bitter blue stones to hurl at a person, like stainless steel surgical instruments. I could try and fight her, but in the end, she was the Teacher. She took complete control of me and ruled my world with an iron fist.

"Come along," she said. "This room is bugged. We'll go to the solarium. You push the chair. Keep your glasses on. I'm glad you thought of that. Very clever, Miranda. And keep your mouth shut. Don't say a word. I'll do all of the talking."

And so I sealed my doom. I clutched the handles of her chair and began to push. I assisted the wheels in their rotation and out we went, me and my captor. We turned left and kept going, past the medicine carts, the laundry carts, the cleaning carts; we wove our way through nurses in scrubs, doctors in scrubs, maybe even a ward clerk in scrubs, all colors of scrubs. For a moment, I thought about dying here, surrounded by nothing but these boxy, baggy, nameless scrubs.

When we passed the nurses' station, people behind the desk glanced at her but continued with their work. I noticed the clock said 10:35. Ole had gone to work at 8:15. Not even three hours ago. I remembered our kiss, likely my last kiss ever.

Finally, an aide noticed us. "You going to the solarium, Mrs. Vic? That's good, honey. I'll make up your bed real nice while you're gone."

We were both very quiet while we continued on. Despite the wheelchair's flimsy appearance, I needed all my energy to push her in it. She hit the wheels with her hands occasionally to help me out. Rounding a corner, we came to the big cheerful solarium next to the phone booth, but it looked gloomy today, with little sunlight. I began to turn the chair into the doorway, but she stopped me cold.

"Not here, you ninny," she hissed. "Keep going."

"But . . ."

"Just shut up and keep pushing."

Although I'd taken two Darvocets at Ole's, I'd hidden the bottle in the Gold Medal flour bag when I returned home. I'd been so flustered in getting ready that I'd forgotten to bring it along. Now, pushing this wheelchair in silence, I wondered when I'd collapse from the pain cramping my legs and low back, as well as my incision area.

We came to a service elevator in the bridge between the two towers.

This section of the hospital had been built after I was expelled. It was not familiar to me, but instinctively I knew this elevator was not for live passengers. It was for dead bodies; the next one would be mine. Mrs. Vic was taking me down to the MORGUE, sure as spitting. She wanted to get even with my mother. She'd hack me up, leave me on a cold slab and be off.

I debated a quick turn-and-dash. There was no reason for me to be in this mess. I knew exactly where to locate Jackson. And Dr. Azadi was likely in the house.

Mrs. Vic saw my hesitation. "Don't leave me, Miranda. I do have information about your family that you need to know. I'm not as nutty as you think I am." She reached up and hit the call button. The door opened immediately, as if this elevator had been trained to stand ready for her. "Come along."

Despite every foreboding, I was still the metal dog roving about on Mrs. Vic's field of play. I pushed her in while straining to bump the wheels over the uneven levels in the door space. She ordered me to place her chair so she could reach the control panel, then she hit the letter B. When we stopped in the basement, she kept her hand poised. "Peek out," she said. "Is the coast clear?"

"I don't see anyone." I looked every which direction trying to spot the morgue, but it must have been hidden around the corner.

"Look at the outside door. Is my cab there?"

"There's a cab. That same driver is waiting."

"Good. If someone had come, we would have zipped back upstairs."

Within moments, the dark man had both of us tucked into the back seat, her wheelchair in the trunk. "Sydney Jones always picks me up at this door," she said. "I'm not about to come and go in the lobby as if I were a common patient. Don't look so frightened, Miranda. It's all right. I have this all figured out." Her voice was a hot wind on my face.

I was not surprised when we pulled into the drive of the dark old fairy-tale house. "Home sweet home" she said, patting my knee. "You'll enjoy my house, dear. Ed and I traveled extensively. We accumulated treasures from around the world."

Sydney Jones soon had us out of the cab, up the ramp and into the house. After he closed the door, Mrs. Vic turned the deadbolt with a theatrical flair.

—So there we were, locked up and alone.

We stepped into a literal jungle in both the living and dining rooms, which were separated only by a high, wide arch.

"Holy shit!" The phrase shot from my mouth as if I'd been thwacked in the stomach.

Across every surface grew long green vines from nests of viper-like plants. They slithered up walls, over windows, across furniture. Reptile leaves clustered on the ceiling and slept in the chandeliers. Vegetation crawled along end tables, trailed down chair legs and coiled onto the floor. There were no blossoms in this jungle, just a hundred shades of green. Trust me, you don't want me to start naming them all.

Under all of this primordial foliage lurked the animals—carved and ceramic elephants, lions, tigers. Maybe a panther or leopard. Some were almost life-sized. Green and yellow cat eyes gleamed at me. A great gray elephant arched its trunk over one side of an upright piano; a giraffe stretched its neck and peered down at the keyboard from the opposite side.

Beneath it all, old wooden slats formed an uneven floor in raw-dirt colors. Garbanzo-bean-yellow wheelchair tracks led to distant haunts in Mrs. Vic's domain.

"Don't touch anything, Miranda. This collection is worth a fortune. I have the finest ceramic and porcelain pieces from around the world. The elephant tusks are genuine ivory."

Something screeched above our heads. "Yes your majesty. Right-O your majesty." I looked up and spotted yellow, orange and green feathers above me. Birds were alive in here!

And Buddy thought I was nuts, with my nursy dolls sitting around?

She looked up at me from her chair and beamed. "Collectors from around the globe are envious of what I've accomplished. I began when Margo was still a baby. Are you impressed?"

I was tempted to ask who came in here to water and clean up the bird poop. "Your child grew up in this?"

"Oh, it wasn't so lush at that time. Just a few pieces and two or three plants. Margo learned to play the piano right there under the watchful eye of the giraffe from Kenya, although we have a Steinway in the upstairs sitting room."

She reached out and rubbed the head of the panther with a cloth from a bag on her chair. Then she smiled at me in triumph. "They make your little dolls look rather puny, wouldn't you say?"

'Puny? *Puny?* Well good heavens, if your junk is so grand, why didn't burglars march in here and shoot up your collection? They could have had a regular African safari. Why did they have to kill my helpless little dolls? Did you know they smashed my doll collection to smithereens? Out behind the A&P? With BB guns? Did you hire them to do that, you crazy old—"

She stared at me with smug unconcern. "Stop yelling, Miranda. When this is over, we'll buy you some new dolls."

I lunged at her, but she had already turned her wheelchair toward the back of her house. I tripped on a lion's foot and fell to my hands and knees. Pain cramped me into a ball; I collapsed and rolled over onto my back in agony.

"Just wait right there. I have to pick up some bank notes from my safe. And don't touch anything."

I was on the floor, knees to chest, feet waving in air. Another screech and I looked up. The parrot gawked down. I was hurting so much I could not possibly get up, even if that damn bird pooped all over my face. Mrs. Vic would have to call 911 to get me out this mess.

I wondered where she kept her phone. If I could crawl to it, I could call 911 myself. I took a few deep breaths and poked at my abdomen. Everything was still intact. I could not believe how strong the human body was.

That gypsy tooth might be giving me power. I rolled over with great care and pulled up onto all fours. I needed to call Ole or Buddy—Buddy! That was it. Buddy would march in here and take care of this lunacy lickety-split. I should have called him from my house, but I'd been way too worried about laundering my underwear.

The phone was likely in the kitchen. I clutched a lion's mane and pulled myself to my feet, then stumbled through the dining room by grabbing the backs of chairs. I stopped at a shelf of photos above the sideboard.

Margo popped out at all ages. In one, she posed with a man who must have been Ed Vickerstromm—I wondered what poor old Ed had actually been. Margo's father? Or the duped?

Margo's photo in Dr. Tormentor's magazine had looked familiar and now I realized why. Her childhood pictures looked like my childhood pictures, except that she was dressed up in satins and laces, whereas I had been relegated to cottons and denims. I shivered and looked at her mouth. It was smaller than mine. Her eyes were maybe larger than mine. In one colored photo, however, they were green like mine. A coincidence, surely.

Behind Margo stood a ceramic-framed photo of two young people in turned-up jeans and saddle shoes, holding hands. I stared into the smug face of Peggy Greene, the nasty, horrid Make-out Queen.

"Your father was a charmer," Mrs. Vic said from behind me. "I'm not surprised you spotted his photo. He drew the girls to him."

I waved the picture in her face. "Is this why you kicked me out of nurses training? Because you're a jealous, conniving, raving—" I threw the photo across the room and heard the glass break. I hoped it also shattered some weird object with claws, like hers. Slumping against the wall, I tried to catch my breath.

She smiled. The audacity! To sit there in her flimsy little wheelchair and smile.

"I'm sorry. I didn't mean to upset you this much, Miranda. I'm not trying to persecute you. I'm trying to catch my son-in-law, who murdered my daughter and wants to be governor of this state. I'm not jealous of your parents. And I did not kick you out of school because of them or your . . . well . . . less than adequate nursing skills. There was something else. We don't have time for it now."

She glanced at her watch. "I need you to tell me about the diary on our way to the bank. I'm sure you have it; you've probably read it. Mr. Cross told you to guard that package with your life, and I think you did exactly that. That's why I chose you, Miranda. You're Beau Smothers' daughter. I can count on you. Now tell me where you've hidden it, dear."

"I'm not telling you one damn thing."

"Oh, I think you will, sooner or later. Right now, we have to get going."

"Going is right. I'm walking out of this loony bin this instant and finding the police. I should have done it the night you gave me that butcher knife." Hoisting my bag higher on my shoulder, I pulled the ridiculous scarf from my head, waved it in her face and turned to the door.

"Stop right were you are, Miranda." Her voice was so cool she could have been some mob's hired woman in a wheelchair. "Turn around, very slowly."

I turned and looked. Her current weapon of choice was an enormous, stainless steel, sturdy-as-an-ox, meat cleaver. Yes, a meat cleaver. In the tight grip of a woman with great upper-body strength. She could hurl it at me and hit her target dead on.

Not taking her eyes from me, she passed the cleaver to her left hand and withdrew a tiny pistol from a bag on her chair. It was a silvery snub-nosed weapon—the kind that women like to carry in their purses. The sturdiness of the meat cleaver and the feminine look of the handgun spoke to the craziness and the cruelty of Mrs. Vic's power. The *ying* and the *yang* of it. I was beyond astonishment.

"Now walk past me, through the kitchen and out into the garage. We don't have much time. Eventually those idiot nurses will realize I'm missing. Not that they'd particularly care."

The parrot screeched, "Yes your majesty. Right-O your majesty."

Mrs. Vic rolled behind me, down a ramp through a dimly lit and covered breezeway, into an even darker cavern that housed a hefty black van. When she flipped on a light, the vehicle flashed as if it were a fly in the sunlight, a glint of purple and green in its wings. "Do you remember the Green Hornet?" she asked.

I clamped my arms to my sides. "If there's a hornets' nest in here, I'll die of anaphylactic—"

"You ninny," she barked, "the Green Hornet! On the radio!" She raised the meat cleaver and threw it like a tomahawk into the rotting floor, where it stuck on point a second before collapsing in the dirt. I figured she aimed that message directly at my head.

"*The Green Hornet* was a radio program when I was with your father. Now it's been made into movies and TV series, but we listened to it on a portable Philco in our basement." Her voice lowered to the same spooky whisper used by Digger O'Dell the friendly undertaker from Grandpa's radio days.

"Stepping through a secret panel," she said, "Reid and Kato went along a narrow passageway that led to an adjoining building that fronted on a dark side street." She painted an imaginary path by dragging the tiny pistol through the dust motes in the air.

"Though supposedly abandoned, it served as the hiding place for the sleek, super-powered Black Beauty, streamlined car of the Green Hornet. A section of the wall in front rose automatically and then closed as the gleaming Black Beauty sped into the darkness."

Mrs. Vic shook herself out of her bizarre drama and zeroed in on me. "Close your mouth, Miranda. I have it memorized. Those were the best days of my life, down in the cellar with your . . . well . . . and now I have my own Beauty." She nodded toward the tall dark van, which pointed nose-out for a quick escape.

"It's technologically superior, this vehicle, a weapon to fight evil with good. I bought it from my rehab center two years ago. Sydney Jones and his friends made alterations so it won't be recognized. New paint and a new license plate. Higher roof, more efficient lifts and driving mechanisms. They backed it in. You won't have to use reverse just yet. The shiny green-black color is perfect, don't you think? It gleams in the sunlight just like the Green Hornet's."

Mrs. Vic pulled a remote control from a leather satchel on her lap. "Have you had any experience with karate or judo, dear? No, I don't suppose you have. The Hornet's sidekick Kato was an expert in the martial arts." I halfway expected a fierce, black-belted chieftain to jump from the shadows and thwack me across the neck.

Keeping me in her sights, she aimed the remote control at a slatted panel in the back of the van. With a great clamor, the door separated, rolled up and disappeared into the roof.

Another click of the remote and a metal lift rumbled forward and lowered itself to the garage floor. She pushed her wheelchair onto it and ordered me to follow. The technology of this thing—I was just dumbstruck. She must have gotten NASA to design it for her.

It was a tight squeeze, but we both fit. Mrs. Vic hit a button and up we went. I expected to blast through the roof. When we stopped, she shooed me into the van. Another firing of the remote and the lift retracted; the awesome door rolled down and shimmied shut.

"So Kato," she sang out like a little kid playing cops and robbers, "we're ready to flush 'em out! That S.O.B. better be prepared. He's about to feel the sting of the Green Hornet!"

— 22 —

When Mrs. Vic clicked her remote, interior lights blinked on. Pretty much everything—the sides, the roof, one seat—was padded in coffin-green upholstery.

"I just can't thank you enough for helping me out here," she said while I bent my head and stumbled toward the passenger seat, the only actual seat in the van. "No, not there, sit in my power chair."

While giving this order, she did a wheelie in her portable chair to get herself into position for lockdown. Then, as I remained halfway standing—still dazed and amazed—she waved the gun at me as if she shot people every day. Her black leather power chair waited on a track just behind the empty space for the driver's seat—this chair that had secreted a butcher knife under the battery a few days ago.

"Why would I sit in that?"

"Don't ask questions. Sit down and fasten the safety belt."

So I sat—her obedient pupil. Thinking about her paralysis and loss of bowel/bladder function, I wondered if she'd soiled the gray cushion I sat upon. While I fastened the seat belt, I also thought I might be strapping myself into my own chair of death. Had she maybe stashed a bomb in that black battery box?

"Look at the controls by your right hand," she said. "Push that joystick forward and you'll roll right into the driving area." I glanced at the lever in the right armrest. If I pushed, would it blow up the bomb?

"Go on. The battery is all charged up. Push the lever."

Scarcely breathing, I pushed the joystick forward and was amazed to feel the electric wheelchair roll itself up to the steering wheel and lock into place. In the meantime, she fastened her lightweight chair to hooks on the floor behind the passenger seat.

The steering wheel was equipped with a standard gearshift and a small lever to move through P-R-N-Drive! This, at least, was something knowable and comfortable. On the other hand, two steel poles with bicycle-grip handles rose up from the gas and brake pedals; one handgrip was black, the other red. I gaped at them. With the engine still off, she told me to practice pushing the black gas grip down and forward until I felt its long steel pole apply pressure to the accelerator; then the red brake grip, which I pushed down and backward toward the dash until I felt it move.

"It's not difficult," she said, hitting another button on her remote. The enormous garage door rumbled to life in front of us and began to rise up slowly and fold into the rafters, revealing gray skies and neighboring trees.

At the same time, a long metal rod slid across my shoulder. Its claw-like pincers dangled the Beauty's keys. "Okay, take these and turn on the ignition."

"Mrs. Vic . . . I've never . . . driven . . . anything like this. I'm not supposed to be driving . . . at all."

"I know, I know, but it can't be helped. I don't want to be spotted too soon. Push the gas grip and we'll start to roll. You can practice in the alleys before we head downtown. Use that steering knob on the wheel with your left hand. Makes it pretty simple."

And so the Magnet moved me again. I pulled the black gas grip with my right hand and we began to roll down into the alley. It was a short driveway with an immediate left turn. My left hand clutched the steering knob and turned the wheel sharply; the van scraped the edge of a trashcan and made a terrible racket. My right foot sprang for the brake automatically, but it whammed the long steel pole and dropped into silent pain. My heart raced toward fibrillation. I would need her pacemaker before this was over.

While I tried to manage it all, the Beauty swerved down the alley. When we came to the street, Mrs. Vic ordered me to drive around a block to my left, another to my right. I passed a grade school at 10 mph and hoped I'd get busted for speeding. Instead, Mrs. Vic said I'd had enough practice on side streets. She told me to pull out into heavier traffic. I increased the pressure on the gas grip and noticed the speedometer arcing all the way up to 20 mph.

I tried to slow for a yellow light near the railroad tracks, but we bucked to a stop when I pushed the brake too quickly. Fortunately, no one rammed us from behind.

"Go on across," she ordered.

"I can't go across. There's not enough room. We'll be stuck on the tracks."

"Who has the gun here, Miranda, you or me? There's room. Go on across. I'll be damned if I want to be sitting here if a freight train comes along."

As I feared, the Beauty's tail did not clear the tracks.

"The rear wheels are stuck on the tracks!" I yelled. "A train's coming, I know it. A train's bound to be coming!" I looked for an escape route. Too many cars to my right and a big Ford truck to the left. I wondered where Buddy was. I could have used him and his truck right now.

Fortunately, the light turned green. I eased my fingers off the brake and pulled at the gas until we lurched forward and almost hit the Ford. "Slow down," she growled.

By the next traffic light, I was woozy, nauseated and in a cold sweat. I tried to catch enough breath to hiss out a few words. "Please. I don't feel good. I can't do this."

"What's wrong now?"

"I'm going to puke . . . my blood sugar's low . . . I'm probably bleeding." I took my hand away from the brake long enough to touch my abdomen. I was surprised when it came away with no blood. "I'm so weak . . . I think it's shock. Don't you have oxygen in this contraption?" I turned a little to show her how deathly ill I was.

"Oh for heaven's sake, don't you suppose I know shock when I see it? You're not in shock, Miranda. When did you last eat? And how long has it been since you've had a pain pill?"

"Early. What time is it?" I remembered breakfast in bed with Ole. Dear, sweet Ole. Would I ever see him again?

"It's a bit after twelve. You need some food, I presume. So do I. Pull into that McDonald's over there when the light changes."

The light changed. I eased us forward but missed the McDonald's driveway, with its handy microphone. I had to drive out the exit, circle under the golden arches and head in again; it was all just awful. Eventually, I arrived at the speaker box. "Can I help you?" someone asked in a sweet, innocent voice.

Mrs. Vic growled from behind me. "Tell her two vanilla shakes, medium, and one glass of water. No ice. And don't try anything funny. I'm the one with the gun here."

The clerk passed the shakes and water from her window to ours. Mrs. Vic had me pay with change from an open compartment in the dashboard. Then she ordered me to pull forward and park along the street. Before I turned off the ignition, she told me to put the chair in reverse and roll back so I could hand over her milkshake. It was a big fuss, but that gun kept me compliant.

Because I was about to drop dead, it seemed odd that I was hungry, but the shake was helpful. Wasn't that something? My last meal on earth would be a McDonald's vanilla milkshake. I would have preferred chocolate, but . . .

"Do you have your pain pills with you?" she asked, after we'd both taken a few gulps.

"I took two before I came to the hospital. I put the bottle back in the Gold Medal flour bag."

"Gold Medal flour? God, what a ninny. Fortunately, I've brought along some extra-strength Anacin." Shortly, the claws came over my shoulder and offered me a small plastic bag with four tablets. "Four?" I asked. "You want me to take four of these?"

"Of course. Doubling up won't hurt you for a single dose. Let's stop this pain."

The milkshake braced my blood sugar and ignited one spark of fight left in me. "Okay your majesty, you're the nurse." I swallowed the pills with the water she'd ordered. "I'm surprised you'd even know about fast food. How come the nurses won't notice you're missing when you don't eat lunch?"

"I made arrangements to cover myself for a few hours." She slurped the bottom of her shake. "Let's get rolling. I want you to drive to First National on the corner of Fifteenth Avenue and 15th Street. Pull into the parking lot at the side where the old Woolworths used to be. There's a new handicap entrance."

I was appalled by the thought of a bank. Was she going to make me stumble in there and rob the place, the way the SLA coerced Patty

170

Hearst into robbing a bank after they'd kept her locked up for an eon, brainwashing her until she committed an armed felony and got herself sent to prison. President Jimmy Carter finally let her out. They said she had the Stockholm syndrome. Remembering this, I told myself to be careful here. I did not want the Stockholm syndrome, under any circumstances. I had enough syndromes to worry about.

"This is where it will start to get interesting," Mrs. Vic said while I angled into the straight-in parking place. "Did Sebastian Cross put in the note about the certificates of deposit and treasury bills maturing today? I have the paperwork in my satchel here.

"Just remember, a cool head will be essential. I'm sure Tom has these banks watched. He knows about the money—all you have to do is sit here. Don't move, but keep your eyes open. You're the watch person. I'm counting on you."

She fumbled about and prepared to disembark. "And Miranda dear, let me sweeten the pot. I'll have close to a million dollars in cash in this satchel by the end of the day. It's my lure for The Honorable Tomlinson Grenadier. I'd be most happy to share a bit of it with you . . . if you cooperate. You won't have to depend on that lame-ass husband of yours. By the way, give me the keys to the ignition."

The claws came over my shoulder and waited with crab-like cunning for the van keys. She clicked her high-tech buttons, opened up the vehicle and pushed her own wheels getting out. The lift rose, the door closed, and then it locked. I glanced out the window and was grateful for the cloud cover that would keep the sun from baking me in this metal box.

The van did become stuffy, but the warmth, the milkshake and the pills actually helped; I finally leaned back and took a good deep breath.

In the silence, I realized that I was already in the Stockholm syndrome, like it or not. I was depending on my captor. I did make a feeble attempt to dislodge the right arm of the chair so I could ease my way out, but it was bolted down. And truthfully, I was exhausted. Closing my eyes, I wondered what a million dollars in cash would look like. How much of that would she actually share with me?

Trust me, it was greed, as much as pain, fatigue and disbelief, that held me captive while Mrs. Vic was in that bank.

I glanced up at the building. When I was a kid, my grandpa would bring me here. I'd always bump my head on the marble counter when I jumped up to see what was going on inside the golden teller cage. Then we'd descend in a creaky elevator to an underground vault filled with safety deposit boxes. The place had been ripe with mysterious keys, clanging doors and creaking, grinding pulleys and chains. I'd always thought of Centerville First National as the Marble Dungeon.

I also noticed two sleazy-looking men who leaned against the red brick wall. They were your cliché kind of young thugs, with tight jeans, leather jackets and cigarettes dangling in their mouths. Perfect for Mrs. Vic's melodrama. Were they watching her? Wouldn't it be something if the Bumblebee—high and mighty in her delusions—was in the bank with her tiny pistol, loading up her satchel with cash, when two thieves strolled in and robbed her cold? I managed a slight smile.

Eventually she came rolling out. She pulled out her remote and pointed it at the Beauty during her approach. Voila, the door slid up, the lift descended and in she rolled. She locked her wheelchair to the floor; all of her electronics shut us up tight again.

"Were we spotted?" she asked, sliding the keys across my shoulder and telling me to pull off the emergency brake.

"I don't think so. How would I know anyway? There were two sleazy types leaning against the building for a while. I don't see them now. Do you have cash in that satchel?"

"Two of them, huh? Were they on cycles or in a car, do you think?"

Her voice was excited in a sick sort of way; the looniness of it brought me back to my fearful state. I felt like Patty Hearst again.

"Whew, this is exciting," she said. "You drive on to Heatherton and then I'll take over. People won't recognize me in that godforsaken place—how you could live there is beyond me."

"If we're going to Heatherton, we'll have to take another route. The sign back there said the onramp is closed for repairs. We can go up 20th Street."

"Fine. Just step on it, time is flying. I'm glad you're beginning to think, Miranda."

Yes, I was. I was coming to my senses and driving the new route while she counted her loot. Eventually, dead ahead, I came to the Pine Woods Mall. The Parking Structure.

When she spotted it, she began hollering. "Don't you dare! I'm ordering you! Turn north! We're on our way to Heatherton."

Not me, lady, I thought, fighting that nasty syndrome, focusing my eyes and applying the gas. We headed into the Pine Woods Mall right through the green light and past the ticket-taker stalls. I bit my lip while I clutched the left-hand steering knob and maneuvered us up the zigzag ramps to the third level, until at last I spotted the back door to the mall manager's office. Beulah would know how to get me out of this mess. My mother-in-law was as tough as Mrs. Vic any day. I could picture them in a confrontation, Beulah's electric cart in a chariot race with the Bumblebee's electric wheelchair, swords clanking.

"Where the hell do you think you're taking this thing?"

"To somewhere that's as nuts as you are."

Beulah's slinky black Lincoln sat in her reserved parking space. I pulled over to the curb and honked the horn while I groped for the door handle and made ready to heave myself up and over the left arm of the wheelchair. I got halfway and fell back.

Where *was* the door handle? Why didn't I know where the door handle was? Why hadn't I checked?

"Where's the door handle?" I yelled, groping along the panel for a nonexistent lever. "What have you done with the damn door handle?"

I heard a quiet chuckle from behind me. A demented, sinister chuckle.

But my ESP must have been working because the Mall Manager came careening out of her back office door. She was in her cart and headed down the sloping ramp. I banged on the glass window; she was talking on a portable phone and did not look up. "Beu . . . lah!" I screamed.

Beulah twisted in her cart as if she thought she heard something; she quickly spotted my illegally parked van. A look of smug glee crossed her face. Beulah Blight reveled in catching wrongdoers. She pulled the beeper from her waistband and waited for security to answer.

I did not think Mrs. Vic could see Beulah, but she guessed at what was happening. "If she calls security, your daughter's a cooked goose. I'm sorry, Miranda, but remember what happened to your dolls? Well, I know where Darcy is. I have her phone number. I told you about my brother in San Francisco. He's far crazier than I am."

"What do you mean? You wouldn't . . . you couldn't . . . you've got to be bluffing."

"Do I ever bluff? No, Miranda, one phone call. Your daughter is my ace in the hole. She just broke her leg. She's helpless . . . but I am not."

Mrs. Vic's intimate knowledge of Darcy's condition filled me with a fear beyond anything I'd ever known. Scarcely paying attention, I revved up the engine, turned it around in an open space and left Beulah in the dust. The powerful van and I careened, screeched and leapt over solid concrete, down the zigzag turns and through the dark cement tunnels; we bounced over the ramps and right on through the money-collecting gate.

In what seemed like an instant, the Green Hornet, the Black Beauty and the terrified sidekick Kato burst forth from the Parking Structure.

With wild determination, we made a break for it.

— 23 —

As soon as we crossed the bridge over Dinky Creek, Mrs. Vic ordered me to drive to the Heatherton Country Bank at the east end of Rosemary Avenue. She intended to repeat the entire money-grabbing process. I tried to remember how many banks Margo had mentioned in her note.

This was my own little bank, located two blocks east of Beulah's Red Bosom Mall. The place was part of a one-block strip mall made to look like an old frontier town. The buildings came with saloon faces, hollow-sounding plank sidewalks and poles out front where you could hitch your steeds to small metal horse heads. Inside, you could plant a foot on a brass rail at the teller counter or sit in a maroon-colored chair to sign up for a new home loan. A spotless public restroom was a bonus. I'd deposited money and more at this bank, precisely because of these facilities. I called it the Bonanza Pee-lotza Bank.

Mrs. Vic quickly rolled herself into daylight and locked me in. Two elderly people had to step aside when she charged the front door; otherwise, all was quiet on the western front, so to speak. I studied the parking lot and spotted two men sitting in a long silver car with fins—probably a Cadillac built during the Sixties. Buddy would know exactly which brand and model it was.

I wondered what Buddy was doing at this moment. Whatever, he would remember it. Until the day he died, Buddy would remember exactly where he was when Mrs. Vic and her crazy people murdered his wife and daughter. "Get her good, Buddy Blight, you owe me that."

While I waited, I checked myself in the rearview mirror. After one quick look, I jerked away. Dark circles rimmed my eyes; my skin was the same dreary fog as my underwear. The wild lipstick was long gone. My only comfort was that if she shot me, I'd be wearing a bra and panties laundered by dear Ole.

When Mrs. Vic returned, she looked a little peaked herself, although her satchel was healthy enough. "Whew!" she said, locking her wheels into place. "I was going to take over the driving, but it's too much commotion. And frankly, I don't dare take my gun off you."

"Promise me . . . please . . . promise me you won't hurt Darcy. I'll drive you to the ends of the earth and back if you promise not to hurt Darcy."

"Then do as you're told. Just one more bank and you can go home."

I longed for home, even covered in fingerprint dust. Clinging to that tiny hope, I drove all the way out Rosemary to the Dinky Creek Splurge on the west side of town. Centerville First National operated a small branch in that mall. Wealthy people who lived in hillside estates frequented the establishment, which was faceless, dark and terribly silent. Money crept in and out of that bank. Lupe and I called it the Slinky Dink.

I pulled into a parking place across from the front door. A few people waited at the ATM. "Lean back and relax," she said. "Take deep, slow breaths. You don't look too well, but this will soon be over. I'm leaving my trail and he's following, just as I planned."

"Could you leave those power windows cracked a little? It gets hot in here."

She scoffed and got herself to the rear. "I won't be long." Out she went, ready to wipe out the Slinky Dink's supply of cash.

During this wait, my concern for Darcy almost turned me inside out. The poor girl, immobilized by a heavy cast. I prayed Percy would be near to protect her, should this old lunatic shoot further off her rocker. But when I tried to picture this Percival at Darcy's side, I could only glimpse a shadow. After all, I knew nothing about him. Not even his last name. Maybe he was actually one of Mrs. Vic's henchmen. Who else could have informed her of the broken leg?

The Beauty's interior felt like a spider's nest padded in insanity-green. I began to question Lupe's actions, and even Ole's. Could Lupe be her spy?

Could Ole be part of some convoluted scheme to get back at my mother? After all, what did I really know about those two? Absolutely zip.

Panicking, I grabbed the cup of McDonald's water and drained it, even though it would shoot right through to my bladder. I would pee in her chair if necessary, but I had to stop terrifying myself with wild notions.

I glanced out the window and saw that the two young men in leather jackets sat in their silver car next to me. They gave me a grin and a V sign for victory. Up close, they were unattractive oafs with pimples and beard stubble, a nose too big on one of them, a chin too small on the other. They climbed out of their Caddy, shifted their jeans low on their butts and stationed themselves behind the Beauty. I figured they were going to grab that bulging satchel when the Bumblebee rolled from the Slinky Dink. They'd likely have enough dough to head for Mexico.

But oh, she foiled them. Upon her exit, she waved at a new line of ATM people and picked up speed crossing the drive. It was amazing how fast she could push that chair. Fast enough to make her lose control. She plowed right into those two men and knocked them down, one way and another. Bystanders rushed over. I thought I heard someone scream, "He's got a gun!"

During the commotion, the Bumblebee rolled up and in, then tossed me the key. I glanced at her in the extra-wide rearview mirror. Her clamshell-beeswax hair stood straight up. Her eyes popped with excitement.

Under orders to step on it, I drove through empty parking spaces and back onto Rosemary. "Have you got all your loot now? Can I please go home?"

"As long as you have the diary. That's essential."

"I told you I was robbed."

"Miranda, please. Don't play games with me. It's not . . . it's not practical."

"Practical? I'll tell you what's practical! I don't have the damn diary! I took it up to Stony Ridge when I rode along with Ole. We left it in an old cabin on his property. You'll have to send Sydney up there to get it."

"Stony Ridge? Up past Precipice Point Road? You took Margo's diary up that horrible mountain?"

"Yes I did. I had Ole stash it in a hole in the fireplace."

"Good God, Miranda, don't you have a brain in your head?"

"You told me to protect it—it wasn't stolen during the robbery, was it?"

"No, but my God, you've just driven away from that end of town. Stop right now and turn around." She ordered me to pull in behind the A&P. "Come on, move it!"

I turned into the supermarket parking lot, the large one in back for delivery trucks and dumpsters. And then I gasped. This is where my dolls had been shot. Straight ahead was the concrete wall where they'd waited for their execution. Clara, Florence, Sue Barton, the Bennet sisters, the March girls. What terror they must have felt when the ugly boys stood like a firing squad and hoisted their BB guns.

And then the worst happened. I saw Darcy sitting among them on that bloody wall. She wrapped her arms over her chest in self-protection. The dolls were on either side, lined up like schoolgirls; their little legs dangled over the scratchy concrete and their tiny hands stretched forward with palms turned out, as if to shove away the horror. Their ceramic faces were full of fear and disbelief.

And then Darcy smiled.

An ugly black gap separated her teeth. My beautiful daughter was missing a major front tooth!

Oh Holy God!

"Miranda, wake up. Come on, girl, wake up." Her vicious claw-on-a-stick was poking at me from behind. "Wake up, you ninny. We have to keep moving."

I gradually came to and saw that we were still ensconced in our coffin of green in the A&P parking lot. I felt like a baby bird that had conked into the window and knocked itself out.

"Put the lid on that cup you vomited in."

"What cup? Where?" Yes, I'd vomited and then passed out. Still confused, I pushed the lid onto the milkshake cup.

"Hurry up, time is running short."

"For what?"

"We have to drive up that mountain. To Stony Ridge. We need that diary."

The thought of driving up Route 71 almost put me out again. "I can't do that. That Jones guy will have to . . . in his taxi."

"There's no time. We have to do this now. Go on, get out of here. Head back out Rosemary to Panic Place."

"Can't you do it? You said you'd drive in Heatherton."

"Absolutely not! I can't drive anywhere near Precipice Point Road. Ever since Margo's accident, I can't even think about it. If you hadn't been such a fool and taken my package up to that mountain, we'd be at your house by now, where he's sure to make his move. Instead, we'll have to take this detour. So step on it! That hospital's going to send out a search party if—oh never mind."

I struggled to figure out what I was supposed to do with the poles shooting up in front of me.

"Don't forget about my gun, Miranda. Or my brother waiting for orders in San Francisco. If you don't believe me, try me."

"Please . . . is Darcy all right? Did you hurt her?"

"Of course not, you ninny. But I will if you don't get that diary for me."

"Why can't the police go out there?"

"I've told you repeatedly. They're owned by the Grenadier bastards. I made a vow to Margo that I would do this myself, and by God, I will. If it kills us both."

"Could we call Ole? It's his property. He could drive us up there."

"Miranda, stop stalling! I told you, there's no time. Get a move on. Before it rains."

When I turned the key, her voice switched with it.

"You know . . . if I'd married your father . . . I would have been your mother. You are like a daughter to me. We need each other."

My mother? *My mother?* But there was no point in arguing any longer. So I collected my wits, revved up that van and retested the hand controls while driving from the lot.

"Driving is good for you, Miranda. It gives you something to concentrate on."

I entered the afternoon traffic. At the intersection of Whiskey, Bourbon, Scotch and Panic, I thought of one more harebrained thing. The Reverend Bob's church rose up in that maze. He said to call anytime—maybe not by crashing through the sanctuary door in a high-powered, hand-controlled—but Mrs. Vic would not dare shoot her gun in a house of God.

Then I saw preschoolers playing outside. With my luck, I'd ram right into them. So I sucked in my breath, passed the church and headed on up the steep, winding road that is Panic Place.

Even with my wretched fatigue, I was getting the hang of this thing. All of that practice on Grandpa's tractor and Buddy's trucks was paying off. This huge van was as sea dark and unfathomable as the Loch Ness Monster; and yet she was becoming familiar and friendly. I began thinking of her as Nessy.

On straight stretches, Nessy and I got all the way up to 25 mph. The knob made steering much easier. If I could just keep us together up the winding road, I could reach Ole's lakebed, pull the package from the fireplace and go home, call Darcy, account for all of her teeth, fingers and toes, and be done with this insane nightmare.

I glanced again in the rearview mirror. Mrs. Vic was quiet behind me, but her eagle eye was roving. She watched out the windows.

When we came to a sharp turn, I braked and slowed to 20 mph. We were climbing and losing speed. I glanced at the gas gauge. Almost full. She'd thought of everything.

"Miranda?" Her voice was low, steady and spooky.

"Yes?"

"Someone is following us. You'll have to lose them."

"What?"

"There's another car following us. A black sedan. I was afraid of that. Step on it, girl. We need to lose them."

I checked the side-view mirror and saw a black car behind us. There were a couple of young fellows inside. It would be dangerous for them to pass us, but they seemed in a hurry. I sped up to 25 mph and hoped they would be satisfied.

On the next curve, I pushed backward on the red brake grip. We almost jerked to a standstill. The black sedan squealed and spun to avoid plowing into us, but stayed right with us when we came to a passing lane. Why didn't it zoom on by?

A little farther on, Mrs. Vic ripped into me again. "Hurry up, you ninny! We've got to lose them."

"Okay, okay. I'll turn off up here so they can go around."

"No! That's a shortcut to Precipice Point Road. Don't you dare go near Precipice Point Road!"

"I don't care, they're making me mad. Let me—"

I pressed the gas grip. Nessy made a left turn across traffic at 33 mph. We just missed a truck, which blared its horn at us. We scraped a mailbox on the smaller road but continued on. When I pushed the brake, we came to a near-miss stop. The evil car was still behind us. Those guys had managed that same turn; they began to move in.

My heart galloped and my focus blurred, but I was perched in that powerful wheelchair on the back of the roaring Loch Ness Monster; I inhaled its fumes of might and power. I wove across both sides of the road, headed for a cow and swerved just in time. I was terrified but lost the black sedan in the rearview mirror.

"Oh God," I said, huffing, letting go of all the grips and knobs. I wiped my forehead with my right hand. "I almost hit a cow. Did you see it? Did you see those big cow eyes?"

"Forget the bloody cow—you just drove onto Precipice—you'd damned well better find a place to turn around."

I hadn't meant to turn left again. I really hadn't. I'd planned to turn right and reconnect with Panic Place—but that cow—that stupid cow had muddled me.

As the road became more treacherous, I slowed Nessy to a crawl. If I remembered correctly, the sheerest drops were just ahead. If I plunged us to the bottom of the chasm, I'd be dead and who knew what would happen to Darcy. I wondered if Mrs. Vic had to phone the people in San Francisco and signal them to call the whole thing off. How could she signal them if she were at the bottom of the abyss?

When I slowed, the black sedan came back in sight. The fellows on board looked to be the same pimply hoodlums who'd watched us at the banks. I did not know how they got away from the uproar at the Slinky Dink and switched cars so quickly, but they did.

Aware of their steady presence, I put more pressure on the gas. I screeched along at 35 mph and then 40, and suddenly—I don't know how—my right hand flew up, stopped in midair, and fell back to the red grip far too quickly and firmly. In a nanosecond, we shook, jerked, jolted and swerved like a monster gone berserk. But Nessy was a heavy creature. I clamped both hands firmly on the wheel and was able to bring her under control.

Ah, but the villains had no such luck; when they slammed on their brakes, they wobbled, bucked, plowed through the guardrail and headed over the cliff.

There it was! I'd killed two people! Exactly where Margo had died.

At that point, all thought and reason left my mind. I drove on and on and could not stop. I grabbed the curves and shot ahead on the straights. Demons controlled the Loch Ness Monster now. As punishment, we would come to the end of the earth and be forced to drive right off the precipice into hell itself.

I glanced in the rearview mirror and saw that Mrs. Vic was as white as a sheet. She stared straight ahead, but her eyes did not register.

Eventually, the road entered a plateau and spread out. I found the courage to pull over in a wide turnout and steer us around. Then I had to face the return trip, back to the horror where I'd sent two young men into the deadly chasm.

There was no choice. I had to drive and drive and drive until I came to Ole's lakebed, and then I had to retrieve the diary and deliver Mrs. Vic to a phone booth so she could call someone to come to her rescue and signal whomever in San Francisco. Then I could go home, die and descend to my just reward. That was my new plan.

Along the way, we passed the black sedan. I could not believe my eyes. It was not in the abyss at all—at least not yet. Its front wheels had plowed through the guardrail and were hanging over the rocky cliff. But its hind end still clung to the road. The two thugs had somehow crawled out of the swinging front door. They sat at the picnic table and looked dazed.

I should have stopped for them. There's no doubt. I should have stopped. But I, too, was dazed beyond all reason.

So I kept on driving.

– 24 –

The *No Trespassing* sign hung askew on the ramshackle bridge to Ole's property. Such a sign was almost comical, I thought. As if trespassing could hold a candle to my criminal acts—almost killing those two poor souls back there and then driving away. Hit and run. A felony! God might not send me to hell, but the Arm of Justice would surely send me straight to prison.

Pulling to a stop in the weeds, I finally let out my breath and summoned courage to look down at my lap. No blood was yet escaping from my incision. Despite the lunacy of that wild car ride, my staples still held me together.

"Miranda?" Her voice was puny but I had no sympathy. Mrs. Vic had caused my descent into the underworld. She had ruined my life. I was going to rot in a putrid, claustrophobic jail cell for the rest of my years. She was too disgusting to be answered.

"Miranda? Please, come back here. I've released the power track. I need to tell you something."

Sighing, I rolled the chair backwards, unbuckled my seatbelt, swung my legs sideways and stood up as best I could—hunched and facing her. There was no sign of the rouge she'd smeared on her face earlier. Her skin reminded me of flaking candle wax. Her shirt was askew, its bumblebee floppy and cross-eyed.

"Miranda, I think I may have gone too far."

"Yes ma'am," I said sarcastically, "considering everything, I think you've definitely gone too far." I reached into the passenger seat and retrieved my cable-car bag. I wanted Clara with me when I walked back into that creepy cabin. Just holding the doll gave me a bit more nerve. But first I had to ask the question I was desperate to ask.

"Mrs. Vic, has anything happened to Darcy? There was a tooth. A stray tooth . . . in my carpet. It might have fallen out of the package. Is it . . . is it hers? Did you send it? Have you already hurt my daughter?"

Her eyes enlarged and her breathing hitched for a moment. She stared at me. "A tooth? What kind of tooth? Was there a . . . oh my . . . was there a *tooth* with the diary?"

"Maybe, but please tell me the truth. Have you let those people hurt her because she's alive and Margo's dead? Is that why you're doing this to me? Punishing Darcy and me simply because we exist?"

She shook her head in the negative while her entire body trembled. "No, no. Actually, I lied to you. I haven't told anyone to hurt Darcy. But that horrid man hurt my daughter. He knocked her tooth out. She tried to tell me it was a skiing accident, but I knew better." Her voice suddenly drizzled into the loony Green Hornet mode. "I know all of the evil that lurks in that man's twisted soul."

I pressed my hand to my bra and wondered whose tooth this was—Darcy's, Margo's or my gypsy grandmother's? I feared I might never know.

Mrs. Vic's face began to sag while she retreated into her own dark world and left me standing at a loss. I'd seen this type of absent, eerie look on patients' faces during my three-month nursing rotation at the state mental hospital. In a sudden role reversal, I realized that I had to take charge of this bizarre abduction. Somehow, I had to transport this lunatic woman back to the hospital. The term *firm kindness* came to mind. This technique was the best drug we had before the arrival of effective medications for the mentally ill.

Firm kindness for the insane.

"Come along, honey," I heard myself saying. "Work your gismo there and let me out. I'll get your package, and then we'll find a phone booth and send someone to pick up those two men. Haul their car off the cliff. We both need to get home." I patted her shoulder lightly.

Her hand trembled when she pushed the button. The clanking of the rising door jolted both of us. Mrs. Vic regained some semblance of her normal self. "Yes, but hurry. Be careful. We're in grave danger here. He'll figure this out. We should have gone to your house in Heatherton. I planned it. Sydney Jones and his friends are down there to protect us. I should have had them drive up here."

"Mrs. Vic, please stop. This is a wild goose chase. Can't you see that?"

"Who do you think those two men were back there?"

"Probably two more kids who spotted a patsy old woman coming from the bank with her satchel bulging. Of course they'd try to rob you. That doesn't mean they deserved to crash into the chasm. It's no thanks to me they didn't."

"Oh no, Miranda. They had it coming." She unhooked her small chair from the floor and turned it toward the rear opening, then hit another button and shot out the lift for me. Working her gismos reignited her. "All right, get going. Shoo! And for heaven's sake, be careful of your incision."

"My incision?" I asked. I hobbled onto the lift and began my descent. "That's the least of my worries at the moment."

"Are you sure there's no one out there?" she whispered.

"I don't see anyone. I'll go as fast as I can." I stepped off the lift and crossed the clearing, feeling both jubilant that Darcy was safe and furious that Mrs. Vic had so abused me. And I was tremendously weary. The muscles around my incision throbbed, even though I propped them with my hands. The muscles in my legs felt as if I were plowing into the resistance of swirling water. I wondered how I'd climb the rotting porch to the cabin. How would I stretch and reach into that hole? And maybe I should squat behind one of these bushes and pee before I went any farther.

Suddenly, a long stick shot from behind a poison-berry bush, as if the pincers were coming over my shoulder. For a second, I imagined a long stinger on her goofy bumblebee outfit. But how would she get stingers or pincers out here? What the hell was going on now?

In the next second, I realized it was neither. It was a man's arm and hand, with five strong fingers that clamped across my neck. "Hold very still," a male voice said into my ear. The tone was similar to Mr. Surrey's, the hospital administrator's.

The mere sound of a hospital executive brought enormous relief. Thank God, they'd sent people out to find her. I did not have to be the savior after all.

But I could be in trouble if they'd located the missing butcher knife with my fingerprints all over it. Maybe Joanie had squealed on me. Maybe they thought I'd kidnapped Mrs. Vic, that *I* was the mental patient here. I'd certainly been acting like one.

Still immobilized by his grasp, I felt his hard finger poke into my ribs.

"Can't you let go of me please?" I asked. "I'm on your side. I can explain all of this." While I stumbled forward, I wondered why Mr. Surrey would come out here himself and not send Security. Or was this Security? Or the State Patrol? The FBI? What about those two young men dangling off the cliff? Had a helicopter been following us? Had they witnessed my hit-and-run?

Or could she be right, after all? Was this the son-in-law? The murdering son-in-law? *Lordy, who was this?*

We reached the clearing and saw her sitting in her flimsy wheelchair just inside the back door of the van, the lift suspended before her. She stared at us, her lips curled into a sneer. "Well, Governor, you've made it to my little party, I see."

"Wouldn't have missed this one for the world, Nora dear. You've come up with some doozies in your time, but this beats all."

Whoever he was, his voice was deep, strong and reassuring. He sounded sensible. Logical. I had to agree with him. I thought she'd come up with a doozy, too.

"Thank God you're here," I said, wriggling to free myself. "You can let go of me now. I'm not with her. She forced me. Please!" The harder I squirmed, the more firmly he held me. "She threatened to hurt my daughter. I had to. It was the Stockholm—"

"Hush up, Miranda!" Mrs. Vic rolled her chair onto the raised lift and hovered like a waiting cat. I could almost hear its yowl.

While she resettled, the man withdrew the hard object from my ribs and pointed a long, black barrel at Mrs. Vic. It was a humungous gun compared to hers, probably what they called a semi-automatic, although I knew zip about guns.

I was dizzy with fear, but the evil creeping into his voice held my attention. "Lower yourself down and hurry up about it."

"What do you plan to do with us?" she asked, not lowering the lift at all.

The situation was still beyond my grasp, and yet it looked more and more as if the Green Hornet were indeed in a face-off with a corrupt politician, their two guns aimed at each other, although she did not seem to have hers at the ready.

"I plan to obtain whatever evidence you have stashed away up here, and then we'll see. No point keeping you around to spoil my plans any longer. I know you've redeemed the money."

"Miranda, dear, meet the next governor of our fine state. I suspect you and I won't be here for the inaugural."

I tried to wriggle away from him. "I'd suggest you hold still, young lady." His thick fingers pressed into my ear, and the long barrel returned to my ribs. "Nora, lower yourself before she gets hurt."

"Why the hell should I? You'll kill us both anyway, just like you killed Margo."

"You're jumping to some fine conclusions."

"Before you shoot me, could you give me a minute to talk to Miranda? I haven't been honest with her. I need to tell her something vitally important before she . . . well . . ."

He loosened his hold slightly so I could straighten my head and look at her.

"Two minutes," he said, jiggling the gun in my ribs. "I wouldn't trust her to tell the truth, if I were you."

"It's the truth. Miranda, I'll try to say this quickly. You've always thought I expelled you because you were a less than adequate nurse. That's not true. Nor did it have anything to do with your parents, although I had to think long and hard about letting Beau Smothers' daughter become one of my nurses.

"It was something else, something Buddy came and showed me during your senior year. He wanted to marry you and this was his way of manipulating it. He came to my office with photos of you in a very inebriated state."

"What?"

"Stoned out of your mind, as they say. He said it started with pot but moved on to other things. LSD even."

"I never smoked pot. Well, maybe once, but it just made me giggle. And I sure never used LSD!"

"Maybe not, but the pictures were quite damning. They were of a young lady doing things, in poses, that I found intolerable. I hated to let you go because I loved your father. And I did make exceptions about how slowly you learned your clinical skills. But the day I saw those photos—I was so angry with you. So disappointed."

"Buddy showed you pictures? We were just fooling around. Just once. We were only kids. It was nothing! And he said I used LSD?"

"I'm sorry. I realize now it was probably just some teenage nonsense. I should have confronted you, given you a chance to defend yourself. But in those days we weren't open-minded like we are nowadays."

"Buddy did that? Had me expelled? He's known it all these years and never told me?"

"Actually . . . to be honest . . . it was more than that. The Blights donated money for the new wing of the hospital. I was courting the Blights in those days. I wanted to keep them happy. They thought if their son were married, he'd settle down. Beulah didn't see any point in you outshining her with a nursing career."

I tried to lash out at Mrs. Vic, but she waved her hand for me to stop. At the same time, the man put his knee into my butt and hurt me badly enough to shock me back to the moment.

"At any rate, I don't have people in San Francisco. My brother was keeping an eye on Darcy. He spotted her with a cast on her leg. But I would not hurt your daughter. She was Margo's niece. Can you understand that? I did have a brief affair with your father. It was my fault. I went to his base, just for a few hours. So Margo was your—where is that tooth, by the way?"

I began to move my left hand to my chest and then thought better of it. "I threw it away. I flushed it down the toilet."

"God, what a ninny. It's evidence against him. That's why she kept it. Can't you understand?"

No! I could not understand anything. So I decided to find out at that moment, right from the source. I took a deep breath, angled my head and spoke directly to him. "Did you really kill your wife?"

His voice was snide when he answered. "Your dear Mrs. Vic thinks so." He pressed the huge gun in and out against my ribs, almost playfully. "She'd tell you I had everything to gain from it; quite a lot of money, as you've learned today." His body tensed, as if he'd thought of something that excited him.

"That list of women," Mrs. Vic growled, glaring at him, "I know who those girls were. Margo did too. Eventually the world will find out. You'll wear your mask one too many times. You'll be caught and roast in hell for it, unless I kill you first."

Mrs. Vic reached for the tiny pistol in her lap, but the man pulled the handgun from my ribs and fired at her before she had a fighting chance, straight into her heart. A terrible look of astonishment crossed her face. Her eyes and mouth expanded and then collapsed; she slumped forward in her seat on the lift.

The explosion stunned me. Maybe my heart stopped along with hers. How easily he'd killed her.

He dragged me forward, reached up, took the satchel from her lap and inspected it. "Crazy old cow," he growled.

I could not help but look. Wads of hundred dollar bills fell into his hands. Maybe she could have shot him first if she hadn't had so much loot in her lap.

He found her gun dangling in her limp hand and tossed it, along with the satchel and the money, into the center of the van. "I'll come back for this," he said, tightening his grip on me. "Now I believe we were on an errand into the bushes. Let's go see what you've hidden back there."

And so we left the Bumblebee dead on her lift. I followed orders, too stunned to have any kind of emotion for what had just happened. He would surely kill me also, but I was almost too exhausted to care. With the gun in my back, I led him through the woods to the decaying cabin. We climbed the steps carefully. I debated stepping on a rotten board to stun him, but it all seemed so hopeless now. Dead-on hopeless. None of my other schemes had worked. My only comfort was in knowing that Darcy was in no grave danger.

But once inside, I mustered up an ounce of strength and begged for my life. "If I give you the evidence, would you let me go? I swear I'll never tell a soul. I'll go out through the woods and make up a story about Mrs. Vic killing herself. Or I'll tell them *I* did it. But please, I don't want to die up here."

He let go of me but kept his handgun pointed at my temple. I saw him clearly for the first time. He wore an expensive charcoal-gray suit with a red tie. His black wavy hair was receding—he must have been wearing a toupee for interviews on the news. His dark slitty eyes were without emotion. It was odd that he could be so composed, considering he'd just killed his mother-in-law. But sweat stood out on his forehead. He pulled the red handkerchief from his breast pocket and dabbed at his face.

Watching him, I remembered Mrs. Vic's words. "You'll put your mask on one too many times." I'd thought she meant his political mask, but now the phrase *red ski mask* exploded in my mind. The red ski mask! The foreign college students on the news. Were they the women in the diary? A man in a red ski mask had raped and killed those girls! Was I standing face to face with a serial killer? One who was out campaigning for votes?

He saw my questioning and raised his eyebrows. "So, little detective, just what do you think's been going on in my life?"

I tried to sit down, but he held me up and shook me a little. "Go on, tell me!"

"You . . . killed . . . those college girls?"

"My wife thought I did. That bitch of a mother put that notion in Margo's head. Paranoid schizophrenics, the two of them."

He squeezed my arm with painful force. "Releasing you now is not an option. But I can offer you a couple of choices. A nice clean easy death for the evidence, or a not-so-nice rape and torture if you give me trouble, since you think that's what I've been up to." He ran his hand under my faded starfish sweatshirt, clutched my breast and squeezed.

I jerked away, determined to keep my little talisman away from him. "I'll get the package for you."

He loosened his hold and dropped my shirt. I turned, moved toward the fireplace and found the stone with the X that Ole had scratched in. But I could not let myself think about dear Ole. I jiggled the rock and felt it move under my fingers. Maybe I could lift it out quickly, raise it and bash it down on his head.

Instead, he pressed hard and trapped me between him and the fireplace. He clamped his hand over mine and guided me while I pulled it out. I could not even drop it on his foot.

"It's in there," I said, not wanting to reach into the dark hole.

He made me do it anyway. "Go on, find it. Stop stalling."

"There might be spiders."

"Ha! You're a regular comedian, you know that? I have a gun that will blow your head to smithereens and you're frightened of spiders?" He slid his hand over my abdomen and whispered, "I wonder what it would feel like to lay you on this floor, then rip out those staples, one by one."

How did he know I had staples? Had he been peeking under my gown in the hospital?

I plunged my hand into the fireplace hole, felt around and pulled out the diary wrapped in the chicken-clucking tea towel. He grabbed it and shoved me toward the door. "C'mon, out into the light."

He stood me against the outside wall and tried to wrap my hands in the towel but could not manage with the gun. Frustrated, he shoved the end of the cloth into my pants pocket and ordered me to put my hands over my head.

He opened the diary, read the note, sneered over the list of dead girls and then poked his finger into the lining cover. And yes, he found more. Another scrap of paper. He held it in front of my nose. "You missed the important one. Another reason I had to get Margo off my case."

I briefly read a couple of male names. Arty something. Pete Bucken . . . something. And Rolph. "Did you kill those men too?" I asked in amazement.

He snickered. "Those goons wanted to kill me. Loan sharks. The world won't miss them." He slowly folded the loose sheets and then slammed shut the diary, shoved it in his inside jacket pocket and stared at me. He held the big gun to my head with one hand and ran his thumb along my cheek with the other. "You're very attractive. It's a shame to kill you, too."

"Did you torment your wife this way, before you shoved her over the cliff? Did you hit her and knock out her tooth?"

He scowled at me and shrugged his shoulders. "So Margo leaned over to see the view. Who's to say if I gave a little push with the toe of my—she screamed for a long way down, tho'."

I was looking over his head, up to the highest hill visible through the trees. *I look to the hills to the hills, the hills . . .*

"Good old Nora did not scream. Not a sound. I had to kill her too quickly. I've dreamed of holding that bitch at gunpoint for years. But you're an enticing substitute. Do you know what I'm going to do now?"

"Maybe." My teeth chattered while I said it.

"And what is that, little darling?"

"Sh . . . shoot me. Stu . . . stuff me in the still."

"Ha! What a splendid idea! That woman must have done quite a job on you. She has you thinking the way she does. So where is this still we're going to stuff you into? Behind the cabin?"

191

He shoved me through the scratchy bushes. I saw the tangle of pipes and rusted boilers wending their way through the brush. Ole would find me in chunks here.

Dear Ole. Why hadn't he sensed this? Figured it out? Now! Right now!

The place was completely silent. I heard no insects, no birds, no cars from the highway, no Ole. When this man finally pulled the trigger, the sound might bounce off the hills, but no one would hear. *I look to the hills, I look to the hills, I look to the hills . . .*

My voice returned. "They'll catch you sometime, just like she said. If you kill me, they'll find my body. Ole will come up here sooner or later and find my body."

"Ah yes, I see your point. Good thinking, Miranda. Maybe we won't put you in the still at all. Maybe we'll put you in the van with your friend before I shove it over the ravine."

"You're going to push Nessy over the cliff?"

"Do you want to be dead or alive when I do?"

"She was right. You are a monster. But they'll still find us. Those men who were following us . . . they're not dead. They'll shoot off their mouths. The police will figure it out."

"If they do, this Browning Buck Mark will be with the two of you. I stole it from Nora's house two years ago. It's registered to her dear, departed Ed. They'll simply think she turned it on you and then shot herself. The money and her girly pistol will be tucked safely away, plenty to run my campaign. I will be governor, Miz Blight."

Lordy, he'd figured it out so carefully.

"Now let's walk—very slowly—back to the van. Look around. It's lovely out here, isn't it? Maybe I'll have the state purchase this land. We'll make a park out of it. In memory of Nora Margaret Vickerstromm and her odd little assistant, Miranda Blight." He held the gun in his left hand while his right clutched my shoulder. Cunningly, he walked his fingers down to my breast. He was very cocky—to hold me so carelessly.

My right hand pressed against the cable-car bag hanging over my shoulder. I could feel poor little Clara lying inside. It would be easier to die if I could hold onto her. I carefully let my fingers go to the bag's opening, slide inside and squeeze my doll, the same way I'd reached for the firecrackers under Darcy's pillow. I scratched my hand against Clara's jagged leg and let my fingers play with her strong thighs, her tendons, muscles and bones. Then I grasped her tightly around her waist.

At the same time, the man's fingers were discovering the hard imprint of the tooth in the left cup of my bra. While he was distracted, I moved faster than I've ever moved in my life. I spun toward him, pulled Clara from the bag, raised her to his face and slammed her jagged leg into his left eyeball. I continued gouging all the way down his face.

I think we both screamed. Blood from his eye socket smeared his face and squirted over mine. At the same time, I hit him in the crotch. I'm not certain if I used my knee or my fingers, but I think my other hand found the gun. It exploded between us and maybe hit him in the chest or his stomach or his foot. I know he was shrieking, dropping to the ground, writhing like a fish, then, plop. Dead like a fish.

Still boiling with rage, I tossed off my bag, picked up one of the long rusted pipes from the old still and whammed him over the head many times until he was good and dead.

Then I dashed from the woods and stopped cold at the van. For a second, I had forgotten about Mrs. Vic.

Mrs. Vic was also dead.

– 25 –

She was slumped in her chair before me. I froze and stared at her—if she'd just trusted the police, the FBI or anyone but me. A choking pain hardened in my throat. Bitterly awful cramps spun in my gut and filled me with nausea. I spewed tears within a nanosecond. I was alone in poor Ole's lovely lakebed, surrounded by dead people. One way or another, I'd killed them all. I leaned against the corner of the van and sobbed with grief.

An unexpected noise made me jump. "Miranda? Is . . . is that you? Oh dear . . . are you weeping again?"

I jerked around and saw Mrs. Vic struggling to raise her head. "You're alive?" I asked, astonished. "How can you possibly be alive? He shot you. I saw him shoot you."

"Of course I'm alive. That silly gun . . . a mere twenty-two. Anyway . . . there's armor . . . sewn into my corset. Metal supports. You ought to know. All paraplegics . . . wear corsets. Mine had extra security. Oh my."

She righted her head with her hands, wiped her brow and then checked her pulse. "The impact . . . goodness . . . far more than I expected. I think that bullet might be stuck in my pacemaker." She worked at focusing and then looked around. "Where is he? What have you done with him?" She looked at me and recoiled. I was covered with Grenadier-red eyeball blood.

I pointed my hand, slimy and dripping. "Back there near the cabin. We fought and his gun went off. Please, let's get out of here. I need to talk to Darcy. Are you sure she's okay?"

"Was he dead?"

"I don't know. Probably. He fell down. I put out his eye and bashed him with a pipe. Shot him, too."

"Where is that stupid gun? I think he stole it from Ed."

I looked at my hands. They were bloody but empty. "I don't know, everything's—"

"The diary?"

"In his pocket."

"Oh God, Miranda, don't you have a brain in your head? He might not be dead. Look at me—am I dead?"

"No." I continued to stare at my empty, blood-smeared hands. Why hadn't I brought Clara?

"They'll need his gun to compare the bullets. And the diary is our best evidence. Have you figured it out yet? About the rapes? Sebastian Cross figured it out. Told me everything before he was killed."

"I don't know. There were loan shark people. Anyway, I can't worry about that right now." My beloved doll was with his wretched dead body. Clara Barton might have seen a lot of battlefield duty, but this was way beyond the call. "I have to get Clara!"

"Where's my money?" Mrs. Vic looked about until she spotted her loot on the floor behind her. She released the brake on her chair and rolled backward. "Ah! Here's my pistol. Forty-five caliber. It would have killed him." She was able to reach it. "Take it with you."

When she looked up at me, she scowled. "Good grief, wipe that blood off your hands. Use that towel hanging out of your pocket."

I stepped back. "I'm not getting his blood on Grandma's chicken-clucking tea towel."

"My Lord, what a—here, I have baby wipes." She pulled out the wipes from a bag on her chair; I swiped at my hands and face. Next, she produced a long rubber tourniquet. She stretched it and let it snap back into place. "I use this for bicep exercises. Even if you think he's dead, don't take any chances. Tie him up. Move!" I tossed the bloody wipes at her feet, then took the pistol and tourniquet from her.

Thus armed, I hobbled back into the bushes, tourniquet stuffed in one pocket, chicken-clucking tea towel in the other. I held Mrs. Vic's snub-nosed pistol tightly in both hands. I stretched out my arms, held my finger on the trigger and prepared to fire. I thought about the women in *Charlie's Angels*—the Angels were some of my all-time favorite television characters.

I wondered if the man was slithering around. I heard nothing, but maybe he and I were like two snakes in the bushes, coiling for one another. I listened again. Nothing but the crackle of brush under my own feet.

After creeping toward the cabin, I ducked behind a pine tree, pulled down my pants and splattered. Half of it ended up on my shoes. But I felt greatly relieved when I stepped into the clearing and saw that he was lying where I'd left him. Clara lay next to him. He was so still. Not even a finger twitched. It seemed a shame that he was dead, after all the anguish he'd caused everyone. I suddenly wanted to see him alive, going to prison forever. I wanted some monstrous jailhouse stud to toy with him, the way he'd toyed with me.

I held the small pistol firmly with both hands and inched forward. When I was near enough, I touched his body with the toe of my bloody urine-soaked Reebok. He did not budge. I cautiously lowered myself to my knees. I would have pulled the trigger if he'd so much as twitched a finger, although I did not know if this thing was loaded or cocked, or whatever prep had to be done to a gun before it would shoot. But he lay still.

I shoved the little gun into my waistband and then grabbed Clara, wrapped her in the tea towel and slipped her into the cable-car bag. I picked up the larger black gun with my headscarf and put that in my bag, as well. I was careful to preserve his fingerprints. Next, I had to get the diary.

He lay face down with his arms behind him. Although I was terrified, I knelt and picked up his two hands. I quickly wrapped the tourniquet around them, making it as tight as I could without cutting off his circulation—if he had any. I got him rolled onto his back by pushing, as if he were a patient needing a linen change.

His jacket was covered with sticky blood, but not a torrent of it. The bullet hole was below and to the left of his heart. Putting two cautious fingers into his pocket, I pulled out the diary. While I dropped Mrs. Vic's precious evidence into my bag, I saw a shallow breathing motion. I felt his neck. There was a slight pulsing under my fingers, but the beat was thready and way too fast. I wondered if he was fibrillating. I would have known such things if I'd made it to ICU training. Instead, I had to rely on what I'd seen on television.

So I studied his face.

He was cyanotic for sure—the color of death—but his bad eye was not as repulsive as I'd feared. It had already swollen shut. I opened the other. The pupil was not dilated. Trust me, this was scary business. *Was he looking at me?* Mrs. Vic was correct again. He was not dead yet, but he might be if I did not act quickly.

"You dirty bastard," I whispered, wiping blood from his face with a clean part of my shirt. "I'll be darned if I let you have a nice simple death."

Setting my bag aside, I leaned down, pulled up his chin, opened his mouth, took a deep breath and blew. After a few puffs, I stopped and punched his chest. "Come on, you slime bag, live. I want you alive."

Push! Push! Push! I pushed on his ribcage as hard as I could, one hand on the other, arms stiff, the way I'd seen on television. I did not care if I fractured his sternum. A broken-chested governor. Exactly what he deserved.

I'll huff and I'll puff and I'll blow your chest in. Adrenalin and boiling blood invigorated me. *Wham! Wham! Wham!* He gasped and then gulped out a life-giving breath. I placed my fingers on his neck and found a pulse. An actual lub dub pulse! I was amazed. I'd brought this murdering son-in-law back to life!

He did not come fully awake. From the looks of the rust streak across his brow, I suspected a concussion, but he was breathing with some regularity. If I could get Mrs. Vic out of her wheelchair, I could use it for him, haul him back to the van and then somehow get him down this mountain and to a hospital. I was going to save this man. Yes indeed, I was going to save this man so he could watch the elections from prison. And never be governor. He could jolly well be strapped into his own electric chair.

My plan was almost successful. I grabbed my cable-car bag, hurried back to the van, sat on the edge of the lift and told Mrs. Vic she would have to roll out of her chair and over onto the floor.

"You're as crazy as a loon," she snarled at me.

"I'm crazy? You're the inventor of crazy!" I pulled up my legs, then clung to her chair and got up on my knees. We were pretty much eyeball to eyeball.

Crazy or not, I retrieved her snub-nosed pistol from my waistband before it could go off in my pants, which I'd just begun to worry about. I tossed it into the front seat. The big gun was still in my bag. I remained in control. "Sorry lady, but this isn't going to be a very nice ride for you. I'm the one sitting in the power chair, and I'm driving us down this mountain on my terms."

I lowered my voice to the undertaker's pitch. "You thought I was a drug addict? And sold me out to Beulah Blight? *Scared me to death about Darcy?* Well, you can ride on that bumpy floor all the way back to Loving Memorial and think about it. Just think about what you've done to me. And to my mother! Forcing my poor father to cheat on her. Your Margo was the product of cheating! You crazy, revengeful . . ."

She stared at me while I caught my breath. Then I took control of the portable wheelchair, pulled myself to hunched upright, tilted the chair and braced it against my knees. I put my hands under her arms and pulled her forward until she slid off and crumpled onto the floor. I straightened her out and put the seat cushion under her head. Handing her the remote, I ordered her to lower me and the wheelchair to the ground. My gut and my back were both in severe spasm, but it would not be much longer. She was yelling something about her shot-up pacemaker as I left the van.

Pushing the chair back through the bushes, I wondered how to lift a two-hundred-pound man into the seat. There must be some trick with leverage or something, the way the Druids put up Stonehenge, maybe. I cast about for a wide enough plank to roll him onto, which I could then inch up toward the chair by putting stones under one end—

I heard a sudden noise in the bushes, a hollering noise. Someone else was out here with us. Maybe those two fellows I'd hit and run from. I pulled his big black gun from my bag and held it with both hands. She'd said it was only a .22, but I didn't know what the hell that meant.

Trust me, the trigger was itching to be squeezed, and I was ready to squeeze it.

Two large men charged through the bushes; they resembled the police, but I could no longer trust the police. The police were corrupt, everybody knew that. They were probably imposters. Very handsome imposters, not the pimply—I kept the gun on them. "Stop right there," I yelled.

"Your friend Ole thought you might be here," one of them said, holding out both hands to show me it was safe. At the mention of Ole, I took a breath.

"Are you okay?" the other asked.

I nodded and pointed to my conquest. He was beginning to rouse. They dropped beside his body, rolled him onto his abdomen, cuffed him and stared in wonder at my tourniquet binding.

When they turned him over, I dropped the gun and retrieved Clara Barton from my cable-car bag. "Lordy, Clara, I'm a nurse!" I shouted at her. "I saved a life today! Can you believe that? On the battlefield! Of all places!"

Something went bonkers in my brain. I forgot my incision, my surgery, my cramping. My dizziness and fatigue. I ran in circles, lifted my knees high, held crippled Clara aloft and leapt like a football player who'd just caught a thirty-yard pass and then run forty yards for a touchdown.

"Yes Clara! I can do it! I'm Cher! I'm Sue Barton! I'm what's-her-name, from Australia! I am woman hear me roar!" Jumping with pride, I ran from the bushes at the same time I saw Ole running from his car.

Before he could reach me, my victory cry became a shriek of horror. The bands of adrenalin that had been holding me together finally snapped. I broke in the same way that my doll Janie Belle broke. Everything in my gut sprang loose.

I exploded. The pain was hell itself. I fell into his outstretched arms while my body split in two. "Ole, Ole, I love you. So much. But it's too late! I just . . . just killed myself . . . jumping for joy."

I looked down and watched my blood pour out onto Ole's gray shoes. Sir Galahad gray, they were.

At that moment, the clouds burst. The rain poured.

— 26 —

I sat at the throne of God.

One gold chrysanthemum arched from a crystal vase on an altar of glossy stones. The distant hillside appeared in shadowed light through the north window.

Sunlight shone through the open door in the east wall, an arch adorned with yellow rose petals tinged with pink. The name of the rose was Peace.

Organ chords were as alive as the altar stones. The notes were tall like the gladioli, full like the white mums, dripping sweetness from the syrup of the maple trees. Ole had never played the organ but he practiced every morning; I came to listen.

My face was cemented shut. I had dry heaves. I tried to pound on the side rails with a heavy stainless steel emesis basin that came with me from surgery; I could only rattle the rails with my head. An entirely new pain seared through my gut.

A nurse came to offer help. Or was she an angel? "Miranda, it's me, Kathy. You need to deep breathe and cough," she said.

"I need to pee."

"No, darlin', we have a catheter in you."

"Well . . . I can't . . . pee straight anyway. I'd miss the pan."

She chuckled. "I'm giving you something for pain and nausea. Go back to sleep."

I relished the woozy wave of Demerol—my favorite drug—and then I slept again.

The Peace rose wilted. Sweetness turned bitter. The witch shrieked. "I've asked you repeatedly to tell me where you've put Miranda Blight. Does she have a private room? You know I've insisted on a private room for her."

"She's right next door, in 302. She's just fine. Now go back to sleep, honey. Your friend is sleeping like a baby. That's what you need to do, too."

"Don't you dare call me honey."

Odd, I thought. Didn't bumblebees like honey?

"Randy? Hey, old buckaroo! God, I'm so proud of you. You caught a rapist and a murderer all by yourself. You're in the news, babe. I've been doing interviews for you, serving as your spokesman. I always knew you had it in you."

"Buddy? Is that you, Buddy? Come closer. I can't talk very well. Closer, Buddy."

The stainless steel emesis basin was on the sheet by my head. My snake-like hand clamped around it. "Closer, Buddy. I need to tell you something."

I smashed the heavy steel basin into his nose. "You dirty rotten son-of-a-bitch. How's that for the mother of all nosebleeds?"

A warm hand rested on mine. Something brushed my forehead. The nausea was gone. The pain in my abdomen was vanishing. Someone very quiet, very gentle, sat beside me.

I forced open my eyes and looked up. Ole smiled at me.

A big gangly smile. His eyes sparkled in wedgewinkle blue.

"Hi sweetheart, are you ready to wake up?" I felt the warmth of his fingers intertwined with mine. Then I realized someone else was holding my other hand.

"It's me, Mom. Me and Percy." Precious Darcy, safe and sound. "Mom? Can you open your eyes? I want you to meet Percy."

I opened an eye and had my first look at Percival. He was a hunk. I was a mess. "Darcy, I'm a mess," I advised them.

"Oh no, you're such a hero, Mom. The hero of the world."

How I loved her. Darcy in a cast from her knee down, but otherwise whole and well and lovely. All of her teeth. A big wide smile like mine.

Ole held one hand. Darcy held the other. Percival held her. We made a chain, a strong connection, a family force that was all set for some powerful healing.

"Am I in one piece?" I asked.

"Just barely," Ole said. "Dr. Azadi had to do some fancy stitching to put you back together. So lie still, Humpty Dumpty. Lie still and we'll take care of you."

"I will." My eyes shut and I was drifting off again.

Ole hummed the Humperdink song, the one about the fourteen angels at your head.

Darcy and Mama sang along. Beau Smothers dribbled a basketball across my vision. He was good at it. And Lordy, wouldn't you know? Here came Mrs. Vic and her precious Margo strutting right along behind.

My sister Margo.